PRAISE FOR *STEALING PARKER*

"Another engrossing romance from Miranda Kenneally with a hero who will melt your heart."—Jennifer Echols, National Award-winning author of *Such a Rush*

PRAISE FOR *Breathe, Annie, Breathe*

"*Breathe, Annie, Breathe* is an emotional, heartfelt, and beautiful story about finding yourself after loss and learning to love. Her best book yet."—Jennifer L. Armentrout, *New York Times* bestselling author of *Wait for You*

PRAISE FOR *Things I Can't Forget*

"Kenneally's books have quickly become must–reads." —*VOYA*

"Entertaining and poignant."—*School Library Journal*

"[A] compassionate and nuanced exploration of friendship, love, and maturing religious understanding."—*Publishers Weekly*

PRAISE FOR *Catching Jordan*

"A must-read! Whoever said football and girls don't mix hasn't read *Catching Jordan*. I couldn't put it down!"—Simone Elkeles, *New York Times* bestselling author of the *Perfect Chemistry* series

"*Catching Jordan* has it all: heart, humor, and a serious set of balls. Kenneally proves once and for all that when it comes to making life's toughest calls—on and off the field—girls rule!"—Sarah Ockler, bestselling author of *Twenty Boy Summer* and *#scandal*

"Sweetly satisfying."—*VOYA*

BREATHE, ANNIE, BREATHE

MIRANDA KENNEALLY

sourcebooks
fire

Published by Sourcebooks Fire, an imprint of Sourcebooks, Inc.
P.O. Box 4410, Naperville, Illinois 60567-4410
(630) 961-3900
Fax: (630) 961-2168
www.sourcebooks.com

Library of Congress Cataloging-in-Publication data is on file with the publisher.

Printed and bound in the United States of America.
WOZ 10 9 8 7 6 5 4 3 2 1

For all the girls looking for a new beginning.

PART I

An Ending

Today's Distance: 5 Miles

Six Months Until the Country Music Marathon

As a kid, I had the worst mile time ever.

Our gym teacher made us run the mile a few times a year for something called the *Presidential Fitness Test*. I'd huff and puff and wonder why the hell President Bush cared how fast I could run laps around the playground. I always came in dead last.

Most of the boys could run a mile in eight or nine minutes. The girls usually came in around ten. And there I was, scooting in at over thirteen minutes. Truth be told, running bored the hell out of me. I'd rather have been doing word problems.

Today, I'm running five miles along the Little Duck River. If I finish, this will be the farthest I've ever run. I know I'll finish— there's no way I can give up.

Because I'm doing this for *him*.

At mile 3.5, my running coach rides up next to me on his bike. Matt Brown is twenty-four and owns a program that trains people to run marathons. Some people on my team are running because it's a lifelong dream, some want to lose weight, and the others, like me, haven't told anyone why they're doing this.

"How's it goin', Annie?" Matt asks.

"Oo-kkay." Great. The lack of air is making me stutter. I can't breathe.

"You're Jordan's friend, right?"

If you consider the school's new football coach my friend. "She s-signed me up for your program, y-yeah."

He hops off his bike and pushes it along beside me. I can't believe he walks as fast as I run. "You need anything? Water? Tylenol? Vaseline?"

"*Vaseline?*"

He shrugs. "Yeah, for chafing. Are you having any issues?"

Never in my wildest dreams did I imagine a man would ask if I'm chafing. "No, thanks."

I shuffle, one foot after the other, trying to run like Matt taught me at the beginning of today's session. Keep my toes facing forward. Move my arms back and forth. Breathe in through my nose, out through my mouth. Pain pierces my side.

"What's your pace so far today?"

I glance at my new watch, tempted to lie and say I'm doing nine-minute miles. "About twelve minutes a m-mile."

"Not bad. When you're doing these long runs on the weekend, make sure you run your miles a minute slower than you usually do on your short runs."

I can't imagine going any more slowly than this, but I nod as Matt climbs back aboard his bike. "See you at the finish line."

I must've accidentally inhaled glue or something when I signed up for the Country Music Marathon.

• • •

I'm at 4.5 miles.

In through my nose, out through my mouth.

In through my nose, out through my mouth.

Point my toes.

Check my watch. I've slowed to a 14-minute mile. I'm going about as fast as that cloud, lazily inching across the blue sky. Half a mile to go.

A gorgeous woman with olive-toned skin, bouncy brown curls, and a pink ID bracelet jogs up next to me. Matt makes everybody on our team wear the bracelets so he can identify us and get in touch with our emergency contacts *just in case*.

"Damn. Our coach is fine."

"Maybe that's the point," I reply, sucking in a breath. "He trains us by making us chase after him."

The lady chuckles. "You're probably right." She speeds up and within the minute, I can't see her anymore. Not a surprise. Every time I start running, I get a great lead, but then it's like a parachute opens behind me.

Swaying willow trees and trickling water lead me along the dirt path back toward my car, which is parked at the mouth of the Little

Duck. Today's run is peaceful, but not boring. Considering how much stuff I have to think about, like drinking the right amount of water, looking for mile markers, and studying my watch, there's not much time left to obsess about graduation, or college, or him.

Instead, I can focus on this new CamelBak water-hydration device I'm wearing like a backpack. It kind of looks like a bong. I slip the plastic tube in my mouth and sip some water, pretending I'm taking a hit. Kyle would laugh at how ridiculous I'm being.

Stop thinking about him. Stop already.

Breathe in, breathe out.

I bet that when I start the longer distances this summer, running upward of fifteen to twenty miles on a Saturday morning, I'll have even more stuff to obsess over to distract me. Like chafing and Vaseline and continent-sized blisters.

One foot after the other. In through the nose, out through the mouth. I inhale the springy smell of dandelions. They dot the grass like gold coins.

"On your left!"

A boy streaks by me, running backwards. He settles directly in front of me and goes even faster. Wow, he has such vivid light blue eyes—I nearly lose my footing at the sight of them.

"Are you freaking kidding me?" I gasp.

He grins and slows to a jog. "What?"

I look for his pink bracelet, and finding none, I blurt, "You're running faster than me and I'm going forward!"

"So speed up then!"

What an ass.

"C'mon." He tosses his head from side to side, acting like one of those macho guys on a cheesy exercise show. "Let's go. Faster now. Work it out, girl! Let's go."

I flip him the bird. He throws his head back and laughs.

"Stop that!" I say.

"Stop what? Laughing at you?"

"Running backwards. It's unsafe."

"No it's not. Besides, I have to. I'm training for the RC Cola Moon Pie ten-miler. I'm running it backwards this year."

My mouth falls open. It shocks me that 1) he's running a race backwards; 2) it's named after RC Cola and Moon Pies; and 3) he's running a ten-mile race more than one time.

The guy has messy, light brown hair, seriously muscular arms and legs, and an outline of his abs peeks through his thin white *Delta Tau Kappa* tee. Is he in a frat?

Even though I usually can't hear Southern accents, I notice his. One time when I was little, my mom, brother, and I took a road trip to Chicago. Everywhere we stopped to eat, waitresses kept telling me I had the most darling accent. That's how I know people in Tennessee have an accent even if I can't hear it; it's weird I can pick up on the twangy countryness in his voice.

He keeps shuffling backwards. Our eyes meet, then he checks me out. It's been a while since a boy has straight up stared at me.

His gaze trails over my long, strawberry blond hair tied up in a ponytail, to my legs, and then settles on my pink bracelet. He smiles at it.

"See ya." He increases his cadence, continuing in reverse. I glance down at my watch. I bet he's running eight-minute miles. And he's doing it fucking backwards.

Being pissed at Running Backwards Boy carries me for another couple minutes.

But soon I'm alone again. Just me and the sky. Kyle's grin flashes in my mind.

A quarter mile more.

One foot after the other.

Breathe, Annie, breathe.

• • •

For all of last year, Kyle had been training to run the Country Music Marathon in Nashville.

Every Saturday, he would jog anywhere between five to twenty miles as he worked his way up to the full twenty-six. All throughout his training runs, I would drive to different meet-up points along the trail and give him water so he could stay hydrated. Month after month, mile after mile, I was there with an energy bar, a smile, and a kiss.

During one run, I brought him chilled Gatorade at mile ten. "I love that dress, babe," he said, gulping his drink so fast the orange liquid trickled down his chin and onto his white shirt. "What do you call that color again? Perihinkle?"

"Periwinkle."

He grinned and took another sip. "Like I said, periwinkle. Can I have a kiss? To get me through the last five miles?"

"You're all sweaty and gross!"

He pulled me to his chest. "You don't care."

And he was right. I kissed him long and slow, running my hand over his buzzed blond hair, then patted his butt to make him start running again. He finished his fifteen-mile run easily that day and kept up his training over the next couple months.

But Kyle only made it to twenty miles before I lost him.

And then he was gone, and snow covered the leaves, and then sun melted the snow, and all my regrets aside, I couldn't stand that all that training was for nothing.

He never got to run a marathon, which had been his dream since he'd started running track in middle school. He couldn't get the idea out of his head.

So early one Saturday morning, I tied on my sneakers and went to the school track. Kyle had told me four laps around equaled a mile, and during his training, he ran about a bazillion miles, so I knew I had to start logging some huge distances if I was going to do the race on his behalf.

But during my first run, I only made it around the track twice before the cool February air burned my lungs and throat, and my shins felt like somebody had kicked soccer balls at them for hours. I rested my hands on my knees and spit onto the pavement, tears clouding my eyes. *Two fucking laps? That's all I could do?* I quickly did the math—a marathon is the equivalent of 104 laps around the track!

On wobbly legs, I hobbled toward my car, passing the new football coach, who was setting up little orange cones for drills. Guys at school were still cursing the Sports Gods because the school board had hired a woman to coach football, and the girls wouldn't stop talking about how hot her boyfriend was—we had all sneaked a peek at the picture of him on her desk, but that's not what I was thinking as I passed Coach Woods.

She must've seen me horribly running those two laps. She knew how pathetic I was, that I would never be a runner. That I could never finish what my boyfriend had started.

I turned the ignition, my engine rumbling and groaning to a start, and got the hell out of there before anyone else saw me. After that first run, I didn't expect to go back. But I couldn't stop thinking that Kyle needed me to finish it for him.

The next Saturday, I went to the school track even earlier—the sun was barely up—so I could run without anyone else around. And Coach Woods was already there doing sprints and exercises of her own!

Up and down the fifty-yard line, she did high kicks and lunges and sprints. She waved at me, and I started running horribly again—like an ape in a zoo, flailing my arms and legs.

I finished two and a half laps, then knelt on the grass,

wheezing, working to keep the tears from falling. And Coach Woods sat down beside me, tossing a football to herself. She was my health class teacher, but we hadn't talked much, at least not about anything except the usual mortifying health class topics—safe sex and bodily changes and the importance of flossing.

"Are you trying out for the track team next week?" she asked.

"No…"

"Then what are you doing out here?" She looked me straight in the eye, and I kind of hated her for that. I didn't want anyone to know I was attempting to run, especially not the best athlete our school's ever seen. Coach Woods used to play football here when she was my age. Unless you count chicken fighting in a pool or beer pong, I had *never* played sports. If people knew I was training to finish the marathon on Kyle's behalf and I ended up failing miserably, I would feel more lost than I already did.

"I'm not a bad runner," Coach Woods said. "Well, I used to be a lot better than I am now, but I still know the basics. Can I help?"

She stared at me expectantly until I admitted, "I'm training for a marathon, okay?"

"Okay." We sat in silence. I counted as she tossed the football up and down, up and down, twelve times. I waited for her to laugh in my face. But she didn't. She stood up with the ball, launched it down the field, and we watched as it bounced to a stop beside the goal post.

She nodded once at me. "I'm not sure I could ever run a marathon. That's a big commitment, and I have no idea how to train for one… But one of my friends might be able to help you."

• • •

26.2 miles.

That's longer than the drive to Nashville.

Kyle would've been upset if he'd known how I spent most of my senior year: eating lunch alone, wearing his flannel shirt to sleep every night while I cried, watching movies alone at the drive-in. I wanted to do something that would make him proud. Something to honor who he was.

I told Coach Woods, "I want to run the Country Music Marathon in October."

She knew a guy who trained people to run marathons and triathlons and any kind of race, really. Matt's program isn't cheap. I picked up more waitressing hours at the Roadhouse, so I could pay for my training, the entrance fee for the October marathon, new sneakers, a watch, athletic clothes, and the water-hydration device that could double as a bong.

And here I am, running every Saturday morning.

Running for *him*.

Marathon Training Schedule~Brown's Race Co.

Name _Annie Winters_

Saturday	Distance	Notes
April 20	3 miles	*I'm really doing this! Finish time 34:00*
April 27	5 miles	*Stupid Running Backwords Boy!!*
May 4	6 miles	
May 11	5 miles	
May 18	7 miles	
May 25	8 miles	
June 1	10 miles	
June 8	9 miles	
June 15	7 miles	
June 22	8 miles	
June 29	9 miles	
July 6	10 miles	
July 13	12 miles	
July 20	13 miles	
July 27	15 miles	
August 3	14 miles	
August 10	11 miles	
August 17	16 miles	
August 24	20 miles	
August 31	14 miles	
September 7	22 miles	
September 14	20 miles	
September 21	The Bluegrass Half Marathon	
September 28	12 miles	
October 5	10 miles	
October 12	Country Music Marathon in Nashville	

Today's Distance: 6 Miles
Six Months Until the Country Music Marathon

I'm halfway through my six-mile run when Running Backwards Boy flashes by. But he's going forward this time.

"Let's go!" Running Backwards Boy yells to the man on his heels. "Pick it up, pick it up!" The man looks like he's fixin' to die, but RBB is in top form.

"Are you training for the Olympics today or something?" I holler, but he doesn't slow down. He's in some sort of super-runner zone and disappears from sight.

Today's run is going a little better than last week's. I'm not as tired, but my feet feel slimy inside my socks and I know another blister is forming. Breathe in through the nose, out through the mouth. It's amazing to think that the fastest ladies in the world can finish a marathon in two hours and twenty minutes. I'd be glad to finish in five hours.

Matt jogs up next to me, his backpack bouncing against his back. "How you feeling?"

"Good."

"Keep your arms moving. Pretend you're a pair of scissors."

I slice air with my hands.

"You got it now. Need anything? Water? Candy? Tylenol?"

"You're a mobile drugstore."

He grins, maintaining my pace. "Need any Vaseline?"

"Gah! Stop asking me that. I do not have chafing issues."

Matt laughs, and then another guy from our team passes us. "Andrew! I told you not to use an iPod on the trails! It's not safe! …As if he can hear me." Matt jets off to catch Andrew, leaving me behind. Damn, Matt's fast.

I saw him run for the first time at Wednesday's training session. Until then, I wasn't aware Usain Bolt was my running coach. I bet Matt's even faster than Running Backwards Boy. Who now runs forward. I shake my head, trying to forget how he checked me out. I admit I've thought about it a few times in the past week.

It's not that I'm desperate for sex. I'm desperate for Kyle to push my hair behind my ears. To scratch my back when I've got an itch. To watch reruns of *The Big Bang Theory* and laugh at all the same parts as me.

I focus on moving my arms back and forth like Matt showed me. Point my toes.

Breathe, Annie, breathe.

• • •

The 0 mile marker comes into view and I sprint toward the finish. Sweat drips down my face. It takes all my energy to keep my arms moving. My calves burn. Matt and his assistants are screaming my name and clapping for me as I near the end. "Go, Annie! Push it!" Twenty seconds later, I pass the mile marker and slow to a walk.

I wipe the sweat off my forehead with my T-shirt and grin up at the sky. Everything hurts, but it's a good hurt. I finished the entire six miles!

"Great job," Matt says, patting my back. He hands me a cup of Gatorade. "Drink it all, and then you can have a banana."

My hand shakes as I lift the cup to my lips. I breathe deeply to combat the dizziness. Don't pass out, don't pass out.

"How did today feel?" he asks.

"Okay. I only walked for a m-minute or s-so in the middle."

Matt watches me finish my Gatorade. He has a group of fifteen runners at the trails this morning, but he makes me feel like I'm the only person here. He reminds me of my big brother. After I finish my drink and eat a banana, he leads me through a series of stretches and gives me instructions on how much water to drink this afternoon and tells me I need to run two miles tomorrow on my own.

His training program is tougher than two-dollar steak: during the week, I run or cross-train over short distances, but then we keep upping the ante on the weekend runs. For instance, if one Saturday we run four miles, the next weekend Matt makes us try for five. Over the next six months, I'll work my way up to twenty-two miles before race day.

"So I'll see you at the gym for cross-training this Wednesday?" Matt asks, and I nod. I love the structure this program brings to my life; I don't like having to figure out how to fill the empty days and hours when I'm not at school or working. Not only do I have to work out every day of the week, but Matt also gave me a meal plan that shows when to drink water and what foods to eat when. I swear, all this planning and thinking about my body and what I'm putting into it is harder than rocket science.

But I like it. When I'm not running, I'm thinking about it constantly: planning my meals, psyching myself up for the next weekend's long run, drinking tons of water, icing my sore legs, sleeping. It exhausts me to the point I don't lie awake staring out my window at the streetlight, hating that I have no strong chest to curl up against anymore. The minute my eyes close at night, I pass out.

I say bye to Matt and limp toward the parking lot. Running Backwards Boy is sitting on the back of a Jeep. Crap. I'm parked right next to him. Luckily he doesn't seem to notice I'm wad- dling like a pregnant lady who needs to use the bathroom real bad—he's fully immersed in texting and listening to something through his headphones.

I hobble over to my tiny red car, a 1984 Audi GT. She's a piece of crap, but it's all I could afford on my own. I saved for two years, and I love her. I pop open the hatchback, sit down, and kick off my sneakers. Then I peel my socks off one by one. The foot odor could knock somebody out.

"Damn," the guy says. Shit, can he smell my feet or something? He slips his earbuds out, stands, and starts rummaging in the back of the Jeep. I expect him to Febreze the area, but seconds later he kneels before me, opening a first aid kid.

Why is he so close to me? My feet stink!

"That is one hell of a blister."

That's when I see it. My skin is stretched over a blood blister that's bigger than a quarter.

"So that's why my foot was killing me."

The boy unscrews the top from a brown bottle. "What's your name?"

"Annie."

He grins. "Hi, Annie. This won't hurt."

"What are you doing?" I blurt, but it's too late. He's poured something on the blister. I don't feel any pain, but there's some kind of scientific reaction going on. Little bubbles appear, like he mixed baking soda and vinegar together.

"It's just hydrogen peroxide. I'm cleaning that blister. Or is this some sort of unborn twin attached to you?"

"I do not have an unborn twin."

"That you know of. Did you ever have this thing checked out? It looks big enough to be an unborn twin." He lifts my foot by the ankle, staring the blister down. It tickles. Oh my God, my foot stinks and he's touching me! "Is it okay if I lance it?"

"Do what?"

He reaches into his kit and pulls out a needle, dipping it into a bottle of alcohol.

"Are you a doctor or something?"

"No, are you?" He beams up at me for a sec. This boy might as well wear a nametag that says *Trouble*. "I've been running a long time. I know how to deal with injuries."

"Oh yeah? What's the weirdest injury you've ever seen?"

"One time I was running a race dressed as Elvis."

"Elvis."

"Yeah, Elvis. And I was doing pretty well too, until this other guy dressed as Elvis tripped in a rut and tore a ligament. I helped him until the medics could get to us. Everyone was pretty impressed to see one Elvis treating another."

I bite into my lip, barely able to contain my laughter.

"I'm gonna lance your blister now," the guy says. He sticks the needle into my skin and I rear back when it stings. The fluid trickles out as I bite into my hand. It's about the grossest thing I've ever seen, but this guy doesn't even react. He pours more hydrogen peroxide on it, making more bubbles.

"You want a *Little Mermaid* Band-Aid?"

I raise an eyebrow. "Disney?"

"I have two little sisters."

I watch as he bandages the blister, taking notes so I can do this next week when I grow another Manhattan-sized blister. The boy pats my foot when he's done and stands.

"Good as new."

His eyes meet mine, and he gives me a little smile, and I find I like the way it makes me shiver even though it's a rain forest outside. When he brushes the hair off his forehead, I get the sudden urge to do it for him, to push it back behind his ears. Uncomfortable, I turn away from his smile to shut the hatchback, and I'm fixing to make a break for it, away from the shivers and weird want to touch his hair, when Matt stalks over.

"What's going on here?"

"Just helping Annie with her blister."

Matt looks at my foot, then motions for the guy to follow him. But they don't move far enough away—I can still hear them.

"I've told you not to hit on my clients," Matt whispers.

The guy steps back like he's been slapped. "I just wanted to help."

"He didn't hurt anything," I start, and both guys glance over at me. "It's not a big de—"

Matt interrupts me. "Jeremiah, I'm trying to build up my reputation—"

The boy holds up a hand. "I get it, I get it—"

"Do you? This is my work, my job, and I'm trying to give you a chance here—"

"Then don't give up on me before I even start!"

"Guys," I interrupt, looking between them, but they keep right on arguing as if they've forgotten I'm here. Matt smacks Running Backwards Boy on the face with a T-shirt and RBB bops Matt on the head with a water bottle and puts him in a headlock. Matt escapes and puts RBB in a headlock of his own. It's hard to believe they're adults right now. They're baboons.

"Boys!" I exclaim, and they jerk their heads up and stop acting like cavemen. "What in the world?"

"This is my little brother, Jeremiah," Matt says.

"Little?" Jeremiah snorts.

Matt ignores this. "He just started working for me, pacing people that are hoping to up their game and improve their speed."

"What do you mean by pacing?" I ask.

Matt says, "It's like, if somebody wants to finish a marathon in a certain amount of time, Jere will run alongside them and keep them on pace so they finish before their goal time—you need a certain time to run big races like Boston. Pacing is what Jere does best."

Jeremiah looks pleased at the compliment. That must be why the man was chasing after him on the trails today.

"But I'll still be working with you sometimes," Jeremiah tells me. "I'll be helping Matt with the Saturday and Sunday long runs."

"So I have two running coaches now?" I ask.

"Something like that," Jeremiah flirts, eyes flickering up and down my body, earning him another nasty look from his brother.

"Jere, I'm serious. If you don't take this job seriously, that's it. You won't get another chance from me." Matt gives his brother a pointed look. Why would Matt chastise him in front of me?

Is he warning me too? I've only known Matt a couple weeks, but he always seems even-keeled. Why's he so strict with his brother?

Jeremiah's face clouds over. "See you next week, Annie." He gives me a curt nod, then follows his brother over to help pack up the water coolers and towels. He doesn't look back.

Given how by-the-book and prepared he is, training with Matt has been calm and cool so far.

Jeremiah makes me feel anything but.

• • •

I climb the crumbling, concrete steps and push open the screen door to our trailer.

A stick of butter, a loaf of bread, and a block of cheese sit on our counter, away from the brownish section where the egg-colored plaster has flaked away.

My older brother is cooking a grilled cheese and listening to the Braves game on the radio. Nick sets the spatula down to kiss my forehead. He smells like grease and exhaust fumes from doing oil changes down at Caldwell Auto Parts.

He flips his sandwich. It sizzles in the frying pan and makes my stomach rumble. I'm starving, but I don't think I can hold any food down. Running screws with my stomach—I can't tell if I need to eat or use the bathroom.

"How'd today go?" Nick asks.

"I finished!"

"All six miles?"

I nod, and he beams. I'd never seen him so happy as when I told him I was training for the marathon.

He scoops the grilled cheese onto a plate. "You hungry? I'll make you one of these."

"No, thanks. Matt's meal plan says I'm supposed to have pizza and salad for lunch today."

At that, Nick flips the gas off and drops his pan in the sink, then pours a mound of potato chips onto his plate, flicks off the radio, and hustles to the living room to watch the game on TV.

Mom flits into the kitchen, brushing her wet curly brown hair. Nick got his dark, floppy hair from her; my straight strawberry blond must come from my father's side.

She searches under a stack of old newspapers, a hand towel, and the teetering pile of mail. I grab her keys from the hook where Nick undoubtedly hung them up and pass them to her.

"Thank you," she says, pocketing them. Our eyes meet for just a second before we both look away. "How'd your run go, sweetie?"

"I finished it."

A small smile appears on her lips. "I'm so glad."

I nod.

"Kyle would've been—"

"Mom, just stop!" I say before I'm able to stop myself, and then she's rushing out the door to make her shift at Quick Pick, to get away from me. I close my eyes for a sec, to calm down. I don't like talking about him, but I can't keep blowing up like that. When I open my eyes, I realize Mom left her cashier's apron and coupon envelope on the counter.

"Mom, wait!" I yell, but she's already gone. She forgot them again. I'll ask Nick to run them over to the store after he's finished eating his lunch.

I run my fingers over the apron's stiff, black fabric. I lift it to my nose, inhaling her scent, the same way I do with Kyle's flannel shirt. His smell is long gone, but her lavender and the Windex she uses to clean the conveyer belt are loud and clear. The smell makes me want a hug. Mom and I used to hug all the time, but we haven't in months. Not since Christmas.

Not bothering to peel off my sweaty shorts and tank, I go to my room and flop down on the bright purple comforter stretched across my twin bed. I point my toes at the ceiling, trying to get rid of the lactic acid build-up in my calves. Sweating on my bed makes me cringe, but I'm too sore and tired to do anything besides wallow. Before Kyle, I never made my bed, but his firefighter dad drilled the habit into him and I picked it up somewhere along the way. Other than the stacks of twenty-five-cent paperbacks I buy at the library and at yard sales, the rest of my room is somewhat bare now.

Before Kelsey and I stopped hanging out, we loved collecting cows. A cowbell alarm clock, cow curtains, cow picture frames, cow candles, and even a cow rug decorated my room. I packed the cows away to make room for the teddy bears Kyle won me at the Coffee County

Fair and the seashell cedar boxes and wind chimes he bought on our road trip to Myrtle Beach. I packed his stuff away so it couldn't make me sad, but now my room feels empty.

After I lost him six months ago, Mom started begging me to go shopping with her for new bedroom décor to fill the blank space, to try out her yoga class, to do *anything* really. I knew she meant well, but I didn't want to do anything.

I snapped at her several times: "If one more person tells me what I need to do..." Being a bitch made me feel better and shittier all at once.

"I don't know how to help you, Annie. Tell me how to help you," she cried into her hands.

If she'd invented a special potion to erase memories and mistakes, I would've been all ears. But nothing she said could fix what I'd done.

I met Kyle on the first day of ninth grade, when kids from the two middle schools in Williamson County came together at Hundred Oaks for freshman year.

I hated him at first. On day one, we were playing volleyball in gym and he picked me for his team. I served, the ball smashed him in the back of the head, and he fell to the gym floor.

I sprinted to him. "I'm sorry!"

I thought I'd hurt him bad, but I discovered him giggling like a little girl. The rest of the day, he and his friends covered their heads every time I passed them in the hallway.

"It's the volleyball vixen!" Kyle cried.

Fourteen-year-old me was mortified. So I got revenge. The next day in gym, I served the volleyball and whacked Kyle in the head again.

He invited me to the Back to School dance that Friday.

Before long, we were serious, and my mom wasn't pleased. "You're gonna end up pregnant at sixteen just like Willa down the street." She said that every time she caught us making out. She thought if I stayed with him, I would never get out of Oakdale trailer park. "Never depend on a guy, Annie. You depend on yourself, understand?"

But I loved being with him. We enjoyed curling up together with a bowl of popcorn in front of the TV. Or he'd sit on the couch playing Assassin's Creed, and I'd lean against his side and dig into the latest mystery I'd picked up at the library. We always felt at home with each other, like we didn't need anything else.

We dated for over three years, even though we were different people: I did my homework every single night and worked hard as a waitress to make money for college. He lived over in the Royal Trail subdivision, did his homework in the ten minutes between classes, ran the mile in the regional track finals, and wanted to work as a firefighter like his father.

He wanted "forever" to start right after high school. He wanted to marry me.

That's why we had the big fight.

We were at the place where we shared our first kiss: the drive-in movie theater that showed old movies. It's still one of the most popular places to go in Franklin. As freshmen, we were too young to drive so we walked there all the time. It became our spot.

When he got older, Kyle worked concessions there on weekends and would sneak me in. That weekend in September, we had just started senior year. We were watching *Forrest Gump* at the drive-in, and during his favorite part, when Forrest decides to run across the country for no apparent reason, Kyle whispered in my ear, "Marry me?"

We were in love, and I didn't want to lose him, but I couldn't imagine getting married before going to college. My mom has been working as a cashier at the Quick Pick since before I was born—my dad ran off when I was little—and I wanted more for myself. If Kyle could have had his way, he would've moved in and had babies with me the week after we graduated.

"We've talked about this," I replied with a shaky voice. "You know I'm not ready."

He slowly pulled his hand out of his jeans pocket. Was there a ring in there?

"You're saying no?" he whispered.

"I can't. You know I want to—"

"If you wanted to, you'd say yes!"

"Kyle, I want to wait until I've gone to college and have a job—"

"I'll take care of you!"

"That's not what this is about—"

"Either you love me and want to marry me, or we're over—"

"How can you put me in that position?" I cried.

He felt so betrayed, so hurt, that he broke up with me.

And I missed him so much, my stomach twisted up and it hurt to breathe. Pizza tasted like broccoli. Music hurt my ears. I didn't know what to do between classes. Who was I supposed to walk with? My bulletin board had long since morphed from pictures of me and Kelsey playing with our moms' makeup to me and Kyle snuggling and kissing. Who was I supposed to say good night to before I went to sleep?

At the same time, the breakup really pissed me off. How dare he throw away three years just because I wasn't ready for marriage? Why couldn't he respect my dream of going to college, getting a job where I could make money, maybe buying a house one day? I didn't want to live in a trailer all my life.

Sometimes when I would talk about college, he'd get a sad but happy face. Like a wince when you have an ice cream headache: it hurts so bad, but the taste is so good. Mom said he might've proposed because he was desperate to hold on to me—he was scared I'd forget him when I left for college. I hated her saying that. I would've kept dating him! Other than working at the Roadhouse, doing my homework, and reading thrillers about hot FBI agents and lady CEOs that partner to solve mysteries, he'd been my whole life for three years. Besides, he dumped me.

Why would he do that if he wanted to hang on to me? None of it made any sense.

A month later, he was gone. He never got to run his marathon. I was alone. And for a while, Mom rocked me to sleep every night like when I was a baby, but then she started pushing, wanting me to go out with my brother and his friends. I could barely sleep through an entire night or do my homework, and she wanted me to go shopping with her?

That's when I blew up.

"He'd still be here if it weren't for you!" I screamed, even though it wasn't true. "If you hadn't pushed me into wanting to go to college, I would've said yes to his proposal. It's all your fault he's gone!"

The blood left Mom's face. She slammed her coffee mug into the sink. In all my life, I'd never seen her cry like that, the tears streaming down her face.

My brother rushed into the kitchen, ordered me to get out of the house for a while, and hugged Mom long and hard. When I came home from my walk up to the empty basketball court on Spring Street, passing a bunch of barefooted little girls playing tag, Mom had gone to work, and the relationship we'd had was gone too.

I knew what I'd said was a lie. I wanted college for me just as much as my mother did. I didn't mean to lash out... And now I don't know how to get back to what we once had. How could she forgive me? I blamed her for my loss. For something that was completely my fault.

It's my fault he's gone…

I cringe at the memories.

I wish I could run from them.

• • •

Every Saturday night, I wait tables at Davy Crockett's Roadhouse.

I work a couple nights during the week and Sunday brunch too, but Saturday is the big date night in Franklin. It's the night when I make nearly all of my money, which I desperately need for college and gas. I wiped out the $600 I had to buy new tennis shoes, running clothes, and the first two months of training dues. Matt's program costs $200 per month, which Nick said was outrageous, but considering I get a gym membership and all the Gatorade, energy bars, fruit, and candy I want at the trails on Saturdays, I think it's worth it. Not to mention I get the support and expertise of a guy who's run over thirty marathons and is a certified personal trainer. That's a billion times better than flailing around the school track by myself.

The only negative to Matt's program? In the gym locker room, old ladies just love walking around naked for some reason. I pray that when I'm old, I don't have any sudden desire to flaunt it.

I hip-check the vestibule door open and head out onto the restaurant floor, passing rusted road signs and paintings of Davy

Crockett in his coonskin cap. My boots crunch peanut shells every step of the way. That's what makes the Roadhouse so famous—we serve free peanuts by the bucket and guys can throw shells at each other, acting like Neanderthals.

I drop beers and Cokes off at one of my four tops and move on to my round. The table seats seven and I generally make big tips off it on Saturdays.

Tonight, Nick is sitting there with a group of friends and their girlfriends. My brother is barely a year older than me and graduated last year, so I know them all from school.

"This is my best table, so you better leave me a good tip," I tell Nick, and he responds by throwing a peanut at my forehead. That earns him a prompt slap on the arm from his girlfriend, Kimberly. "And you're not getting any free food either."

"You'll serve us beer though, right?" Evan asks.

"Hell no. I'm not losing my job over you." I open my notepad and pull a pen from my apron. "What do you want to drink?"

"Beer," Evan says with a wide grin.

I respond by grabbing a handful of peanuts and dropping them on his head.

"Hey!" Evan shakes them out of his shirt as everyone laughs. Nick has been friends with Evan since elementary school, and now they do oil changes together at the auto parts store. Almost all of Nick's friends stayed in Franklin and didn't go to college, and now they work at places like the Buchanan Ford dealership and Total Billiards. Kimberly got a receptionist job at a realty company. Nick takes night classes over at the Motlow community college. Compared with the rest of the kids who grew up in the Oakdale trailer park, I'm pretty different in that I'm moving to college this fall and will be living in the dorms.

I take their drink orders for real this time—a round of waters, Cokes, and sweet teas. In the back, I scoop ice into cups and let out a long breath. Today took a lot out of me—the six-mile run zapped me energy-wise while finding Jeremiah attractive hit me guilt-wise. I'm sure he's a great running coach and all, considering he blasts down those trails like a bullet, but I don't know that I want to see him again. I need to concentrate on making it through this marathon. But I also liked feeling a spark of *something*.

"Hey, where are you?"

I glance up to find Stephanie, the manager of the Roadhouse, scanning the floor. That's when I notice I've been pressing the dispenser for so long, ice is tumbling off the counter. I let go of the lever as Stephanie grabs a broom and sweeps the ice over to a drainage grate.

"You okay?"

"I'm good. Just tired," I lie.

Stephanie gives me her worried-mom look. She learned that expression from my mother—they've been friends since middle school. They both work in the retail/hospitality business, so they often get together and bitch about bitchy customers.

"I'm *fine*," I say again and press the Coke dispenser to fill the glasses, then evenly distribute them on my tray, add lemons to the rims, and carry the drinks out onto the floor.

I serve Nick and his friends burgers and chicken strips as fast as I can, to rush them away from my money-maker table, but of course they end up staying a couple hours and throw at least five buckets of peanuts at each other. When they finally pay the check, they split the bill four ways. So annoying.

Evan gives me a 30 percent tip but won't meet my eyes when I say thank you. He just pockets his wallet. "You should come out with us after you get off work. We're camping at Normandy."

My face flushes hot. After what happened with Kyle, everybody gave me distance for a few months. But once New Year's rolled around, life went back to *their* normal. Guys knew I was single and started asking me out. Did Kyle even cross their minds when I said no?

Anyway, Evan has been acting weird since February, and I've been wondering when this would happen. It must've taken him a while to garner the guts, and it makes me feel terrible. He's a good-looking guy: his brown hair hangs to his eyes and he has great arms, roped with muscles from working in the garage. But I can't.

"No, but thank you," I reply. "I need to sleep in a bed tonight—I'm so sore from running."

Evan looks crestfallen. "Maybe next weekend then?"

I take the damp rag from my apron pocket and start wiping

down the round, working to scrub dried, brownish-yellow mustard away. "Maybe."

But I know I'll say no. I already have to listen to my brother doing his girlfriend when I'm at home; there's no way I'm going camping with them—tents have thinner walls than our trailer.

"I guess I'll see you soon, then," Evan says in a quiet voice. I can't look him in the eye.

Nick stops fawning over Kimberly long enough to give me a quick hug. "I'll be home tomorrow."

"Thanks." I lean into the hug. He subtly stuffs more tip money in my apron, and I give him a smile.

I wait tables until midnight. Then it's time for side work. It's my turn to scrape gum off the bottoms of tables, which is just about the worst task ever. The worst is refilling all the glass ketchup bottles; a good night is when I don't drop a bottle on the floor. Next, I roll a hundred sets of silverware for tomorrow's brunch shift, and then I clock out.

I pull my apron off and search my bag for my keys as I enter the parking lot, and soon I'm tucked in my car. I swipe my cell on, hoping to find messages, even though I don't really want to deal with anybody. The only text is from Mom, asking me to pull her blue shirt off the clothesline when I get home. Ok, I text back, then scroll through my contacts. I always flick past Kyle's name quicker than anyone else's. Really, between him and Kelsey, there's nobody in the Ks that I can talk to anymore. But that's sort of true for the

As, Bs, and Ws too. I drop my phone in my tote and start the ignition. I drive past Sonic, where kids from school are hanging out over Cherry Limeades and onion rings. My heart pangs when I spot Kelsey's bright blue Mustang convertible.

I head to the drive-in movie theater, to the spot I shared with Kyle. I make it in time for the last half of the late showing of *Clueless*, that Alicia Silverstone movie from the nineties. It's about this rich, hilarious girl who does nice things for people.

I buy some popcorn from the concession stand, then sit on the hood of my car and laugh at all the funny parts, wishing he was laughing along with me.

Marathon Training Schedule–Brown's Race Co.

Name *Annie Winters*

Saturday	Distance	Notes
April 20	3 miles	*I'm really doing this! Finish time 34:00*
April 27	5 miles	*Stupid Running Backwords Boy!!*
May 4	6 miles	*Blister from HELL*
May 11	5 miles	
May 18	7 miles	
May 25	8 miles	
June 1	10 miles	
June 8	9 miles	
June 15	7 miles	
June 22	8 miles	
June 29	9 miles	
July 6	10 miles	
July 13	12 miles	
July 20	13 miles	
July 27	15 miles	
August 3	14 miles	
August 10	11 miles	
August 17	16 miles	
August 24	20 miles	
August 31	14 miles	
September 7	22 miles	
September 14	20 miles	
September 21	The Bluegrass Half Marathon	
September 28	12 miles	
October 5	10 miles	
October 12	Country Music Marathon in Nashville	

Today's Distance: 5 Miles

Six Months Until the Country Music Marathon

Today is what Matt calls a "rest" day.

This means our team has to run five miles before we do seven miles next Saturday. Five miles does not seem like rest to me. I'm beginning to think a radioactive spider bit my running coach.

I wonder if it'll be a Jeremiah-free day—I didn't see his Jeep parked near the rest of our cars this morning. Maybe he's off working with runners training to run the Boston Marathon or something fancy.

Matt's making us run around downtown Nashville this weekend, because we're all sick of the trails; plus he wants us to get used to running in the city since we'll be doing that during the marathon itself. He made us memorize our route today—it's important to understand a course before you run it. You need to know where the hills are, so you can steel yourself. It's also crucial to know which coffee shops are runner-friendly and will let you use the bathroom if there aren't any porta-potties nearby. And just in case we get lost, Matt hung a bunch of orange ribbons on various light poles and street signs. Like Hansel and Gretel and their crumbs.

Our team started out at Music Row, home to all the country music labels, and now I'm coming up on mile 4. The largest building in Nashville—the AT&T building—looms over the city. Everyone calls it the *Batman building* because its spires stick up like Batman's mask.

I run past a smattering of trees that surround LP Stadium, where the Titans play. Titans tickets cost a few hundred apiece, so the only time I've ever been to a game was when my brother won a pair of tickets from a radio station contest. I loved the cheering crowds, the cotton candy. It was just an overall good day. Remembering the energy in the stadium gives me the extra oomph I need to push through this mile as I head toward Bicentennial Park—the finish line.

When I see the final orange ribbon, I sprint toward Matt and arrive to cheering and clapping from the people who finished a few minutes before me. Matt hands me a cup of Gatorade, checks his watch, and writes my time on his clipboard. "You did good today, Annie."

I lick Gatorade off the cup's rim so it doesn't get my hand sticky and then take a sip. "Am I getting faster?"

He grins. "No, not really. But all that matters is that you build the stamina to finish the race, okay? Your goal is to finish."

Queasiness suddenly rushes over me. I squat to the ground. Sweat rolls off my face and splatters on the concrete.

"Up you go," Matt says, pulling me to a standing position.

"We gotta walk it off. Let's move." He leads me in a wide circle like a circus elephant. After I've caught my breath, stretched, and clapped for the runners who came in after me, it's time to go home. Since we ran from one place to another today, not out and back like we do at the Little Duck River, Matt said he and his assistants would give us rides.

"Who's taking me back to my car?"

"I'll take you," a voice says.

It's that slow, twangy accent again. I look up from wiping sweat off my face with my tank top to find Jeremiah grinning his ass off. Did he appear out of thin air?

"No," Matt says, rolling his eyes. "Bridget'll give her a ride."

"Why can't I take her?" Jeremiah says. "I'm a good driver. I've been driving for four years…six if you count the time I borrowed Dad's truck freshman year of high school."

"You mean the time you stole his truck to go fool around with Melody Andersen at that potluck supper at church?"

"I *borrowed* it."

"You *stole* it."

"That's just semantics."

I interrupt, "I'm glad I only have one brother, not two. All y'all do is fight."

"That's not true," Matt replies. "We don't fight when we sleep."

"Sometimes we do," Jeremiah says.

What goofs.

"C'mon, I'll drive you," Jeremiah says, jingling his keys, and I shrug okay. Matt doesn't look pleased, but I'm eighteen now. I make my own decisions. And even though getting a ride from Jeremiah is sort of like running into a burning building, I like the way I feel when he makes me laugh.

I need to laugh.

I say bye to Matt, follow Jeremiah over to his Jeep, and he opens the door for me. My knees tremble as I step up into the Jeep. He shuts the door and my hands shake as I buckle my seat belt. It smells like *boy* in here. Cologne, sweat, muskiness. I suck in a nervous deep breath as he climbs into the driver's seat.

I peek at him while he turns the key. A dusting of golden hair covers his strong hands and tan arms. Just like the light stubble on his face. Does he not shave on weekends? Jeremiah's face is tan and his eyes are a pretty light blue, but I wouldn't call him traditionally handsome. Something about him is too jagged. He's cute though. Three black, circular tattoos the size of quarters race up his left forearm. A scar runs along the right side of his jaw, matching the scar on his right arm. There's one beside his eye too. God, I hope he doesn't get into knife fights or something.

I decide to ask about it. "Jeremiah?"

"Call me Jere. Only my Granny and PopPop call me Jeremiah."

"But I like Jeremiah better."

He flashes me a smile. "Jeremiah it is, then."

"How'd you get that scar on your jaw?"

He starts telling me about how he loves Adventure Races, these crazy races that involve anything from running a half marathon and jumping over huge holes throughout the course, to running beside fire pits that spit out smoke like volcanoes. He explains he got the scar on his jaw from a race through a thick forest in Georgia: "A tree branch got me."

"What's been your favorite race?" I ask.

At a stoplight, he pops a piece of gum in his mouth and chews. "I had to do an obstacle course with rock climbing and inner tubing down a river, and then I rappelled off a mountain, and then I had to run a 10K after that. I came in fourth."

"Fourth place?" I exclaim.

"I'm still pissed. I would've won it if I hadn't lost control of my inner tube after I hit a rock in the water."

"Do you do a lot of races?"

"I do normal races all the time, but I haven't done an Adventure Race in a few months," he says in a soft drawl.

"Why not?"

"I promised my mother I wouldn't."

"Huh? Why? If you were doing well…"

"She said I was addicted…I dunno."

Jere turns down 6th Avenue in silence, glancing at me. He hasn't said a word in a few blocks. He kinda went gloomy.

I can't just sit here. "So did you train somebody today?"

"Yeah. I paced for this guy who's training for the Ironman

Triathlon in Wisconsin this fall. We only did fifteen miles. It was a rest day."

I swear, these genetically enhanced brothers are gonna be the death of me.

He drums the steering wheel. "I'm thinking I'll do a ropes course this afternoon."

"Don't you ever get tired?"

"Oh yeah. I'm so beat at night, it takes like five minutes for my parents to wake me up in the mornings. Alarm clocks don't work for me."

The image of his parents shaking him awake makes me giggle. "Your parents have to wake you up? How old are you?"

He turns left, grinning. "Twenty. You?"

"Eighteen. Did you run downtown where we did today? I didn't see you."

"No, the Stones River Greenway. We needed room to stretch the run out."

"But then Matt asked you to drive downtown?"

"No." He glances over at me. "I came down here 'cause… I wanted to say I'm sorry. I didn't mean to make you uncomfortable last week or whatever. With the blister and the Band-Aid. I saw the look on your face when you left."

"No, no. Everything's good." I'm such a liar.

"I don't believe you," Jere says with a smirk. "I realized later it was weird that I gave you first aid when you didn't even know who I was."

"I thought it was nice of you."

"Yeah?" He grins widely. "I can't wait to tell my brother that I didn't traumatize you. He said that I did."

"Do you really not get along with Matt?"

Jere pauses. "He's my best friend. I love him. He's giving me a chance… you know, with this job and all."

I wait for him to elaborate, but he goes silent again. "But do you guys seriously fight a lot or something?"

"We're brothers—we fight all the time. But I've heard that if you fight about all the little stuff, then you're less likely to blow up big time."

"Doesn't that more apply to couples?"

He shrugs. "I think you can apply it to all friendships."

I gnaw on my pinky, pulling the skin away from the nail. I told Kyle so many times that I didn't want to settle down right after high school, that I had a lot of things I wanted to do before marrying him. But we never had a big fight until I refused his proposal. If we had had more arguments, would things have turned out differently? Would we have understood how to move past our problems without Kyle having resorted to a full-on breakup?

The five-minute drive goes by in a flash. Jere pulls up alongside my ancient Audi and puts his Jeep in park. He hops out, jogs around to the passenger side, and opens my door. Hello, über gentleman.

"I hope you have a nice rest of your weekend," he says, helping me down.

"You too."

He waits until I'm safely in my car and backing out of my parking spot before waving and climbing in his Jeep. I return the wave, flick on the radio, and crank down the window for some fresh air.

• • •

It's brunch time at the Roadhouse.

Sundays before and after church are always busy. Besides Saturday nights, this is when I make my best tips. And I need every cent I can get before college. Financial aid from the government will cover my tuition and my dorm room, but I have to cover my meal plan and incidentals. As it stands right now, I might be able to afford one book.

I refill the coffees of this little old couple that comes here every week. They must be in their eighties, but they always sit on the same side of the booth to work the crossword together. He pats his wife's spotted brown hand and smiles down at her. I used to wonder if that would be me and Kyle one day.

I spend a few minutes listening to a trucker tell me how a concrete truck overturned on I-40 near Knoxville, causing a three-hour traffic jam. No one was hurt, thank goodness.

At around eleven, the hostess seats Kelsey Painter, Vanessa Green, and Savannah Barrow in my section.

Great.

Kelsey grew up in Oakdale with me—her trailer sat two doors

down from mine, and we had a lot in common. We both had single moms, only mine worked nights at the Quick Pick while hers worked days down at the Co-op. Her mom watched Nick and me while we slept, and my mother made sure Kelsey got to school, picked her up, and took care of her afterward. We shared a bed for years—it was like a never-ending slumber party. In all ways except blood, we were sisters.

Until eighth grade, that is, when Kelsey's mom married a man who owns a landscaping business. They moved into a four-bedroom house on the other side of Franklin, and suddenly Kelsey had new jeans and an iPod while I still had the same flip-flops from Walmart and the radio. Every time I hung out at her house, all I could think about was how clean her kitchen was, how I could see my reflection in the stainless steel appliances. I wondered if the trailer park had a smell I didn't notice, because I sure as hell could smell the lemon Pledge and dryer sheets in her new home.

Going there made me so uncomfortable, so unsure of myself, I stopped accepting her invitations to spend the night. Then she joined the cheerleading squad and became friends with the new girl, Vanessa. By the time high school rolled around, we didn't have much in common, and we started arguing over little things, like when I accidentally lost a T-shirt of hers. And I didn't have as much time to hang out anymore since I'd started dating Kyle. Then a rumor went around that Kelsey had a thing for him and I started dating him anyway. I never knew she liked him. If I had, I wouldn't have dated him. If your friend—your *sister*—likes a boy, you don't date him. But by the point the gossip started, Kelsey and I hadn't spoken in months. Why give up the boy I was falling in love with for a friend who ditched me for the new girl? Besides, if the rumor was true, spending time with her could be super awkward.

None of that made Mom too happy; she didn't like that I spent all my time outside of school with him and working at the Roadhouse and never really had girlfriends after that.

"A boy should fit into your life—not become it. High school is when you start to define yourself. Don't define yourself as the girl who has a boyfriend and nothing else."

Problems with Kelsey aside, Vanessa has been nice to me this year. Some days I feel well enough to talk to her in study hall, and we partnered for a history project on pirates.

I pull a deep breath through my nose and charge toward their table, where they're looking at menus and talking loud enough for the entire restaurant to hear them.

"I want cheese fries to start!" Savannah says.

"But I won't be able to try on clothes later today," Kelsey whines. "I'll get bloated."

"I don't trust anybody who doesn't like appetizers," Savannah says matter-of-factly.

I pull a pen from behind my ear. "Hey."

Vanessa and Savannah look up and smile. "Hey!"

Kelsey studies the menu and doesn't acknowledge me. Figures.

All three girls look slightly disheveled, wearing last night's mascara. Their hair is messy and curly, falling out of pinned up buns on top of their heads.

"What's with the hair?" I ask.

"Prom," Savannah says.

Oh yeah. Prom. Now that I think about it, I did see some sparkly girls eating in another section last night. "How was it?"

"Use your imagination. It was a Wild West theme in the cafeteria," Kelsey mutters.

"I wish we could've convinced the school board to let us have prom at a hotel this year," Vanessa says. "Why do they always assume we'll get hotel rooms, have sex, and drink?"

"That's what *you* would do," Savannah teases. "Seems the school board knows what they're talking about."

"You got a hotel room last night!" Kelsey replies.

Savannah's cheeks turn pink. "And you didn't?"

"No, because she's still in a guy drought, remember?" Vanessa says.

"Can I get y'all something to drink?" I interrupt, not wanting to hear about this *guy drought*, whatever that means. "Want an appetizer? It's on me." Anything to get out of this conversation.

"You're the sweetest," Vanessa says, and they order Diet Cokes and the calorific cheese fries. I rocket to the vestibule, enter the order in the computer, and start filling glasses with ice. When I drop off their drinks and get their entrée order, they're talking about graduation and the senior class cruise that's the same night.

"We're going shopping for graduation dresses this afternoon," Vanessa says to me. "You should come with us."

"Vanessa!" Kelsey hisses at her, but Vanessa waves her off.

"I have to work," I say quietly, not really caring about graduation, which is a month away. Mom cries happy tears every time it comes up in conversation, like when I had to order my cap and gown, but to me it's any other day.

"What time do you get off?" Vanessa asks, checking the time on her phone. "We can wait."

I glance at Kelsey, who's still ignoring me. "Three?"

"Cool," Savannah says. "We'll come back and meet you. Then we can drive over to the Galleria."

Maybe it would be nice to have a new dress for graduation. But if I'm being truthful, I can't afford a thing from the Galleria, and I'll probably end up wearing the "perihinkle" dress Kyle loved. Mostly I agree to go because my heart pounded harder when I heard the girls laughing about how they took their prom limo to the drive-thru at McDonald's. I bet that was fun. Shopping could be fun too, and distracting.

As promised, they pick me up at 3:00. Kelsey sits in the front seat and doesn't even turn around to say hello when I slip into the backseat. Fine by me. The girls start chattering about what kinds of dresses they want, about how they went to the roller-skating rink in their fancy prom gear last night, about how excited they are for graduation, about college.

A Middle Tennessee State course catalog arrived in the mail the other day. I'm starting there in August, but I haven't even ripped the plastic off the catalog yet. The college is only about half an hour from Franklin, which is good. It makes me happy I'll be so close to my mom and brother. But that's about all that makes me excited. I mean, I can't bring myself to care about whether I'll take math or politics. College just feels like the next step I'm supposed to take. I'll go to classes, one day I'll get a job doing something, and I will be able to support myself and not live in a trailer park. But the rest of my future feels hazy. Without *him*, why does any of it matter?

At the Galleria, we head straight to Nordstrom and pick out a bunch of outfits to try on. Kelsey carries a rainbow of dresses to the fitting room.

Savannah has been training to be a horse jockey for the past year, and even though she can eat like eight plates of cheese fries, she weighs nothing, doesn't have much of a chest, and is super short. All the dresses hit below her knees. "Jesus! I look like an old lady!" She throws a dress over the fitting room door. Vanessa looks gorgeous in all of the dresses she tries on—the universe blessed her with supermodel genes. Kelsey and I have about the same body type: medium.

"God damn!" Savannah exclaims, and another dress goes flying. Vanessa bursts out laughing at her. I find myself chuckling too.

I strip off my Roadhouse polo shirt and jeans, which smell like onions. I pull a light blue dress off the hanger and try it on. It fits fine. When I turn to the side, I notice my waist is slimming down and my legs are trim. Running over twenty miles a week is bringing big changes to my body.

Vanessa eyes my dress. "That's cute."

I love her green silk dress with spaghetti straps. "Yours is great too."

With a dress under each arm, Kelsey is texting a mile a minute. She speaks as she jabs buttons on her cell. "No, Colton, you can't come dress shopping with me. You. Are. A. Boy."

Still wearing the dresses we tried on, Vanessa and I wander barefoot back out onto the department store floor to browse the racks again.

She holds a silver sequined dress to her chest. "Listen, I wanted to talk to you. I saw in the school newspaper that you're going to MTSU this fall. Right?"

"Right…"

"Are you living in the dorms?"

I was planning on it, considering that's all my financial aid will cover. An apartment off campus seems too much a luxury. "Yeah."

"So am I."

"You aren't getting an apartment?" A lot of kids do that, and Vanessa doesn't hurt for money.

She gives the dress she's holding a dirty look and pulls another from the rack. "My brother is making me stay on campus freshman year. And I'd rather not live with a complete stranger..."

I check the price on a pink halter dress I'd never wear. "Mm-hmm."

"Kelsey and I are getting an on-campus place with her cousin. It's a two-bedroom suite with a little kitchen and a bathroom. But we need a fourth person."

I feel a silky blue skirt. "Uh-huh."

"Would that be something you'd be interested in?" Vanessa asks.

"What?"

"Would you consider being my roommate?" she asks, chewing her lip. "Kelsey and her crazy cousin, Iggy, will be in the other bedroom."

"I didn't know Kelsey had a cousin Iggy."

"It's her stepdad's niece. Apparently their parents are insisting on them being roommates."

I stare across the store at Kelsey. She's browsing through a rack of dresses, throwing confused glances my way. I doubt she likes hanging around me any more than I like being around her.

On the one hand, I don't relish the idea of ending up sharing a dorm room with a crazy girl who sports a faux hawk and plays the accordion or something. I also like the idea of starting anew.

But being with Kelsey doesn't feel new. It feels like reawakening something I want to forget.

When I look up into Vanessa's eyes, they are kind and waiting for an answer.

"That could be good," I choke out.

"So you'll think about it?" She sounds excited. Truth be told, the idea kind of excites me too. It also terrifies me.

"Don't you think Kelsey will be pissed? I mean, would she go for this?"

Vanessa shrugs. "It's my bedroom. I can choose to live with whoever I want."

"When do we need to decide by?"

"July, I think," she says.

"Let me talk to my mom and I'll get back to you," I say, making her smile.

Vanessa yanks a red mini dress off the rack. "This would be great for you for the senior cruise."

I take the mini dress from her. It would look good with my strawberry blond hair. Last year, before Nick and Kimberly left for their senior cruise, Mom snapped a billion pictures of them. She made my brother pose by the birdfeeder, on the porch, by the oak tree. Kyle and I stood off to the side, snickering at Nick's misfortune.

"We'll be posing by the mailbox next year," Kyle said, wrapping his arms around my waist, my back to his front. I settled against his chest, and he kissed the top of my head.

Here in the now, I sigh and hang the red dress back up.

• • •

During lunch, I stop by the table where the student council is distributing graduation caps and gowns. The boys will wear black and the girls get red. With my hair, I'm glad it's not mustard yellow.

I stuff the cap and gown into my backpack, which suddenly feels very heavy. I glance around at the other students, and it's hard to believe that in less than a week, I may never see some of these kids again. We won't come back together after spending our summer at the city pool and cruising around town. Jared Campbell is joining the army and going to basic. Brooke Taylor, the best violinist our school's ever seen, will study music at Brevard in North Carolina.

Soon I'll only see these people online.

I pass by the table where Kelsey, Vanessa, and Savannah are chatting with the guys. If I decide not to room with Vanessa, would I ever see her and Kelsey again? I mean, the school I'm going to has, like, 30,000 students. That's a sea of people. We only have about 500 kids at Hundred Oaks. Savannah says something and everybody at the table bursts out laughing.

And I feel lonely.

I've often wondered if Kelsey and I hadn't grown apart when she moved, would I have been a part of her group? Along with Vanessa and Savannah, she hangs out with Colton Bradford, the mayor's son; Rory Whitfield, one of the cutest guys at our school;

and Jack Goodwin, the heir to Franklin's largest horse farm. With my trailer's ratty orange carpets and the gross brown spot on our counter, how could I invite guys like that over to eat pizza and watch a movie? I know they must be down to earth, because Savannah works on Jack's farm and they are dating, but still. The people Kelsey left me behind for make me feel inferior in all sorts of ways.

I used to eat lunch with Kyle, his best friend, Seth, and Seth's girlfriend, Melanie, but I haven't since Kyle died. In terms of dealing with what happened to my boyfriend, I've heard that Seth is doing about the same as I am: he doesn't want to play video games with anybody else; he shoots hoops alone.

When I walk past their table, Seth looks up and nods. Even though he knows Kyle and I made up and agreed to start dating again right before he died, Seth isn't rushing to invite me to sit down. Another day, same story.

At least it's Wednesday, which means I have my personal workout with Matt tonight at the gym. I never imagined I'd be that girl who comes to love working out, who craves it like a cop wants a donut. But I can't figure out if I like being active or if it's that I love working toward something. Regardless, I haven't even run the race yet and I'm already missing the structure this program brings.

I glance around the cafeteria again as I pop open my Diet Coke. Good luck posters from the juniors hang everywhere.

High school is over. I take a sip of my drink. The more I think about it, what I love most about the running and exercising is the control. I have complete control over me, my body, my future. Which is something I haven't felt since he died.

And I want to keep that feeling.

I find myself barreling across the cafeteria to Kelsey and Vanessa. Their group glances around at each other when I walk up to their table. Kelsey bends her head and whispers to Colton, ignoring me. When Jack Goodwin sees me, ever the gentleman, he immediately stands to offer me his chair.

"Thank you," I tell him. He smiles as he steals a chair from another table.

I take a deep breath and lean over to Vanessa. "I've been thinking about college. If you haven't found a roommate for your suite yet, and you still want me…I'm in."

Marathon Training Schedule~Brown's Race Co.

Name *Annie Winters*

Saturday	Distance	Notes
April 20	3 miles	*I'm really doing this! Finish time 34:00*
April 27	5 miles	*Stupid Running Backwords Boy!!*
May 4	6 miles	*Blister from HELL*
May 11	5 miles	*Ran downtown Nashville*
May 18	7 miles	*Tripped on rock. Fell on my butt*
May 25	8 miles	*Came in 5 min. quicker than usual!*
June 1	10 miles	
June 8	9 miles	
June 15	7 miles	
June 22	8 miles	
June 29	9 miles	
July 6	10 miles	
July 13	12 miles	
July 20	13 miles	
July 27	15 miles	
August 3	14 miles	
August 10	11 miles	
August 17	16 miles	
August 24	20 miles	
August 31	14 miles	
September 7	22 miles	
September 14	20 miles	
September 21	The Bluegrass Half Marathon	
September 28	12 miles	
October 5	10 miles	
October 12	Country Music Marathon in Nashville	

THE TIME OF YOUR LIFE

The radio said this is the first Hundred Oaks graduation to take place indoors in twelve years. Normally students graduate out on the football field, but this year it's in the gym because the rain hasn't let up in four days.

Last year, we had to write a thesis paper for junior English. To determine paper topics, students pulled prompts out of a hat. I chose "Can Coca Cola save the Third World?" which was awesome. Kyle, however, chose "Did the Great Flood actually happen?" I made fun of him, but he ended up loving the assignment. He learned that some Indian tribes believed Noah didn't build an ark; they thought an evil god was eating peanuts in heaven. The god scraped the shells out the window, they fell to earth, and mankind survived the flood by floating in the shells.

Even rain makes me think of him.

In the cafeteria, teachers line us up in alphabetical order to take our seats. Mrs. Lane just made Zack Burns put on a new graduation cap. He wrote IT'S OVER! in silver paint on top of his, but apparently that's against school rules. The minute Mrs. Lane turns her head, Zack makes jerking-off motions to his friends. Do boys ever grow up?

The teachers lead us into the gym like we're back in kindergarten again and a rush of humidity hits me in the face. The gym feels like a sauna. I spot Mom and Nick on the third row of the bleachers. Nick is fanning himself with a program and she's dabbing at her eyes with Kleenex. Regardless that we aren't the same *team* we once were, this is a big moment for her: both of her kids made it through high school. She never graduated because she got pregnant with my brother. Seeing her tear up makes my eyes water, and I scrunch up my face to hold myself together. I don't want to cry. If I start, I won't stop.

I sit in my chair and pick up my program. The cover says *In loving memory of Kyle Allen Crocker.* People throughout the gym are using their programs as fans, just like my brother. I peer through the audience to see if Mr. and Mrs. Crocker showed up. No sign of them. I doubt they'll be here. If they come, the floodgates in my eyes will crumble.

I run my fingers over Kyle's name, and a single tear falls from my eye, spotting the paper. I can't cry. I can't. Haven't cried in months. *Breathe in through the nose, out through the mouth.* I bite into my lower lip hard. So hard I break skin. Taste bitter blood. *Think of happy times. Think, think.*

If he were here, I bet he would've found a silver marker and wrote something on his hat in the middle of the ceremony, just to piss off Mrs. Lane. He would've launched a beach ball into the crowd like Nick and Evan did at their graduation. *Think more, Annie.*

This gym has a lot of memories. I first met Kyle here when I smashed him in the head with a volleyball. Thinking about it now makes me laugh, and since I'm struggling not to cry, it comes out as a snort.

"You okay?" Leslie Warren asks. I'm with other people whose last names begin with W. We had French together.

"Just thinking about how much has happened in this gym in the last four years."

She grins. "Remember during the first football pep rally this year, how the senior guys played tug-of-war against the guy teachers?"

"That was hilarious," I reply with a laugh. The senior boys had been strutting around for days boasting how they were gonna kick some teacher ass, but then they got owned by the teachers. The guys toppled to the floor like bowling pins.

Our ceremony begins with lots of raucous cheering and clapping, and a rumor goes around that crazy Zack Burns is completely naked under his robe. That makes me laugh *and* cringe.

The evening grows more somber during the speeches. During his valedictory address, Mark MacCullum says, "Kyle Crocker was friends with everybody. He always wandered around the cafeteria, talking people up and eating food right off their trays. He also was a pen thief."

Murmured laughter brushes through the crowd. It doesn't really matter what Mark's saying, because everyone is remembering their own Kyle stories. I glance down the aisle to where Kyle's best friend, Seth, is crying.

Even the people who didn't know him are silently weeping. Maybe not for him specifically, but for what Kyle lost: the chance to have experiences, good and bad and crazy and life changing. They feel sorry his mother and father lost their son. And maybe they start thinking of losing their own parents or children or brothers and sisters and how that feels like darkness, a hole that can never be filled. And if they've never lost somebody, what will it feel like when they do? When you finally watch your loved one being lowered into the ground, away from you forever. Before October, I couldn't have fathomed it.

I felt immortal.

Guilt builds up under my skin, because Kyle's the one who lost out on not being here at graduation. Never getting married or having kids. Never buying a house out on Normandy Lake, where he could live on a sailboat on weekends, doing nothing but swimming and snuggling up with me under sunsets. He's the one I should feel sorry for. But I feel bad for me too. Because I can't enjoy my future knowing he's missing out.

• • •

Later that night, I curl up in bed with my phone. I should be getting to sleep considering I have a ten-mile run/walk tomorrow. Matt told me I could skip the run and make it up with him on Sunday since I graduated today. But I told him it was no big deal. It's not like I'm going on the senior cruise.

The entire class is out on the General Jackson Riverboat on the Cumberland tonight. I went back and forth on whether to buy a ticket, and ultimately I didn't. In twenty years, will I look back on this night and wish I'd gone? There's nothing on that boat for me. Sure, I could pose for pictures with Vanessa and Savannah, but then they'd go dance with their boyfriends and I'd be left alone. Kelsey would ignore me…and guys would ask me to dance, and they wouldn't be Kyle. The entire time I'd be thinking: *I'm here, and he's not.*

My mind flashes to junior prom when Kyle and I left an hour early, before Mom would get off work at the Quick Pick. We rushed back to my place and made love, then wrapped ourselves up in my bed sheets. We sat Indian style and talked about the road trip to Myrtle Beach we would take that summer. And I kept thinking, *He is all I could ever want. He's the guy for me. He's my fate.*

But when Kyle laid it out for me and asked me to marry him, I—we screwed everything up. Why couldn't he have waited until after graduation to ask? Or after I graduated college?

If he'd just respected my wishes about college, he'd still be here.

I pull Instagram up on my phone and watch pictures from the cruise pop up. Cute, colorful dresses and dark suits fill my screen: a selfie of Vanessa Green and Rory Whitfield leaning against the boat's railing; a photo of Savannah Barrow and Jack Goodwin kissing in the middle of the dance floor.

I wipe away the tears threatening to roll down my cheeks. Feel a sudden urge to go grab some beers and drink my loneliness away. I'd do anything to make my mind go blank. I stuff my phone under my pillow. Grab the photo of me and Kyle from my bedside table and turn it face down.

Twenty years, my ass. I'm already wishing I'd gone on the cruise.

•••

The next morning, I see him stretching next to the 0 mile marker.

Jeremiah.

He pulls his arm back behind his head and stretches his triceps, causing his T-shirt to ride up, revealing strong stomach muscles. Stubble covers his cheeks and jaw, and his light brown hair is a disaster. When he sees me, a grin breaks across his face, and after last night's loneliness, I'm glad to see it. Really glad.

I adjust my CamelBak as I approach him. "How many miles you doing today?"

"It's a big one," he says. "We're shooting for twenty. And Charlie, the guy I'm pacing, wants to finish in less than two and a half hours."

"Good luck," I say. "I bet I couldn't even ride a bike twenty miles in that amount of time. I could drive it though."

We laugh together and smile. I don't look away from his pretty blue eyes.

"What?" he says, his mouth quirking up.

I shake my head. "Nothing."

And then my finger reaches without my permission and gently traces the long, white scar on his arm. Then I move to the mysterious circle tattoos on his forearm.

"What are these?"

"Crop circles. I saw the design and just went for it. You like them?"

Very much. "Yeah," I say with a thick voice. He watches me touch his skin, and I see his Adam's apple shift. He stops watching my finger and his light blue eyes move to my lips, then chest, then legs. And a queasy feeling rushes through me, sort of a mixture of excitement and feeling like I'm standing on a plank, fixing to tumble into crashing waves.

I stop touching his arm and look away.

"Well," he says, clearing his throat. "Have a good run today." He meets up with a buff-looking guy, takes off on the trail, and disappears within seconds.

Matt gives our team instructions. We're to run/walk ten miles, which means we run as much as we can and take walking breaks when we need to.

"None of you have the endurance yet to run a full ten miles," Matt says to the group. "But I want you to get used to the long distances, so we're going to walk a lot today. Don't push yourself into running too much, okay?"

I've never gone that far before. What happens if I get stranded five miles out on the trail? Will Matt have to cart me back somehow? How embarrassing would that be?

Matt makes us warm up by doing this ridiculous move called "Ali jumps" where we jump around and pretend we're boxing like Muhammad Ali, and then I jog out onto the trail, my sneakers smacking the dirt. Then it's just me and ten miles.

What was I thinking, touching Jeremiah's arm like that? He must think I'm a complete Creepy McCreeperson. On the other hand, he did patch up my blister and give me a Little Mermaid Band-Aid when we were complete strangers.

But isn't that what we still are? Strangers? Sure, he gave me a ride to my car, and I know a few tidbits about him, like he's twenty and only his grandparents call him by his full name, but I still don't know anything real. Is he in college? I never see him with friends, but I did see his Delta Tau Kappa frat T-shirt. Is he a party animal or just addicted to running and working out? Why is Matt giving him a chance? A chance for what?

I take a sip of water and focus on my feet. Point my toes forward. Swing my arms like scissors. Breathe in through the nose, out through the mouth. Pray for the running to make me forget I skipped my senior cruise. I manage to run six miles, but then have to slow to a shuffle walk. I'm proud I made it this far.

Right about then, Jeremiah and his client flash by. I can't believe they're already on their way back in on a twenty-mile run! Damn, he's fast.

I figure that's the last I'll see of him today, but at mile marker 2, I see his wicked smile approaching, his long hair bouncing all over the place. Again that urge to dig my fingers in it. When he rejoins me, he slows to a pace matching mine. He finished a twenty-mile run, then came back out to run with me? He must be certifiable.

"What are you doing here?" I ask, wheezing.

He takes a long sip from his water bottle, looking at me sideways. "I was thinking about you."

I suck in a gasp, scramble for air. I was already panting in the humid morning, but now I can't breathe at all.

His breathing slows to steady, because maintaining my pace is nothing for goddamned *Superman*, and when we reach the wooden footbridge that marks mile 1.5, Jeremiah gently takes my elbow and leads me off the path and way down to the stream. Wait, I shouldn't leave the trail without Matt's permission—and I haven't finished my run yet. But the break sure is nice. Floppy willow tree branches cocoon us, offering much needed shade. Pink, yellow, purple, and blue flowers explode everywhere, like in a psychedelic dream—or *Willy Wonka*.

"It's hotter than blue blazes outside," he says.

I wipe sweat off my forehead. "That water is tempting."

"Let's jump in." He grabs me and starts to pull me toward the water—and I pound on his chest and giggle like a seventh grader.

"Jere—no! If I get wet, I'll have to run back in soggy clothes and I'll get chafed—"

"Wouldn't want that."

"I'd finally get to take your brother up on his kind offer of Vaseline."

"I'm gonna pretend you didn't say that."

My hands switch from pounding on his chest to tentatively exploring it. He's strong. I miss resting my head on a solid chest. I move my fingertips in tiny circles. His eyes flash. He takes my hands, weaving his fingers in mine. Leans forward. Steals a kiss.

He pulls back and searches my face—for what I don't know, and once the shock wears off, I find myself up on tiptoes reaching to return the kiss.

My arms and legs turn against me. My knees sink and he has to grab me to hold me up. His tongue teases mine. I clutch the hair at the nape of his neck. Cup his cheeks with my hands, enjoying the way his stubble scratches my skin.

Our hands are everywhere. He pushes the CamelBak off my shoulders and unclips his water fanny pack thing, letting both drop to the ground. At first I try to push him away because my underarms are sweaty—hell, everywhere is sweaty, but he won't let me go and then I don't care. I don't care about anything but his hand on my jaw and the other kneading my hip. His lips trail over my ear and neck, then hungrily find mine again. He tugs my bottom lip between his teeth and bites until I moan.

God, these kisses are hot, his mouth hard, then soft, then wanting. We lie down on the grass—it's still slick with morning dew, and still kissing me, he presses his body to mine, rocking his hips in a rhythm until I'm seeing spots. It's been so long. So long since I've felt this good, with a guy's heavy comforting weight above me and my body on fire. I let out a sob.

Gasping for breath, he pulls himself to his knees and settles between my legs. "Annie." He swallows. "You okay?"

"Don't stop."

I reach for his waist and we tug at our running clothes until they're heaped beside us. His toned body is sculpted like a statue, and when I set my chin on his shoulder so he can kiss my neck, I discover another tattoo on his shoulder blade—it's a black lightning bolt superimposed over a black circle.

And then his hand dips between my legs. I let my body relax, and he gives me what I didn't know I needed so bad. I cry out and he quiets me with his mouth, kissing me until I feel sated all over, like after a Sunday afternoon nap. I don't think a thing till I feel him pushing against me.

"We don't have a condom!" I whisper loudly, and his eyes pop open and he rolls off. From the corner of my eye, I watch him wipe the sweat from his face and clench his eyes shut. Shit, what was I thinking? I'm not on the pill anymore. I don't know this guy. I haven't even told him my last name. He's not my boyfriend. I don't love him. He's not Kyle.

Another sob, a different kind from before, builds in my throat.

I rip away from him and work to turn my clothes the right side out and jerk my panties and shorts back on. I untangle my sports bra, shove it over my head, and force my arms through the holes. Slap away the blades of grass stuck to my knees and elbows.

"Annie?"

Ignore him.

"Sorry, I got carried away. You're just so pretty," he says, grabbing his T-shirt up from the dirt and wiping his hands with it. "I never do it without a condom. Seriously, I'm sorry."

So he does stuff like this often? I've only kissed one other boy my whole life. I yank my sports bra down over my chest and reach for my tank top.

Following my lead, he dresses quickly, even though he's still raring to go, if you know what I mean.

"Please don't tell my brother about this," he says with a distressed look toward the trail. "I can't mess things up this time. Please don't say anything."

"I won't," I snap, more at myself than at him. He looks taken aback, running his hands through his hair, swallowing.

I leave him behind, hurry back onto the trail, and resume my glacial pace. And of course, two minutes later, he overtakes me, darting through the tunnel of trees, leaving me in his dust, streaking toward the sun.

• • •

At home, I rush for the bathroom.

I peel my damp, sweaty clothes off and let them fall to the tile floor. My panties come off last.

Kyle's laughing voice rings in my mind. *"I don't care what kind of underwear you wear as long as I can get them off you."*

Even so, I always wore cute lacy sets anytime I knew we'd be together. I wanted to feel pretty for him.

I look down at the plain white panties I wore today. They're good for running—they keep wedgies at bay—but they certainly don't make me feel pretty. They make me feel gross. I *am* gross. What I did today was skanky and selfish.

I wanted to *feel* something new, to connect with someone, but all I feel is more confused. And scared. Tired. More alone than when I go to the drive-in by myself.

I turn the shower nozzle to ice cold and climb in. Water rains down on me and I pray it will make me clean. "Forgive me," I whisper.

Guilt changes as you get older. I cheated on a spelling test when I was eight and beat myself up over it for months. No matter how hard I scrubbed, I kept imagining the correct answer was still written on my hand in black ink. Then, freshman year, Kyle touched me down there for the first time on the school bus on our way back from a field trip to the Cumberland Science Museum. He draped his jacket over my lap, unzipped my jeans, and made me feel like a totally new girl. It was exciting until I got off the bus and started freaking out mentally. Was Kelsey looking at me funny? What if someone saw us? What if a rumor went around and people at school made fun of me? What if it got back to Nick? What if he told Mom? What did it say about me that I let my boyfriend touch me in a public place? Was I dirty?

There are levels of guilt, and today I entered the big leagues.

I lean my head against the shower tile as water pounds my back.

I doubted I'd stay single forever. I mean, I want to have kids one day, and that generally requires a partner, but I never thought I'd nearly have sex with a stranger. And that I'd do it on the trail where I'm training to honor my boyfriend.

I turn the water up as hot as it will go, burning my skin scarlet red.

Today's run forced the thoughts out of my head, but they're screaming back now. *Jeremiah. Kyle.* I wish I could go back in time to that Sunday night. Silent sobs begin to shake my body.

When I first heard, I couldn't sit still. Scrubbed the dishes. Poured Halloween candy into a dish. But an hour later, the shock wore off and I cried hysterically. Mom and Nick took turns holding me, to rock me to sleep. But the sleep didn't come.

To get through the funeral, Nick gave me a tiny white pill. It calmed me down enough to sit through the service and hold Mrs.

Crocker's hand as they flashed pictures of Kyle on the wall. I'll never forget how his six-year-old brother Isaac asked his father why I was crying so bad, and his father choked out, "Because she's never gonna see Kyle again." He was too young to understand what was happening, and the more I thought about it, I didn't understand it either.

Nick never told me what the pill was exactly or where he got it. As homecoming and Thanksgiving came and went, I begged him for another tiny white pill because I was so sick of crying. But he said it was a one-time deal. That winter, every time tears filled my eyes, they leaked into my throat and caused a cold. I was sick from November to January. Then I decided I wasn't going to cry anymore. I was too angry. Angry at Kyle for leaving me here all alone, for not taking me with him. Angry at the universe for not hearing my pleas: *Take me, not him. If I can just have him back, I'll say yes this time. Yes, I'll marry you.*

Angry I didn't get to say good-bye.

Today is the first day I've truly cried since. I feel guilty for having shivers when Jeremiah smiled at me. I like how he took care of my blister. Made me laugh. Mostly I loved that glimmer of hope I felt for just a second.

That second before I remembered Kyle would still be here if I hadn't refused him.

PART II

The Last Summer

CROSS-TRAINING

Four Months Until the Country Music Marathon

"Today, I want y'all to do the entire run without walking."

At this announcement, a few people gasp and two women who always run together give each other looks. Matt is giving our team instructions for today's nine-mile run by Marks Creek. Sure, we've gone that far before, but we were allowed to walk. Even so, an older man quit our team after the ten-mile training session. It's getting more and more intense.

"I can run that far as long as I'm chasing him," the lady next to me mutters.

I laugh. We've been running on Matt's team for three months, but I didn't gather the courage to ask her name until a couple weeks ago. It's Liza, and she's definitely older than Matt. I don't think she really *like* likes him. She just likes looking at him. Who wouldn't?

Matt makes us stretch and drink another cup of water before heading onto the trail. I start the run easy and gradually increase my speed as I go along. Having cool weather in June is weird, but I'm grateful for the breeze. I'm also grateful I took a few ibuprofen before the run started. I've found my legs don't hurt as badly when I take it.

When I hit the 4.5-mile marker, Matt's assistant Bridget passes me lemon Gatorade without asking. After three months of training, she knows my preferred flavor. "Are you feeling okay, Annie?"

I work to get my breathing under control. "Yeah."

"Good. Get going."

"I'm not allowed to rest while I have my d-drink?"

She smiles. "Nope. Matt wants you to learn how to run and carry a cup at the same time. You'll be doing that during the race. Just throw the cup away when you see a trash can."

Grumbling, I hop back on the trail, finish the drink, and toss my paper cup. Check my watch. Think about my foot placement. Swing my arms. Breathe, breathe, breathe.

This is the first time we've run this route, the Cumberland Bicentennial Trail. When I told Mom where today's session was, she said, "I've heard the spring dogwoods over there are beautiful." My mother does know a lot about plants even though she has a black thumb. And she was right about how gorgeous this trail is: pink and white flowers are everywhere. It's like Valentine's Day exploded.

Soon I don't have anything else to concentrate on. So I think about the real reason today's run is freaking me out. I haven't seen Jeremiah yet. And he didn't call.

After last week's run, after we hooked up, Jeremiah waited for me by my car. My thoughts were jumbled like multicolored gumballs in a jar, but I was coherent enough to give him my phone number when he asked for it. He gazed around the parking lot before punching the number into his cell. Was he looking to make sure Matt didn't notice? His brother was dead serious about Jeremiah not hooking up with his clients. But he did it anyway.

At the time, I figured he was interested, and I wasn't sure how I felt about that, but it turns out it didn't matter. Why ask for a girl's number if you aren't going to use it? Did he ask because he felt some sort of obligation? Or because he felt guilty? Did his brother find out and get pissed? Is that why he didn't call? I'm pissed at myself for caring. I'm not sure why I do. Probably to give myself a reason not to feel so skanky.

"Gah!" I say to myself.

"What's up?" a voice says. I nearly say the corny joke Kyle always said in response to *What's up?*

Helicopters! he'd blurt.

When I turn to find Liza jogging up next to me, I'm really glad I didn't say *Helicopters!*

"Did you hurt yourself?" she asks.

"Nah. Just talking to myself."

She laughs and nods. "Running definitely gives you lots of time alone with your thoughts. I'm sure I'll be talking to myself soon."

For the past three months, I've had a hard time maintaining the same pace as other people on my team. Either they're too slow for me or I'm too slow for them, but today Liza and I manage to stay together for several minutes. It would be nice if I had company for today's final four miles. It would be nice if I didn't have to run the entire marathon alone.

"How old are you?" Liza asks.

"Eighteen."

"You seem older," she says, looking me over. "You're very mature."

"Oh yeah?"

"My older sister has a couple of teen girls. I went to their house for Mother's Day and my nieces giggled for an hour about absolutely nothing."

When I went shopping at the Galleria with the girls a few weeks ago, we ate a snack at the cookie store, where Vanessa and Savannah giggled for like ten straight minutes about these cookies with Justin Bieber's face on them. I still don't know what was so funny about that.

"How old are you, if you don't mind me asking?" I ask.

"Thirty-two," she says with a sigh.

"You seem younger." That makes her smile. She's very glamorous, with brown curls, full lips, and fancy sunglasses specifically for running. I wanted a pair of those, but I had to decide between them and gas for my car.

"So why are you running a marathon?" Liza asks. "You're the youngest person on our team by a long shot."

I look at her sideways and pull a deep breath. The only person who knows why I'm here is Matt—Coach Woods told him—and I want to keep it that way. When I don't say anything, I guess she takes a hint because she changes the subject.

"I just moved to Nashville in January. I'm from New York."

I've never driven that far north before. "Wow, that's a big move."

"My law firm transferred me down here for a major case."

"And you have time to run?"

She glances over for a sec, then averts her eyes. "I don't really know anybody except people at work. I needed to get back in shape and I wanted a fun way to meet people, so here I am." She wipes sweat off her forehead. "But it's getting harder and harder to make the time for these long runs. Last weekend, I was so pooped after that ten-miler that I just went home and watched TV the rest of the day. I didn't do any work. I better be careful or I'll lose my case."

"Running d-does take up a lot of time."

"You know what the worst part was, Annie? I was watching that movie *Sweet Home Alabama* on TNT. The one with Reese Witherspoon? And I was so tired, I bawled like a baby when Reese gets back together with her sexy ex-husband."

I smile at Liza. I like her personality, and her rambling keeps me nice and distracted.

She goes on, "I guess the movie got to me—the whole realizing-who-your-true-love-is stuff and all that." Liza suddenly goes really quiet, and I get the feeling she has more to say. "The training is good. I'm finding that it's healthy for me to get away from the office. It clears my thoughts."

"Running does that for me too."

Liza chatters on about the case her law firm transferred her for. It's a huge sexual harassment lawsuit filed by a bunch of women at a nationwide communications company.

"I can't discuss the case specifically," she starts, "but let me tell you, Annie, I never thought I'd have to use the word penis so much."

She says it matter-of-factly, and it occurs to me that she wouldn't be telling me about her job unless she thought I was mature enough to hear it. I smile.

"Hello," a voice says. I look over my shoulder to find Andrew, this tall, middle-aged guy on our team. Instead of wearing a fanny pack, like Liza, or a CamelBak, like me, he carries a thick, plastic water bottle in his hand. He falls into step beside us.

"You're gonna get in trouble with Matt for wearing those headphones," I tease.

"Why are all you ladies so into him? *Matt says this, Matt says that*," Andrew jokes.

"Um, have you seen him?" Liza asks.

"He's not my type," Andrew says. "I'm into short, curly-haired brunettes."

God, is he hitting on her right in front of me? She raises her eyebrows at me, and I shrug. He's okay looking, I guess, for somebody who could be my dad.

Matt jogs up next to us. Andrew yanks his headphones out, hides them under his shirt, and Matt smirks and shakes his head.

"Annie, let's finish your run together," Matt says. "We need to talk."

I gasp. Does he know I hooked up with Jeremiah last week? My body tenses.

"You have to breathe while you're running or you'll pass out," he says.

I remember to breathe.

"C'mon, Annie," Matt says. "Let's do some speed bursts. They'll make you stronger." He gestures for me to pass Liza and Andrew, and then he shoots off like a bottle rocket. "Let's go!" he calls, and I sprint after him.

He makes me run at full speed for thirty seconds. Goddamn it makes my legs burn. I'm panting when he lets me return to a jog.

"Control your breathing," he says.

In through the nose, out through the mouth. Breathe. Breathe.

"Good," he says. "Now let's jog for a bit and then we'll do some more bursts."

I give him my *I'm-totally-freaked-out* face.

"You can do this, Annie. I'm pushing you because I know you can do it."

After that speed-burst thing, the jogging *is* easier. But I can't do another one of those bursts. It hurt!

"Relax your arms and shoulders," he says, shuffling beside me. "Let that stress go. It's holding you back."

I roll my shoulders and shake out my arms.

"So I wanted to talk to you—"

And my arms and shoulders tense right back up.

"This week, you need to do speed bursts every day when you run. And I want you to start adding more peanut butter and eggs to your diet. You're getting too skinny and you need to eat more as we start doing longer and longer runs."

Is this what he wanted to talk about? Peanut butter and eggs?!

"I can do that."

He gives me a smile. I'm guessing he doesn't know.

"Ready for another sprint?"

I shake my head. He shakes his head back at me. "Let's go, Annie. Pick it up."

I jet forward through the dogwood trees. Matt stays with me the entire sprint, urging me on. We do three more sets of bursts. They make my chest ache like crazy—my heart doesn't like the repeated starts and stops. Somehow I make it to the finish line, and with sweat dripping down my face, I kneel to the ground.

"C'mon, Annie," Matt says gently. He helps me to my feet. "You did great. Seriously great."

I roll my shoulders and swallow. I glance around to see if Jeremiah's here. He's not.

Matt squeezes my arm. "Relax. Let all that tension out."

Let go, I tell myself.

Let go.

• • •

I barely make it to the toilet before I throw up again.

I had to stop two times on the way home to vomit by the side of the road. I kneel and clutch the toilet seat, breathing deeply. I get sick again. Then again. Why is my stomach so screwed up? Those sprints today made me feel worse than when I first tried to run around the track, when Coach Woods caught me running like a baboon. At least I took those ibuprofen. How bad would I feel if I hadn't?

The bathroom door creaks open to reveal Mom standing there with a towel. She squats next to me and pats my back as I get sick. The lactic acid built up under my skin makes me feel tingly, and not in the good way. If I can't even run nine miles without feeling this awful, how in the world will I make it to twenty-six?

"Did you finish your run?" she asks quietly, patting my face with the towel.

"Yeah. Nine miles."

"Wow. He would've been proud of you."

"Mom, don't. Not now."

I feel her tense up next to me, and we both look away. I hear her sniffle. I feel bad for snapping at her, I really do, but does she have to bring Kyle up *now*?

"I can't help it," she says. "I just know he would've been amazed. Never talking about him isn't healthy, sweetie. You need to let it out."

I lean against the toilet, resting my head on my arm.

"I'll call Stephanie," Mom says quietly, brushing the hair out of my face. "I'll tell her you won't be at work tonight."

"No!" I blurt, and then I get sick again. I clutch the toilet and hate my stomach. Hate it. "I need the money."

"You can't wait tables like this. People like it when their waitresses are healthy."

She's right. If I show up at work all sweaty and red faced and getting sick every two minutes, Stephanie won't let me wait tables anyway. But if I don't go in, I'll lose out on at least $75 in tips. This is my big moneymaker night!

"Mom," I cry. "I won't be able to afford my training. I won't be able to save money for college. I've only got like three hundred dollars right now."

She pulls me over into her arms and hugs me. "I know, baby. But you can't go to work like this. I wish you didn't put so much pressure on yourself...I wish I could pay for everything. You know I would if I could."

I know. I know.

• • •

My alarm clock blares like a fire alarm.

I reach over and slam the snooze button. 5:00 a.m. I got off work at midnight, and now I have to drive to Nashville to go run seven miles? Or as Matt and Jeremiah would call it, a rest day.

The alarm goes off again. There's no way I've snoozed for five minutes already! I groan into my pillow.

The aftermath of last Saturday's run, in which I got sick for four straight hours and missed work, was so spectacularly bad I haven't run all week. I skipped my three short runs and didn't ride my bike to cross-train like I was supposed to.

If I run the seven miles this morning, will I get sick and have to call out of work again? I can't risk missing work again this week…I won't be able to pay for training, much less the gas to get to training. And what about supplies for college, like new sheets, towels, books, and stuff to cook with?

My stomach hurt so bad last week…I don't want to feel that pain again.

When the alarm goes off for the third time, I reach over and turn it off, then burrow back under my sheets.

The next time I wake up, it's to my phone ringing. The clock says it's 7:05 a.m. Matt's name flashes on the screen. Shit. I should've called him.

"Hello?" I say groggily, picking the sleep out of my eyes.

"Where are you?" he asks in a rush. "Are you okay?"

"Umm…I'm sorry, I fell back asleep."

"Are you sick?"

"No…"

"Are you hurt?"

"No."

"Then why aren't you here? Everybody else is."

That makes me feel ashamed. "Look, I'm sorry. I woke up and wasn't feeling up to the run."

"You should've called me."

I yawn into my hand. "You're right. I will next time."

"There won't be a next time if you don't take training seriously, Annie."

"What?"

"You don't show up for my training sessions, I won't train you. It's simple as that."

"Why not? I mean, I'm paying for it."

A long silence. "Annie, you're running on my team, under my name. Every single person I've trained who's made it to the day of a race has finished. I've helped over two hundred people finish a race. If a client doesn't take me seriously, I don't train them. I want to keep my one hundred percent race-day success rate."

"I get it—"

"Now do you want to tell me what's wrong? If something's wrong with the training, we can adjust. If you aren't feeling good, we can adjust. But you have to talk to me, okay?"

I pull a deep breath and clutch a pillow to my chest. "I'm

scared about my stomach. It hurt so bad last week. I got so sick after doing those god-awful speed bursts with you. I threw up like eight times."

Another pause. "We'll change up your diet then. Maybe try some toast and English muffins instead of cereal and oatmeal. Maybe we'll stop giving you Gatorade. The sugar might be making you sick."

"No! I love my lemon Gatorade. I'll give up the speed bursts."

He laughs. "Not a chance. Now, what are you doing tomorrow? You've got seven miles to make up."

• • •

Why can't they just leave it be?

"Do we really have to do this?" I ask.

"It's time," Connor says quietly, looking at one of Kyle's track trophies. How can Connor say that so matter-of-factly?

I swallow as I scan the room. I'm kind of pissed at Kyle's parents for wanting to box up his things. But then I remember how I boxed up the teddy bears and wind chimes he gave me, and I can't imagine walking past this room every day either, so I kind of get how they feel. Probably the same way I do whenever I drive past the fire station.

Kyle's younger brother, Connor, who will be a junior at Hundred Oaks this fall, texted me a few days ago and invited me to come check out Kyle's room, to decide if I want to keep anything.

"I'll be out in the living room if you need me," Connor says. The door clicks shut.

I haven't been in Kyle's room since September, since before he broke up with me. His alarm clock blinks a red 12:00 over and over. I pick up a worn Titans sweatshirt from the floor and bring it to my nose. His scent is gone. It smells like nothing. I fold the sweatshirt neatly and set it on his unmade bed.

I wipe dust off the framed picture of us from junior prom. I set it on top of the sweatshirt, starting a pile. I pat his stuffed bear's head. Kyle had Chuck since he was a baby, and now the bear lives on the bookshelf.

For a while, I'd call Kyle's cell phone just to hear his voicemail message. But then his parents shut it off. I look frantically around the room to see if there's anything I should take in case his parents don't recognize its value. If I had been his parents, I would've kept that cell phone plan forever.

I find a red Nike headband he wore for track and slip it into my back pocket. If I make it to the marathon, maybe I'll wear it during the race. Eighties style.

I sit down on his bed and run my fingertips over his pillow. When I lift it to see if it still has Kyle Smell, I discover a small black velvet box. With shaking fingers I open it to find a gold ring with a small diamond. I gasp. The night at the drive-in when Kyle proposed, he didn't hold a ring out to me. He only said, "Marry me."

The door creaks open and I look up to find Mrs. Crocker, decked out in her apron, the one spotted with a cherry print. Honestly, I've never seen her at home without an apron on— she's always cooking something—but it doesn't fit like it used to. It hangs around her loosely.

"Annie, we're ordering pizza. Do you want to join us for din—" She makes a noise when she sees what I'm holding. She brings her fingers to her mouth. "I'd wondered where he put it. That ring belonged to my grandmother."

"It's beautiful."

"Look under the lid."

I carefully peel the silk lining back and fish out a delicate piece of onion paper. It's so fine, I worry it might crumble in my hand like a Saltine. I slowly open the paper and discover a note dated 1946: *"For Ellen, with all my love, Arthur."*

"That's great," I say with a genuine smile, putting the note back where I found it.

"I'm so happy you found the ring."

I hold the box out to her, and she takes it.

"He would've wanted you to keep this," she adds.

I can't. I wouldn't take it when he was alive.

She must sense my hesitation. "I'll save it for Connor…maybe he'll want to give it to a girl one day."

I clear my throat and nod. Mrs. Crocker opens her mouth again to say something, but she shuts it.

Does she blame me?

That's when Mr. Crocker shows up, wearing a blue T-shirt that reads *Williamson County Fire Department.* He used to have a full head of blond hair, just like his sons, but now it's thinned out.

"Hi, Annie," Mr. Crocker says. "Your mom told us you're training to run the Country Music Marathon."

"To finish on Kyle's behalf." His mother chokes on her words.

I nod slowly, picking at a hangnail, ripping the skin away.

"How's it going?" Mr. Crocker asks, smiling.

I don't have it in me to tell them I got sick as hell after a run, had to miss work, and nearly got dropped by my trainer. Not to mention I'm scared to death of this weekend's eight-mile run. When Kyle was training, he rarely complained and never considered giving up. At least not that I know of.

"I did seven miles last weekend," I say softly. Barely. I had to walk a lot of it.

"Need any pointers? I ran a half one time."

"Have any idea why my stomach hurts all the time?" Even though Matt changed my diet a little this week, I still feel pains.

Mr. Crocker cocks his head to the side. "Never heard that one before."

"Did you want to join us for pizza?" Mrs. Crocker asks.

"I would, but my training plan says I have to eat a grilled chicken salad today."

"I guess we'll leave you to it, then," Mrs. Crocker says, and then I'm alone again, with all his clothes and pictures and tro-phies, with his bed that hasn't been warm in months, with only the sunlight streaming through the window to hug me.

I curl my arms around his pillow. Make myself think about the three-mile run I'm doing tonight after the heat bleeds off. One foot after the other.

Breathe, Annie, breathe.

The Fourth Circle of Hell

Not only does Matt train people to run races, he gives personal training sessions at the gym where he works on the side—or as I like to call it, the Fourth Circle of Hell. During my first session with him, I discovered muscles I didn't know I had. I can't imagine what tortures he has planned for today.

I lean my head into Matt's office at the gym and find him chewing and reading a magazine. He wraps his sandwich back in its baggie, stands up, and high-fives me. "Ready to work out?" he says through a mouthful.

"Yeah."

He chews, studying my face. "You feeling okay? You're all red. Did you hydrate enough?"

"I drank five bottles of water today, like you said to."

"Good."

I let out the deep breath I was holding and follow Matt over to the treadmill, where I hop on and jog to warm up.

Ever since I fooled around with his brother a few weeks ago,

I've been expecting Matt to drop some sort of hint that he knows, but it hasn't happened. I mean, I didn't think Matt would come right out and ask, "Whatever possessed you to hook up with my brother?!" But I expected some sort of reaction—a flash in his eyes or flushed cheeks. Either he has the best poker face of all time or Jeremiah kept his mouth shut.

It's three weeks later, and I haven't even seen him at training. Maybe he decided to use trails where I specifically wouldn't be? He still hasn't called. He won't, and that's just fine.

"Hey!" Matt says loudly over the sound of my feet pounding the treadmill. "Where are you?"

"What?"

"I've been trying to get your attention."

"Sorry, my mind's all over the place today."

He increases the treadmill speed to six miles per hour. "Oh yeah? So's mine. My big sister went into labor an hour ago."

"What?" I shout. "Why aren't you at the hospital? Why are you here?"

Matt grins. "It's her first baby and considering my mom was in labor with all of us for, like, days, I don't think the baby will be here anytime soon."

"So will this be your first niece or nephew?"

"Yeah. It's a boy," he says proudly.

I can't help but smile at his giddiness. "Is your brother at the hospital with her?"

He gives me a brief look, but then he's all business again. "The whole family's there. I'll head over as soon as we're finished." He points at my face. "Don't think you can get out of training."

"Darn."

Matt leads me through a series of lunges and squats and other horrible exercises that make my legs feel like they've been lit on fire.

"You're doing really well, Annie," Matt says when I'm done with a load of jumping jacks. "You think you'll be able to run the full ten miles on Saturday?"

I lean over and rest my hands on my knees, panting. "I'm gonna try...but, Matt?"

"Mm-hmm?"

Every week the runs get harder and harder. I sleep more and more. More aches and pains pop up every day. I should go ahead and buy a lifetime supply of ibuprofen at this rate.

Do I have a limit?

"I'm scared that I won't be able to do it all, you know? The last time I ran ten miles, I got really sick."

Matt pats my back. "If you weren't scared, then I'd be worried."

• • •

"Now, who wants to buy the bath mat?"

I groan. It seems bass ackwards that I haven't even picked out which classes I'm taking yet, but I have to decide if I'll supply a crock-pot or an ironing board.

I've been sitting at the Roadhouse for over an hour discussing our college suite with Vanessa, Kelsey, and her cousin, Iggy, a self-proclaimed hipster. She says that anyone who has a bike with more than one gear and claims to be a hipster isn't really a hipster.

Who knew?

When I sat down at their booth earlier, Kelsey's mouth fell open and she glared at Vanessa. "Annie's your roommate?"

"You didn't tell her?" I blurted at Vanessa.

Vanessa looked back and forth between us. "I told you my roommate was coming to meet us, didn't I?"

"You could've told me," Kelsey replied, furrowing her eyebrows. "I have a say who lives in our suite."

"I thought this could be good for all of us," Vanessa said, biting her lip.

"How could living with *her* be good for me?" Kelsey hissed.

My face burned red. "Is this because I live in a trailer?"

Kelsey gave me her *what-the-F* look. "Of course it's not. It's because we're not friends anymore, Annie."

We would be if you hadn't ditched me for Vanessa and spread that rumor I dated Kyle even after you declared your love for him.

"Fine, whatever," I said and got up to leave. Taking my chances with the random roommate lottery had to be better than this.

"I don't want to live with a stranger, Kels," Vanessa whined. "And my brother doesn't want me to either. He'd probably make me keep on living with our papa."

Kelsey looked over at Iggy, who was busy making a house out of sugar packets. "Fine," Kelsey said, and I slowly sat back down, wishing she'd never moved out of Oakdale. If she hadn't, I never would've grown self-conscious and started turning down her invitations to spend the night. I wouldn't have started pulling away from my friend. How would my life be different now if she'd never moved?

An hour later, it's like we're participating in Middle East peace talks.

"I'm not bringing the bath mat," Iggy argues. "I already said I'd bring the shower curtain. I have one with skulls on it."

Kelsey, Vanessa, and I all pause to look at each other.

"I'll get the bath mat," Vanessa says.

"And I'll get another shower curtain," I say.

"Deal," Kelsey says.

"Hey!" Iggy blurts. "I want my skulls!"

Kelsey makes a green checkmark on her color-coded chart that details all the stuff we need to buy for college. Kelsey is bringing everything with an orange checkmark next to it, which so far includes the coffee maker, a broom, and cleaning supplies. Vanessa is green and Iggy is blue. My color is purple. An assortment of Kelsey's colored Sharpies is fanned across the table in a straight line.

"How did you get the name Iggy?" Vanessa asks, shoveling more cheese fries in her mouth.

Iggy peers at us through thick glasses and adjusts the leather bands circling her arms. "My parents named me in honor of the night I was conceived. They were at an Iggy Pop concert getting stoned and they did it in a bathroom. And here I am."

Uh, okay.

Chewing, Vanessa stares at Iggy for a long moment. Kelsey ignores her cousin, seemingly used to such remarks. How in the world is the former head cheerleader of Hundred Oaks High stepcousins with Iggy the self-proclaimed hipster?

At least I'm sharing a bedroom with Vanessa at college.

"Can we get more cheese fries?" she asks me, gesturing at the empty white plate in front of us.

Anything to get away from this table. I jump to my feet and take my time walking over to the vestibule, where I find my manager, Stephanie.

She grins and I give her my *don't-mess-with-me* face. "Can I have another order of cheese fries?"

"Hell, I'll give you free New York strips if you want 'em. Your mom will be so happy to hear you're hanging out with friends."

I lift a shoulder. "We're making plans for college is all. Nothing big."

"I'll get those fries right out to you," she says, pushing me in the direction of our table. Damn. I'd been planning on loitering in the vestibule until the fries are ready. I slip back into the booth as Kelsey is checking her phone.

"I swear, that boy texts me for every little last thing."

"Who?" I ask.

"Colton."

"What did he want this time?" Vanessa asks.

"To let me know he's awake from his nap."

Vanessa looks at me out of the corner of her eye and gives me a sly grin. Huh. Does Colton have a thing for Kelsey? When she and her mom moved in with her new landscaper husband, Colton became her new next-door neighbor. They've been hanging out for years, but I thought they were just friends.

Kelsey puts her phone away. "Who wants to bring the plunger?"

This goes on for a while longer until Stephanie appears with the cheese fries and some potato skins. Vanessa grins widely, and I wonder where she's putting all this food. She's as thin as one of these fries.

Vanessa pops one in her mouth and dusts the salt from her fingers. "We need to discuss suite rules."

"Like whether or not we're allowed to cook fish?" Iggy asks.

"Fish?" Vanessa says, crinkling her nose.

"I know from my job at the library that some people *are not okay* when you cook fish in the microwave. It has a certain odor," Iggy explains.

"O-kayyy," Vanessa says. "No, I was not talking about fish, but we can definitely add that to our list of things *not to do* in the suite."

Kelsey turns to a new section in her leather planner and writes

"Rules of the Suite" in red Sharpie at the top. "I'll record the rules and email them to everyone for your reference."

Vanessa leans over and whispers in my ear, "This is why I asked you to share a room."

"Agreed," I say.

"I was actually talking about having 'significant others' stay overnight in our suite," Vanessa says. "We need to work out some ground rules."

"I'm not even at college yet and I'm already being sexiled," I mutter.

"I say that none of us can have a guy spend the night more than twice a week," Kelsey says.

"But what if Rory comes to stay on a three-day weekend?" Vanessa asks. "He's going to college two hours away!"

"You'll have to decide which two nights matter more," Kelsey replies.

"You can always pitch a tent in the woods and sleep outside with your boyfriend," Iggy says. "I have one you can borrow, but it might have a slightly fishy smell."

Vanessa points at Kelsey with a cheese fry. "Only two nights? You need to get laid, my friend."

Kelsey points at Vanessa with a green Sharpie. "I'm in a guy drought. You know that."

Vanessa mutters to me, "Maybe she wouldn't be in a guy drought if she'd just jump Colton already."

"I have a great guy I can introduce you to," Iggy tells Kelsey. "His name is Chevy Ernesto and he publishes his own newspaper, *The Nashville Newsmonger*. He sells it every day outside Food Lion."

My mouth falls open. Kelsey ignores her cousin and focuses on punching numbers into her planner's built-in calculator.

"I say we make up a signal to let each other know if we have a guy in our bedroom," Vanessa says. "We can tie something to the doorknob, like a necktie or a jump rope."

"What if someone steals the jump rope and we walk in on something we don't want to see?" Iggy asks, pushing the glasses up on her nose.

"Who would steal the jump rope?" I ask.

"Anti-hipsters."

Vanessa and I are now shaking our heads at each other.

"Is there anything else we're missing from our supply list?" Kelsey asks, dragging a pen down a sheet of paper. "If not, I'll email a copy of the list to everyone for your reference—"

I start laughing and find I can't stop, like when Vanessa and Savannah giggled about that Justin Bieber cookie for ages.

It feels good.

Marathon Training Schedule~Brown's Race Co.

Name *Annie Winters*

Saturday	Distance	Notes
April 20	3 miles	I'm really doing this! Finish time 34:00
April 27	5 miles	Stupid Running Backwords Boy!!
May 4	6 miles	Blister from HELL
May 11	5 miles	Ran downtown Nashville
May 18	7 miles	Tripped on rock. Fell on my butt ☹
May 25	8 miles	Came in 5 min. quicker than usual!
June 1	10 miles	Let's just pretend this day never happened...
June 8	9 miles	Evil suicide sprint things. Ran w/ Liza. Got sick.
June 15	7 miles	Skipped Saturday's run..had to make it up Sunday.
June 22	8 miles	Stomach hurt again. Matt said eat granola instead of oatmeal.
June 29	9 miles	Matt says it's time for new tennis shoes.
July 6	10 miles	
July 13	12 miles	
July 20	13 miles	
July 27	15 miles	
August 3	14 miles	
August 10	11 miles	
August 17	16 miles	
August 24	20 miles	
August 31	14 miles	
September 7	22 miles	
September 14	20 miles	
September 21	The Bluegrass Half Marathon	
September 28	12 miles	
October 5	10 miles	
October 12	Country Music Marathon in Nashville	

Today's Distance: 10 Miles

Four Months Until the Country Music Marathon

Kyle wasn't my type.

Right before the Welcome Back Dance freshman year—the night of our first date—I stared in the mirror and swiped on mascara, wondering if I should cancel. I'd said yes because he put me on the spot. And he was kind of cute, I guess, if you liked short boys with short blond crew cuts. Which I didn't. I liked tall skinny guys with floppy hair. Nick made fun of Kyle, saying he was too angelic looking and should go join a boy band immediately. If my own brother didn't think Kyle was good enough for me, what would other people think? I'd always figured that people determined what kind of person you are based on who you date, whether you're cool or pretty or not so attractive. It's not nice, but it's true.

At the dance, Kyle and I sat on the bleachers and talked, and he paid no attention to the guys goofing around, jumping to touch the rim of the basketball hoop. He didn't check his phone once all night. I hated when people did that. He stayed tuned in to me, and the more I considered him, it didn't matter that he wasn't gorgeous, that he wasn't tall. I honestly don't know what clicked in my brain that night at the dance. Something just told me—*this guy is nice; he treats you well. His smile is bright like a waking sun, peeking over the horizon. Who cares what other people think? Just give him a chance.*

I did, and I never got bored with him. It seemed we always had something to talk about. He'd love hearing about my marathon training. It's strange to have something new I'm excited about and not be able to tell him.

Matt doesn't want us to get bored on our runs either, so he changes up our long-run locations nearly every weekend. For our second ten-miler, we're running a trail called the Richland Creek Greenway in Nashville. It connects a lot of the trails to each other, sort of like an interchange. You can tell the Fourth of July was a couple days ago—lots of firework debris and beer cans litter the area. People really partied here, I guess. I partied hard by working at the Roadhouse and making huge tips.

Still, even with the change in scenery, ten miles is a long time to spend alone—I've been thinking about *him* today, even though I try not to.

About half a mile from the finish, I see Jeremiah leaning against a mile marker. I haven't seen him in over a month. How did I miss seeing him on the trails today? Was he coming from another direction and switched onto this trail at the interchange?

As I get closer, I realize his face is bright red and his breathing is rough. I sprint to him.

"Annie, my ankle," he says through gritted teeth.

I drop to my knees and touch his foot, making him wince.

"Shit!" he says. I glance up to find him looking down at me with watery blue eyes. Considering he's got scars all over him and he did crazy races, his ankle must hurt pretty bad for him to have this kind of reaction.

"Are you pacing somebody today?" I ask, looking around for that Charlie guy he works out with.

He shakes his head. "I moved our sessions to Sundays. I was just training myself today—I have a race next weekend," he says quietly.

Did he move his work to Sundays so he wouldn't have to see me on Saturdays or something? *That sure makes me feel good.* It's like he couldn't get away from me fast enough. Was our hookup that bad for him?

"We need to get you back to your brother."

"I can't walk," he whispers. "I don't want to make it worse."

"I'm only a half mile from the end of the trail. I'll go get your brother."

Jeremiah bites into his hand and nods.

"Can I help you sit down first?" I ask, wrapping an arm around his waist. Nodding, he inhales deeply through his nose. I can tell he's in a ton of pain as I lower him to rest on the ground. I yank off my CamelBak and slip it under his ankle, to prop it up.

"I'll be back in a few, okay?" I say softly, then hop to my feet, and I'm fixing to start sprinting when he speaks again.

"Annie."

I look into his blue eyes.

"Thanks."

"Don't mention it." I rush back onto the trail and make a mad dash to Matt. I've never run so hard in my life, not even during suicide sprints at the gym. I imagine Jeremiah wincing and that pushes me even harder. *Run faster.*

When I see the finish line and my teammates cheering, I don't hold my arms up in celebration or yell "Woo!" like I normally do. I run straight into Matt's arms. I'm panting so hard I can't form words.

"Annie, why were you running so hard? You shouldn't push yourself too soon," Matt scolds me.

"Jere," I blurt and lean over, my hands on my knees. "Jeremiah is hurt."

"Where?" Matt asks.

"Half mile that way." I point down the trail. "He can't walk."

"Let's go," Matt says, jerking me toward his truck. "Bridget! Stay with everybody else," he yells to his assistant.

I jog to Matt's truck, hop in, and he drives along the trail, hitting tree branches and running over tree roots all the way to

Jeremiah. When we get there, Matt slams the truck into park, leaves the engine running, and leaps down before I can even get my seatbelt unbuckled. Matt squeezes Jeremiah's shoulder, then immediately starts examining his ankle.

"Annie," Matt says calmly. "Get an ice pack out of the backseat. And an ace bandage. And Tylenol."

I push emotion aside and do everything Matt says, happy to play nurse. I bend down next to Jeremiah and touch his wrist as his brother patches up his ankle.

"What were you doing when you hurt yourself?" Matt asks in a low voice.

"I stepped wrong on a rock."

Matt stops examining his ankle and gives him a long look.

"I swear," Jeremiah says. "I swear." When Matt nods, Jeremiah lets out a sigh, almost as if he was more worried about Matt's reaction than his hurt ankle.

"Did I rip a tendon or break it?" Jeremiah goes on.

"It's just a sprain, I think," Matt says, gently moving the ankle in circles. "We'll know more once we get the X-ray." Matt gestures for me to move closer. "See, Annie? If it were broken, we wouldn't be able to move it at all."

"So it's a sprain?" I ask, in awe of how much he knows about the human body.

Jeremiah wipes sweat off his face. "If it's a sprain, I can run on it next week, then."

Matt nods, but my mouth falls open. "What?" I say. "You can't run on this. You need to get better!"

"I'll push through it."

"You probably can," Matt says. "But you'd better not let Mom find out you're racing on a hurt ankle."

Jeremiah gives his brother a tiny, grateful smile.

"You don't just push through a sprained ankle," I snap. "You need rest and ice. RICE. You know, rest, ice, compression, and elevation. You have to do RICE," I ramble.

"And that's what I'll be doing until next weekend," Jeremiah snaps back.

"I don't want you to get hurt worse," I say, and Matt looks back and forth between us, then gently rests a hand on my arm.

"He should be all right. You did the right thing by coming to find me. You helped him a lot today—he would've been a whole lot worse off if he'd had to hobble back."

"Jere," I say, making fists with my hands. "Don't do this. You should take care of yourself."

His voice is harsh. "I'll be fine."

My mind flashes back. *Kyle flipped the covers back and stepped out of my bed, fumbling for his boxers on the floor. A crack of thunder rocked my trailer. A few minutes later, he was holding a newspaper over his head. He prepared to make a break for his car.*

"Maybe you should wait for the rain to clear out," I said.

He kissed me. "I'll be fine."

But he wasn't.

Jeremiah never called after he said he would. He hasn't made any effort to see me in the past month. And I won't stand by and watch him hurt himself further when there's no reason for it.

"Hope you feel better," I say. "See you around."

I leave Matt to deal with his brother and walk away.

"Annie," Jeremiah calls, but I'm already sprinting, finishing my run for the second time today.

• • •

I sleep in on Sunday mornings.

And by sleep in, I mean I stay in bed until nine.

After working Saturday nights at the Roadhouse, I never get home before 1:00 a.m., and I have to be back at work by ten for Sunday morning brunch. Even if I sleep until nine, my eyes still feel heavy and dry. So that's why I kind of feel like murdering somebody when my phone rings at around seven. I don't recognize the number, but it's a Tennessee area code. No one calls anybody anymore. People send texts. This must be an emergency. Oh hell, what if something happened to my brother while he was camping down at Normandy? I sit up straight and push the answer call button.

"Hello?" I mumble.

"Up and at 'em!"

I rub my eyes. "Who is this?"

"Jere. From the trails?"

"Oh." I so don't feel like talking to someone stupid enough to run on an injured ankle. Or stupid enough to call at—I glance at the clock—7:00 a.m. "I'm sleeping, Jeremiah."

"No you're not," he replies in a slow drawl. "You're talking to me."

I make a face at my cell phone. "I'm fixing to be asleep in about a minute. Now, what's up? Make it quick."

"Why are you still in bed at seven?"

"Because most of us aren't from Planet Krypton. Why'd you call?" I try to keep my voice level, but it comes out totally snarky.

"To say thanks for helping me yesterday…"

"You're welcome."

"…and to see if you want to come over to my house."

"At seven in the morning?"

He ignores this. "My mom is having all her church lady friends over for fried chicken this afternoon, and I was thinking we could crash it. Mom's fried chicken is awesome."

"I don't think that's such a good idea."

"That's crazy. Mom's fried chicken is always a good idea."

I smile slightly, curl back up under my sheets, and pick the sleep out of my eye.

"So how about it? I'll text you directions how to get here. I'd come pick you up but I can't drive today—I need to keep my ankle elevated."

"What you need is a foot doctor. And a head doctor while you're at it."

"I'm fine. The doctor said it's just a sprain. Now, can you be here by two o'clock? If you get here any later, you might miss the best pieces of chicken."

"I work until three on Sundays."

"That's fine. I'll have my little sisters save us some. That's what they're for. I'll make sure you get a chicken leg, I promise."

"Fine," I say, to get off the phone. "I'm going back to sleep."

I hang up before he can say another word and put the ringer on silent. I snuggle back under my covers and fall asleep with a smile on my face. But I wake up two hours later with a frown. I can't believe what I agreed to. Did I really say I'd go over to Jeremiah's house?

Honestly, who makes calls at 7:00 a.m. on Sundays?

• • •

It turns out that Jeremiah's place is forty minutes from mine. He lives over in Bell Buckle, which is on the other side of Murfreesboro, where I'm going to college in August. Forty minutes seems like a long drive to see a guy I'm not that interested in seeing again, so I tell myself I'm going for the fried chicken.

I've actually never been to Bell Buckle before. It's a super rural town that people drive through on their way from Chattanooga to Nashville. I discover there's not much here except for a few gas stations and one of those massive fireworks stores. I've always worried about those. What if the whole place explodes at once? Would you see the mushroom cloud from space?

I turn down a bumpy country road, drive past Bell Buckle Chapel, and come upon a long line of cars. Mrs. Brown must have invited the entire church to her fried chicken fest.

I park beside a ditch and turn off the ignition. Clutching the steering wheel, I blow air out and gaze up at the brick façade. Thank God his house is nothing fancy—the shutters need painting and the sidewalk is crumbling. But the yard is neatly mowed and the tulips pop like Starbursts. Tomato plants and potted herbs are clustered at the edge of the yard.

As I approach the house, I can hear voices coming from the backyard. An old golden retriever with gray whiskers naps on the porch. I climb the steps and discover Jeremiah lounging on a swing with his leg propped up. I didn't know he wore glasses—they make him look sort of rugged geeky. He's drinking an iced tea and reading the comics page from the Sunday paper. A thick ace bandage is wrapped securely around his ankle; his other foot is bare. I've never seen his face so smooth before. Did he shave for church this morning?

Glancing up from his newspaper, he smiles at me and takes his glasses off, hooking them in the neck of his T-shirt. "Annie."

He sets his tea and comics on a side table and makes a grab for his crutches.

"No, no, don't get up," I say, waving a hand. He leans back against the swing, all the while scanning my jean shorts and tee I changed into after work.

"I didn't think you'd actually come," he says, folding his arms behind his head.

"Well, you did say it would be a mistake to miss your mom's fried chicken."

He laughs. Then there's a long silence. I squat to scratch the dog's ears. Its collar reads *Maggy*. Her eyes blink open and she sniffs my flip-flops.

"Thank you for helping me with my foot yesterday," Jeremiah says. "I would be a wreck next weekend if not for you."

"What is this big race?" I ask.

"The Sparta Marathon reenactment over in Sparta. It attracts a lot of runners because sometimes people wear gladiator clothes. First prize is five thousand dollars."

"Holy crap. Were you supposed to win or something?"

He waves a hand. "Nah. But I might could come in third or fourth, or win my age group. And there's money in that. Five hundred or so. I make most of my cash at races. Matt doesn't pay all that well."

Then why does he want to work for his brother? Just to spend time with him?

"And this is how you make money?"

He smirks. "It's better than working at McDonald's."

"But you're hurt…" I look at his bandaged ankle.

"I'll take care of my foot all week, and I'll be just like new for the race. I run through injuries all the time."

"You really just run for money?" I ask.

"I love it too," he says. "I love any kind of rush...hang gliding, BASE jumping..." He pauses to take a slow sip of tea. A grimace flashes on his face, but I doubt it's 'cause the tea is bitter. I can smell the sugar.

That's when the screen door opens and a little girl with Jeremiah's light brown hair appears. She rushes over to him and he kisses her forehead. It reminds me of how my brother kisses my forehead and takes care of me.

"You brought a girl over?" She gapes. Before Jeremiah can respond, she sticks a hand out to me. "I'm Jennifer, Jeremiah's favorite sister." I smile at how direct she is.

"Nice to meet you."

"Where's our fried chicken?" Jeremiah interrupts teasingly.

"I got it, I got it. Hold your horses," she says. "Who's your friend?"

"I'm Annie."

She swivels to face Jeremiah. "Is she your girlfriend?"

"Mind your own business! Go get our chicken, munchkin."

His sister bursts out laughing, clearly pleased she's gotten under her brother's skin. I remember teasing Nick like this when he first started bringing girls around.

Jennifer darts back into the house with Maggy the dog loping after her, leaving me alone with him. It's peaceful out here. The wind blows lazily, jingling the wind chime and rustling the grass. I breathe the warm air in through my nose. This house has no memories of my life, of high school, of Kyle. This place is just *blank*. I like that, the feeling of nothingness.

Jeremiah pats the seat next to him. I sit down and sway back and forth on the swing, listening to church ladies bustling about the backyard.

The screen door swings open and a woman appears on the front porch. "Jeremiah, your sister said—" She takes one look at me, one look at him, then rubs her eyes. I sneak a glance at Jeremiah. He's gazing at her head-on.

"Mom, this is my friend, Annie."

Oh, we're friends now?

Then Matt crashes onto the porch, throwing me a worried glance. "Mom, I need to talk to you. Now."

She gives me another look, then disappears inside. Matt nods at his brother and me before following his mom. What happened to southern hospitality? If this were Kyle's house, his mother would've offered me lemonade and invited me in to chat about my college plans and my work at the Roadhouse. Jeremiah's mother didn't even say hello.

"What was that about?" I ask.

He plays with the glasses hanging from his shirt collar, hesitating. "My summer break from college started a few weeks ago and I moved back in. My mom didn't want to let me live here again… but Matt convinced her I won't upset her."

I can't imagine my mother not wanting me to come home. "How would you upset her?"

"She just didn't want me around my little sisters until I figured some stuff out…and, well, my family's too important to me to fuck everything up again…"

I'm not sure I want to know what's going on. I have enough to deal with. But what could it be? Drugs? No, he's too athletic for that. Steroids? He doesn't look totally muscle man.

When the screen door opens again, Mrs. Brown gazes down at Jeremiah's injured ankle, then approaches me with an extended hand. "Hi, Annie dear. So nice to meet you."

"You too, ma'am," I say.

"I'd love to talk but I have guests." She gestures toward the backyard.

"No problem, nice meeting you," I reply as she leaves as quickly as she arrived. What in the world? I mean, clearly Matt intervened, but what did he say to her? And why was she so distant and somewhat rude at first?

Jennifer comes out of the house balancing two paper plates loaded with chicken legs, mac 'n' cheese, and biscuits. Jeremiah rewards his little sister with another kiss, and she runs off toward the back of the house.

"She's sweet," I say.

Jeremiah bites into his biscuit. "She's only nice to me because I'm her ride to ballet."

I smile at how much he loves her, then take a bite of fried chicken. I groan as it melts in my mouth.

"It's good, huh?" he says, and I nod. We chow down in silence. A freight train chugs by in the distance, and when the sound dies away, I hear him clearing his throat.

"I didn't just invite you over to say thank you for yesterday," he says softly.

"I know. You invited me for fried chicken."

He looks up at me and shakes the hair out of his eyes as he chews. He swallows and takes a deep breath. Wow. I didn't figure a guy like Jeremiah ever got nervous. "I wanted to say I'm sorry about what happened between us on the trails last month."

"It's fine—"

"No, it's not. I let things get out of hand..." Since when do guys fess up for having one-night stands? Or in our case, a one-morning stand. Does that mean he didn't want to hook up with me? That makes me feel relieved...and a bit let down at the same time.

He drags a hand through his light brown hair. "After what happened between us, I was a little freaked out but really happy, and I asked Matt about you. Yeah, he doesn't want me dating any of his clients, but I wanted to ask you out anyway—you're totally worth the risk...and then he told me why you're running a marathon."

I don't want him to spoil this peace I've discovered here. A place that has no memory of Kyle. "Jere, don't. What happened between us was my fault. Please stop talking."

He holds up a hand. "Let me just get this out. I'm so sorry, Annie. I've felt like shit since that day. I feel like, I dunno, I used you or something."

"You didn't. It's fine," I say, even though it's not.

He stretches his leg out and flexes his ankle. Then he speaks quietly, "I've thought a lot about you since we kissed…Honestly, I've thought a lot about you since the moment we met—"

"You didn't call," I say bluntly.

He nods sheepishly. "I wanted to ask you out. I couldn't stop thinking about you—you don't know how many times I started to text you but didn't push send…I figured you were madder than a wet hen that I didn't call, but my brother said I'm the last thing you need right now…It sucks what happened to your boyfriend."

I look up at him. People usually say "I'm sorry, I'm sorry, I'm sorry," and I get so sick of hearing that. It's nice hearing Jeremiah tell the truth: it sucks. That's all there is to it. Living with a hole in my life blows.

We finish our food, then he takes my paper plate and sets it on the little, wobbly table with his iced tea glass and newspaper. He looks at me sideways. "So if I were to call you—"

"You already did call me, remember? You woke me up at the ass crack of dawn and somehow convinced me to come check on you and your foot."

He grins. "But if I called you for real…"

I clutch the swing, thinking of what happened on the banks of the Little Duck, how Jeremiah's lips and hands set me on fire. But he waited an entire month to give me this speech. What if he waits another month before calling me again? Not to mention he's into extremes and has that big scar along his jaw. That's the last thing I need right now. I need white bread. I need vanilla. I don't need a guy who hurts himself running on an injured ankle.

Speaking of extremes, I've seen Jeremiah naked, but this is only, like, the fifth conversation I've ever had with him. And the first *real* one. He is the weirdest guy I've ever met.

Jeremiah scooches closer on the swing, and with a finger and thumb, he lifts my strawberry blond braid and brings it to his lips. Does my hair smell like onions from the Roadhouse? He shyly presses his forehead to mine and his warm breath sends tingles down my neck. God, he smells good, like cologne and boy and the sun.

God, he's making a move on me. I'm not ready for this with anybody. Plus, we're not even alone. His little sister and dog are buzzing around. Not to mention his mom has a bunch of church ladies over. I press a restraining hand to his chest. "I can't do this right now."

"So I shouldn't call you then?"

"You already did, genius."

"But for real…"

I don't know anything about him. I don't know if I want to get close to somebody ever again. "Maybe. I don't even know you. I need time…"

He searches my eyes, then nods. "Fair enough." He wobbles to his feet and grabs the crutches leaning against the house. "C'mon. Let's go play some Ping-Pong."

• • •

I serve.

Jeremiah hits the Ping-Pong ball back toward me. I bite into my lower lip, working to concentrate. I slap it to him, and he rears back and wallops the ball. I lunge to the right but I miss. The ball rockets off the table and into a corner of the basement.

"Yesssss." Jeremiah does the *Rocky* pose. "Another point for me."

"Goddammit," I mutter. Jeremiah's playing Ping-Pong, standing perfectly balanced on one foot, yet he's still beating me. This is stupid. He's going to hurt himself worse. I tried to talk him out of playing, but he's too thickheaded.

I dig the ball out from under a dusty shelf and throw it back to him. He catches it with one hand. He leans his head back and tosses the ball up to serve, and the basement door squeaks open and feet pound down the stairs. Jeremiah rushes to set his paddle down and grab his crutches.

"Don't mention we were playing!" he whispers to me.

His little sister appears along with a very sophisticated looking girl with long black hair and freckles, wearing diamond studs, short khaki shorts, and a cute tank top. Wow, she's pretty. Is she here to see him?

"See, I told you," Jennifer says to the girl.

She raises her eyebrows at me, then turns to Jeremiah. I start to worry that she's pissed at me for being here with him, but then a sly grin pops on her face when she notices the Ping-Pong ball rolling around on the floor.

"Why are you playing Ping-Pong on that ankle, Jere?" she snaps. "You sit down, right now."

He swallows hard.

"Jeremiah Brown!" a voice shouts from upstairs. His mother.

"Great," he mutters. "Why are all the women in my life out to get me?"

"I need you to jump-start Mrs. Englewood's car!" Mrs. Brown shouts.

"Coming, Ma!" Without another word he crutches up the stairs.

"Hi, I'm Kate," the beautiful girl says, stepping forward. "I'm Jere's brother's fiancée."

I shake her hand. "Matt's?"

"Yep. And you are…?"

"I told you! She's Annie," Jennifer says with a grin.

"I'm Annie."

"We didn't know Jere was dating anybody," Kate says.

Where would she get that idea? A girl can go to a guy's house without doing him or whatever. "We're not dating."

Kate and Jennifer exchange a significant look.

"Jere used to bring girls home a lot," Jennifer says. "But not anymore."

"Oh?" Is he in a girl drought like Kelsey's in a guy drought? Given how cute he is, I find that hard to believe.

"Jenn," Kate warns, but it doesn't do any good because she starts spilling all the juicy info.

"He used to bring girls home all the time, but he wasn't serious about them. And Mama and Daddy got so tired of it they said if he brought one more girl home that he wasn't serious about, Mama would stop cooking for him! And that is *serious*."

"Okay," I say slowly.

"But he brought you home!" Jennifer says, bouncing on her toes.

I take a deep breath. This has been an overwhelming day. An overwhelming year.

Kate clucks her tongue at Jennifer. "Your brother's gonna get you for spilling."

"Er, he doesn't have to know. At least I didn't tell Annie that Mama kicked him out."

Kate shuts her eyes. "Now you're in for it."

"Oops," Jennifer says sheepishly.

"Your mom kicked him out?" I ask quietly.

"Yeah, because he kept getting hurt at contests and stuff—he went to the hospital three times in one month! He, like, broke

121

his arm mountain biking and didn't tell anybody it hurt, and the bone grew back wrong and he had to have surgery to make his arm bend the right way again—"

"Jenn—" Kate tries to interrupt, but Jennifer is undeterred.

"And then he nearly lost his eye when he bungee jumped off this bridge and had to get ten stitches." That explains the thin scar beside his right eye. "Mama said he couldn't keep coming home and scaring her like that," Jennifer says. "So he said he won't do that stuff anymore because he loves me so much and he missed me."

"How long did she kick him out for?"

"I didn't see him for like a year!" Jennifer exclaims. "He missed my birthday party at Pizza Hut. And I had a two-tiered raspberry cake!"

My heart begins to speed up. How damaged is he? I touch my throat, swallow hard, and blink the tears away. I'm excited for college, but also dreading it because I won't see Nick every day anymore. And Jeremiah didn't see his sister for a whole year?

Kate senses my distress, I guess, because she whispers in my ear, "He used to do extreme sports, and he was hurt a lot, and their mom didn't want his sisters seeing him injured when there was no reason for it. But Matt's trying to help him get better."

Is that why he works with Matt? Is that why he was so quick to jump to Jeremiah's aid today out on the porch? How bad was it? He went to the hospital *three times* in one month? He broke his arm and didn't tell anybody? Crazy.

I'm glad when Kate changes the subject. "So, Annie, how did you meet Jere?"

"Running on the trails. When are you and Matt getting married?"

"We're planning on next summer."

"I'm gonna be a bridesmaid!" Jennifer says. "And I get to pick out my own dress. It has to be a certain shade of dark red, but I can pick any style I want."

"Sounds pretty," I say. "You'll look good in that color. Do you have any pictures of styles you like?"

She nods and rockets up the stairs, presumably to get pictures of dresses, and I sigh, grateful for the diversion.

"It's so nice to meet you," Kate says, pulling me to sit with her on the couch. "Are you in college?"

"I'm starting MTSU in the fall."

"Do you know what you're studying?"

"I'm not sure yet actually...Are you in college?" She doesn't look that much older than me.

"I graduated from Belmont last year. Now I'm working as a graphics designer at a consulting firm, like, designing logos and presentation materials."

I tell her about how I met Matt and that he's training me to run a marathon. She's really easy to talk to and asks lots of nonintrusive questions. She reminds me of her fiancé.

Jennifer clomps back down the steps and sits to my right,

drops assorted wedding magazines in my lap, and starts pointing out what she likes.

I tap my fingernail on a cute halter dress. "I think you'd look good in this one, Jenn."

"I like that one too! By the way, did you know I'm an aunt now? I'm the first person in my class at school to be an aunt."

"I heard," I say, smiling. "That's really cool."

"Kate, Kate." Jennifer flips frantically through a magazine. "Show Annie your dress."

Then a girl a couple years younger than me appears in the basement: another sister, Lacey. After introductions, she squeezes onto the couch with us to look at pictures.

Kate finds her dress in the magazine, and we all oooh and ahhh over it. Jeremiah crutches back down the stairs and discovers us laughing together.

"Jere, is Annie your girlfriend? I sure hope so 'cause if she's not, Mama's not gonna feed you anymore," Jennifer blurts, making Kate and Lacey snigger.

"Munchkin, you're in big trouble now." Jeremiah chases her on his crutches, and when he corners her, he lifts her and holds her upside down. She squeals.

And all the girls in the room, including me, blurt at the same time, "Get off that ankle right now, Jeremiah!"

• • •

After all the church ladies have cleared out to go—yep, you

guessed it—back to church, Jeremiah and I sit together at the picnic table in his backyard, playing checkers at twilight. It turns out his mother is a youth pastor and does Sunday night services, but she only makes him attend on Sunday mornings.

"It doesn't matter how many times a week I go," he joked, "I could bathe in an ocean of holy water, and I still couldn't get the sin off me."

Hearing that made me feel more comfortable around him; church has never been my thing—I don't believe in heaven or hell or reincarnation. When this life ends, that's it. Poof. When I was little, dying and being buried underground scared the crap out of me. Riding in the car late at night especially terrified me because the darkness made me think of death. It got to the point where I didn't want to sleep with the light out and Mom finally made me admit what I was scared of. Then she said, *You can't remember the world before you were born, right?*

"Right," I agreed.

"When you're gone, it'll be like before you were born. Everything'll be okay, sweetie."

That made me feel better—at least to the point I could deal with it without shaking, but whenever I think about how I'll never see Kyle again, this sick feeling rushes under my skin and I wish I could believe in something bigger, but I'm too much of a realist.

I really should have gone home already, but Jeremiah said, "Stay and play checkers with me. I'll give you some cherry cobbler."

I like bribes that involve dessert. I scoop a bite into my mouth and push a checker forward.

"Sorry about all the drama today," he says, jumping one of my white pieces. "It's pretty standard in the Brown household."

"I can't believe I lost at Ping-Pong to a guy on one foot. I better not lose to you at checkers."

"I reckon we'll find out."

"I hope you're not one of those guys who lets a girl win to make her feel good."

A smile flashes on his face as he spoons cobbler in his mouth. "Never."

I jump over his black checker and he retaliates by jumping three of mine in one turn. I lay my head down on the picnic table. "Damn."

He laughs. "I wish we'd bet on our game now. I could make bank playing you."

"If we were bowling, I'd totally be beating your ass."

He smirks. "Oh yeah?"

"Yeah."

We play the game in a nice silence. Crickets chirp. Warm wind rustles the green trees. It baffles me that we're doing this all backwards: we nearly had sex last month and I've already met his family—his dad grinned at me and firmly shook my hand—but I still know next to nothing about him except that he's addicted to extreme sports. Where does he go to school? What's his favorite book? Favorite movie? And most importantly, do I even want to know these things? I'm not sure. Things must've been pretty bad for his mother to kick him out of the house and his little sister not to see him for an entire year, and like I said, I need white bread, not hot sauce.

But did he feel lost like I do? I haven't seen Kyle in eight months and it's like looking into a black hole.

"Your sister told me your mom asked you to move out," I say.

He nods. "When you were in the bathroom, Kate told me what Jennifer told you. I don't mind that you know…I mean, my brother told me what's going on with you."

I guess it's only fair. "I don't mind that you know about me either."

Our eyes meet for a moment. I briefly wonder what he's thinking, but then I find out. He jumps me twice, ending the game. He pumps his fist, gives me a wicked smile, and I let out a low groan.

"I should be getting home," I say, sliding out from the picnic table.

"Stay." Again, his wicked smile. "Want to play some hide and seek?"

I laugh. "I have to run tomorrow morning 'cause I'm working the night shift."

"Trying to beat the heat by going early?"

"You got it."

"Well," he says, running a hand through his hair. "Maybe I'll call you sometime?"

"For real this time?" I say with a laugh.

"For real."

When I drive away from his house with a plate of leftovers Kate wrapped up for me, he waves good-bye with one of his crutches. It's like a robot arm.

I plan out tomorrow's running schedule and meals in my head on my way home. I think about which of my running clothes are clean and which are dirty. I have one sports bra that fits really well and one pair of underwear that never ride up. I hope they're both clean, because I'm running five miles in the morning. My goal is to finish in less than an hour.

But soon I'm out of running-related stuff to obsess about. So I think of Jeremiah. Will he call this time? Do I want him to? At a stoplight, I look over at the empty passenger seat. When it was my turn to drive, Kyle would massage my thigh, kiss my neck at stop signs, and suffer listening to the country music station, just because he knew I loved it.

Spending time with Jeremiah was good—great even, but the risk of caring is too high.

A friend. He can be a friend, but nothing more.

When I pull into my driveway at home, I check my cell and get my answer about whether he'd call. He texted: You really think you can beat me at bowling? Name time and place.

Marathon Training Schedule~Brown's Race Co.

Name _Annie Winters_

Saturday	Distance	Notes
April 20	3 miles	I'm really doing this! Finish time 34:00
April 27	5 miles	Stupid Running Backwords Boy!!
May 4	6 miles	Blister from HELL
May 11	5 miles	Ran downtown Nashville
May 18	7 miles	Tripped on rock. Fell on my butt ☺
May 25	8 miles	Came in 5 min. quicker than usual!
June 1	10 miles	Let's just pretend this day never happened...
June 8	9 miles	Evil suicide sprint things. Ran w/ Liza. Got sick.
June 15	7 miles	Skipped Saturday's run..had to make it up Sunday.
June 22	8 miles	Stomach hurt again. Matt said eat granola instead of oatmeal
June 29	9 miles	Matt says it's time for new tennis shoes.
July 6	10 miles	Jere got hurt.
July 13	12 miles	Finished in 2:14! Only had to use bathroom once ☺
July 20	13 miles	
July 27	15 miles	
August 3	14 miles	
August 10	11 miles	
August 17	16 miles	
August 24	20 miles	
August 31	14 miles	
September 7	22 miles	
September 14	20 miles	
September 21	The Bluegrass Half Marathon	
September 28	12 miles	
October 5	10 miles	
October 12	Country Music Marathon in Nashville	

IT'S ON

I knew I was in trouble when he brought his own bowling ball.

Who has their own bowling ball?!

Until tonight, I hadn't seen Jeremiah in a week and a half. Against my advice, he ran on his injured ankle and managed to come in sixth place overall, which is just crazy, and based on how he's bowling now, you'd never know he had a sprained ankle. He's beating me 138 to 72. I guess he and Matt somehow knew it would be okay for him to run.

I step up to the lane and eye the pins. I bring the ball to my chest, step forward to roll, and Jere blurts, "Focus, Annie!"

The ball veers sharply to the right. Gutter ball.

"I can't believe you distracted me!" I snap, charging over to wait at the ball return.

He holds his palms up. "I never said I played fair."

After he bowls his second strike of the night, he pumps his fist and I groan.

He doesn't even look like a bowler. I wore khakis and a polo, because I like to dress the part, but he's wearing a gray knitted cap and a white T-shirt. Cargo shorts hang off his hips. Slacker.

He took me to an alley where they do "Cosmic Bowling," which basically means they light the place up with glow in the dark stars and burn incense. Cheesy, yeah, but my inner geek thinks it's pretty awesome.

We're on to the seventh frame. I lift my pink swirl ball and charge up to the lane. I hurl the ball as hard as I can and manage to knock down six pins. "Yessss." Now, to see if I can make the spare.

Waiting for my ball to reappear, I notice the couple to our right. Both seem more interested in their phones than bowling—or each other, for that matter. I hate it when people do that. I glance over at Jeremiah. He's busy wiping his bowling ball with a cloth like it's his most prized possession.

My ball pops out of the chute. I take a deep breath before my turn. I'm gonna ace this spare.

"Don't psych yourself out," Jeremiah says from behind me.

I whip around and point at him. "Quiet, you!"

He drags fingers across his lips, closing his mouth with an imaginary zipper.

Okay. I get in the zone, aim, and roll the ball down the lane. I clasp my hands together and pray for the other four pins to fall. I knock three down easy, but the fourth rocks back and forth like a bobblehead. I jump up and down trying to knock the pin loose, but it rights itself. "Dammit, dammit, dammit!"

When I turn to face Jeremiah, his hands are folded behind his head and he has a smug smile on his face.

"I'm really starting to hate you," I say.

"Who, me?"

"I'm a great bowler! I should be winning."

"But you're not."

I flop down in the seat next to him behind the computer. "Why am I playing like crap tonight?"

"I don't know. It's just simple physics."

"Just simple physics? You ass."

He claps his hands once. "Well, it's my turn."

He leaps to his feet. As he's prepping to bowl, I creep up behind him on tiptoes. He bites his lip, lifts the ball to his chest. And that's when I charge at him and yell "Bugaboo!"

"Ahh!" he screams, but manages to throw the ball anyway. It sails down the lane and knocks seven pins over.

"Gah!" I exclaim, kneeling to the floor. "Why do you have to be so good at everything?"

He puts out a hand to help me up, pulling me to his chest. "Aren't you glad we didn't make a friendly wager on this game?"

That's when I see them. Kyle's best friend, Seth, and his girlfriend, Melanie.

They are three lanes down from us. Seth's ball falls to his side when he sees I'm here with another guy, standing so close I can hear his breathing. Smell his soap.

I rush to step away from Jeremiah, tripping over my bowling shoes, and he gives me a weird look. Seth approaches me, focusing on something over my shoulder. Is he studying Jeremiah?

"How's it going?" Seth asks.

"Not bad," I say quietly. "You?"

He nods slowly. "Kyle's parents told me you're running a marathon. That's really cool."

"Thanks."

"I kinda wish you'd told me. I would've started training to run it with you."

I slip my hands into my back pockets, not knowing what to do with my hands. When I don't respond, Seth says, "My mom was thinking about starting a collection for your marathon. Like, asking people to give a dollar for every mile you run and then donate the money to the fire department in Kyle's name."

I pinch the top of my nose and sniffle. It's nice that people believe in me, but what if I don't finish the race? I don't want to let them down. Besides, this is something I'm doing for Kyle, not for anybody else. I guess it's selfish that I want to keep this marathon all to myself. But it's kind of like the last time I'll be with Kyle—the last hurrah we never had.

Seth clears his throat. "Well, I guess I'll see you around. I'll be there to cheer you on. At the marathon."

Jeremiah walks up behind me. "Is everything okay here?"

I feel a sudden urge to rush into the bathroom, but I stand

up straight. "Seth, this is Jeremiah. Jere, this is Seth. He was best friends…" I can't get the words out.

"Annie's boyfriend was my best friend," Seth says softly.

Sadness flickers in Jeremiah's eyes as they shake hands. Seth sizes Jeremiah up. What's he thinking? That Jere is nothing like Kyle? Sure, Kyle was a runner too, but he combed his hair and knew what a belt is. The thought makes me smile to myself.

"I better get going," Seth says, looking from Jeremiah to me. "See you, Annie."

As soon as he's out of earshot, Jeremiah stares me down. "You all right?"

"Fine." My throat feels scratchy.

He glances over at Seth putting on his bowling shoes and lifts a hand as if he's going to squeeze my shoulder, but suddenly adjusts his knitted hat instead.

"Tell you what," he says. "Let me finish beating you at bowling, and then I'll treat you to a Blizzard at Dairy Queen."

I scowl at him. Then agree to the Blizzard. I do like the kind with Snickers in it.

• • •

Jeremiah decides to order a chicken sandwich and a large fry in addition to a Reese's Blizzard.

"I thought you said you already ate," I say.

"I had supper, but this is my late-night snack."

I roll my eyes at his ripped, six-foot-tall frame. "How do you maintain your girlish figure?"

He grins. "You know how it is with running. It's like I can't eat enough. I'm always hungry."

"I know what you mean."

"My brother says that with my training schedule and working as a pacer, I should eat at least 6,000 calories a day."

That's amazing and disgusting at the same time. "Since I started running, I've been eating two jars of peanut butter a week."

He leans in toward me. "I bet I could eat four jars."

I take a step back. "You don't have to beat me at everything, you know."

At my skittishness, he adjusts his knit cap and focuses on the Dairy Queen worker scooping fries into a paper sleeve.

We get our order and sit at a table outside, watching cars drive by on the four-lane. The summer air warms me like a hug. I scoop Snickers Blizzard into my mouth and lick the spoon dry.

"My brother said you just graduated high school?" Jeremiah asks, biting into his chicken sandwich.

"This isn't fair. You have an inside way to find out stuff about me. I don't know a lick about you."

Chewing, he looks up. "What do you want to know?"

"What else do you do besides race?"

"I go to school at MTSU. I play intramural soccer for my fraternity. I like watching TV and reading the newspaper."

He lifts a shoulder, his face turning a bit pink. "That's about it, I guess."

"I'm starting MTSU this fall."

His expression changes when he hears I'll be going to his school. He finishes chewing a bite, then licks mustard off his thumb. "Do you have any interest in playing intramural soccer? I'll get you on another team, so I can beat you at that too." He laughs and stuffs fries in his mouth.

I give him a serious look that shuts him right up.

"What do you study?" I ask.

"Education. I might be a P.E. teacher. My goal in life is never to have a desk job."

I spoon ice cream onto my tongue. "I don't want a desk job, either."

"What do you wanna do?"

"Not sure yet." I liked helping Jeremiah when he hurt his foot, and I like feeling healthy and being on a schedule. It could be cool to help somebody else the way Matt has helped me. "I've sort of been thinking about physical therapy or nursing."

"I dunno," Jeremiah says. "I don't think you're cut out to be a nurse."

I gape at him.

"I mean, you couldn't even diagnose that you had an unborn twin stuck to your foot."

I throw a french fry at his chest, but it veers off course onto the sidewalk.

He smirks at the fry on the ground. "Clearly I could beat you at darts too...So why'd you pick MTSU?"

"I had to choose a state school. So I could get financial aid, you know?"

He pops a fry in his mouth. "Same here."

"My mom pushed me my whole life to go to college...she made sure I did my homework and studied for tests."

"Mine too." He bites into his chicken sandwich and stares out at the highway. "I just wish she wouldn't push me all the time now."

"I wish mine wouldn't push me either..." We look at each other for a long moment. Then I admit, "My mom had been trying to get me to hang out with friends and go shopping and stuff for months...and she just kept pushing me until I snapped. And I said some stuff—"

Some stuff I regret. I blamed her for my boyfriend's death.

Jeremiah looks at me expectantly, but I don't want to tell him any of my big secrets, my shame. "My mom never talks to me about anything real anymore. And I don't know how to get back to where we were."

"Have you tried talking to her?" Jeremiah asks through a mouthful of fries.

I shake my head.

He swallows the bite in his mouth. "My mom and I didn't talk for a long time...she threw a hissy fit after I hurt myself bungee jumping. "

"And now?"

"Things aren't great, but I know I can go to her anytime I need her. Maybe your mom's waiting on you."

Maybe.

My entire life, Mom always told me: "You're a beautiful girl, Annie, and lots of boys will like you, but never depend on one. You should depend on yourself."

I knew Kyle loved me. I knew he'd take care of me forever. But I had never forgotten what Mom said. She and my father never married—he left before I could crawl, but I don't really care that I've never known him. Who would want to know a father who walks out on his girlfriend and young kids?

Mom has dated off and on over the years, but never serious enough to settle down. And I think she's fine with that—Nick and I have always been her focus. She gave me everything, sometimes working two jobs to make enough money to pay for our braces, my summer camps, and Nick's baseball cleats.

That's why I said no to Kyle's proposal—because I want to go to college, to learn to take care of myself.

Jeremiah's right. I could try reaching out to my mom again. Even though we live paycheck-to-paycheck, clip coupons, and have never flown anywhere on an airplane, she's never let me down. She always makes it work.

Maybe I can try to make it work too.

• • •

I can't stand the idea of not being able to beat Jeremiah at something.

So I agree to hang out with him after my brunch shift on Sunday. While waiting for him in the Roadhouse parking lot, I sniff my T-shirt. Yup, I smell like onions.

He arrives right on time, wearing running shorts and a wrinkled gray tee. I smile up at his face as he walks up to me, and that's when I discover the large welt next to his left eye.

"Oh my God," I say, lifting up on tiptoes to get a better look. Without thinking, I gently push his light brown hair back to check out the greenish lump. The bruise looks a few days old. "What happened?"

"White-water rafting with some of the guys. We crashed."

I thought he was giving up extreme sports. Does white-water rafting count as one? "How big were the rapids?"

"Only class four. Pretty moderate. That's why I figured it'd be okay, you know?" He looks embarrassed.

"What did your mom say?"

"She hasn't seen it…I've been staying at my fraternity house until the swelling goes down. I don't want Jennifer and Lacey to see it and get scared."

"Jeremiah," I say quietly. "Please be careful."

"I'm always careful."

I don't buy that at all. I mean, he ran on an injured ankle, and less than two weeks later, he has another injury. Worried, I touch a finger to the scar on his arm.

He leans down, huskily whispering in my ear, "Careful. Last time you touched my scar, we ended up on the banks of the Little Duck."

I yank my finger away. "This isn't a good idea." I pull my keys from my pocket and stalk toward my car, feeling a shiver shoot up my spine.

"Annie! Wait." He runs to block my driver's side door, not letting me open it. "I'm an idiot. I didn't mean to make you uncomfortable or hurt you or anything."

"Then why did you say that?"

"Because I'm a guy. And sometimes guys say dick things. Because guys think with their d—"

"Jere." I jingle my keys, inhaling deeply. "Look, I like hanging out with you, but what I need is a friend. That's all."

He flexes his hands, looks deep in my eyes. "Will my friend forgive me for saying something stupid?"

I slowly return my keys to my pocket and gesture for him to lead us to his Jeep. "What did you want to do today?"

"Well, it's Shuffleboard Sunday."

"Shuffleboard Sunday? Really?" I ask as he opens my door for me.

"I needed a sport that starts with S. To match Sunday, you know?"

I climb up; he shuts the door behind me and jogs to the driver's side.

"And you could only come up with shuffleboard?"

He throws me a wicked smile. "I figured you'd prefer that to skydiving or Sumo Wrestling Sunday."

"What is Sumo Wrestling Sunday?"

"We'd dress up in those sumo wrestling suits that would make us look real fat. And then we'd wrestle."

"Oh good Lord," I mutter. "Shuffleboard Sunday sounds just fine."

"Good. I had no idea where I was gonna get sumo wrestling suits."

I give him a look.

"We can always do Synchronized Swimming Sunday if you want, but I don't know how we'd declare a winner."

"Would you just drive, Jeremiah?" I snap, working to hold my laughter inside.

He chuckles, starts the ignition, and turns out onto the highway. The scorching summer sun blazes through the Jeep windows; my thighs stick to the duct tape holding the seat together. We sing along to the radio as we dip up and down the hills near Spring Hill. He takes me to, I kid you not, his grandparents' old folks' home.

"Why are we here?" I blurt.

"This is the only place I know with a shuffleboard court."

I accidentally snort, and once the laughter starts, I can't stop. And then he's laughing too. I laugh so hard my stomach hurts. The elderly people loitering in the courtyard give us confused looks.

We laugh until an elderly man with a walker appears. He's wearing a gray pageboy cap and has more wrinkles than a Shar-Pei.

"Jeremiah Brown."

"Hey, PopPop."

PopPop reaches up to pat his grandson's face, gingerly touching the greenish bruise. "You been icing this, young man?"

"Yes, sir."

Seemingly satisfied with that answer, his grandfather then turns his attention to me. "You haven't visited in two weeks and now you show up with a date?"

"This isn't a date. It's a competition. I'm fixin' to beat Annie at shuffleboard."

"You're using your PopPop for his club membership?" PopPop gives his grandson a shifty look.

"He thinks this is an exclusive club," Jeremiah whispers to me. "But it's an old folks' home."

PopPop grabs his grandson's ear and shakes it.

"Ow! Stop it!" Jeremiah says.

"Why do you put up with this clown?" PopPop grabs my elbow. "Come sit with me."

Jeremiah rescues me from his grandfather's clutches. "No, no. Don't grab Annie like that."

"If you're not dating her, I will."

"You better not let Granny hear you say that," Jeremiah warns. "Where is she anyway?"

"She went to play bingo over at the church."

"I reckon you couldn't go, huh? A sinner like you would spontaneously combust the minute he walks inside," Jeremiah says, and PopPop grabs his ear again.

"I'll have you thrown out of my resort," PopPop says.

"It's an old folks' home!"

"PopPop, can you keep score for us?" I interrupt, in case they were planning on arguing all afternoon, and the next thing I know, I'm beating Jeremiah at shuffleboard because his grandfather keeps awarding me extra points.

"You get ten points just for being pretty," he says.

"Yessss," I say, pumping my fist.

Jeremiah rolls his eyes. "Stop hitting on her, PopPop. She's not your type."

"And what's her type?"

"Somebody under seventy."

"I'm cutting you out of my will, boy."

I love their banter. It kind of makes me jealous, to be honest. My mother's parents live in Mississippi and I don't see them much. And I never knew my dad's parents.

I use my broom-paddle thing to push the disk toward the numbered triangle. It stops on the number eight. I hop up and down, smiling.

Jeremiah's turn. He slides the next disk and it lands outside the triangle. "Daggownnit!"

"Don't use that foul language of yours around a young lady," PopPop says. "That's negative five points."

"You can't take away points!"

"I just did."

With the help of PopPop and his special scoring process, I beat Jeremiah by a landslide.

"That was so unfair," Jeremiah grumbles during the drive back to the Roadhouse.

"I didn't take you for a sore loser."

"Hmph."

I enjoyed this afternoon. Jeremiah hugged his PopPop long and hard before we left, and PopPop patted his grandson's back. Jere really is a nice guy; I like how he cares for his family, and he's down to earth and sort of an old-school gentleman. I wonder if he'd ever let a woman open a door for herself.

"Your PopPop is cool."

"He's such a badass," Jeremiah says. "When my mom wouldn't let me come home for Easter, he took me on a fly-fishing trip over in Johnson City. It was cool—he called it a *bachelor's weekend*. And he always tells me I should really live life…you know, because he went to Vietnam and he lost a lot of friends there…He's the one who gave me a gift certificate for my first skydiving lesson."

"You've been skydiving?" I exclaim.

"Yeah, seven times so far…it's the best rush I've ever had…but I guess I won't be going anymore." His quiet smile is happy and sad at the same time. To me, it seems so simple: family would outweigh the need to do something bat-shit crazy like skydive. But it must not be simple for him.

"We'll have to have a rematch," I say to get his mind off skydiving. "I want to beat you at something for real…With all of those extra points PopPop gave me, who knows who really won?"

"Tomorrow is Miniature Golf Monday."

"You probably have your own putter, huh?"

He grins, turning the steering wheel.

"I've got work tomorrow," I say.

"That's fine…I'll beat you at putt-putt some other time. Listen, do you want to run a race with me next weekend? It's on Sunday." He sounds nervous asking.

"I can't run as fast as you. Or as far."

"It's only a 5K. It'll be just like one of your daily runs."

That's only three miles. Matt has me signed up to run a half-marathon in September—he's considering it one of my Saturday long runs. Doing a 5K ahead of the half isn't a bad idea. It would be good to experience what actually happens on race day. I mean, all the information about the Country Music Marathon kind of overwhelms me. I'm supposed to pick up my race number the day before and I have to clip a timer to my shoelace. I have to park my car in a certain place and check my bag at the starting line. Someone will bring it to the finish. I need to memorize charts that show the elevation of every section of the course, along with maps that show the water stops, food tables, and first aid tents. I know where the porta-potties will be by heart.

Matt expects me to remember it all.

"What time is the race?" I ask.

"Seven a.m."

"Good lord, that's early. I can't. I work brunch on Sundays."

He taps the steering wheel and chews on his lower lip. "That sucks."

"Did you want me to come so I can see what a real race will be like?" I ask.

He looks over at me. "I thought we'd have fun together. We're friends, right?"

"I'll have to see if I can get off work."

"You will love this race," he says, smiling.

Nothing wrong with going to a race with him. I need to experience one, after all. And I do like having plans again.

When he drops me off at my car, he taps on my window and I crank it down. "I forgot to mention something about the race. You have to wear a white T-shirt."

Adrenaline Junkie

Work starts to slow down late Tuesday night, so I take the opportunity to page through the MTSU course catalog. Standing in the back vestibule, I dog-ear the physical therapy section. This human anatomy and physiology course looks cool. Working with Matt and discovering muscles I didn't know I had is making me more interested in the human body.

Right then, Stephanie stalks by. Oh good, I need to talk to her.

"Stevens, get out there and clear table twelve already!" she yells, and the offending busboy darts past the vestibule where I'm hiding.

I stow the course catalog in my tote bag, take a deep breath, and approach Stephanie. Sure, she's Mom's friend, but she takes her job as manager of the Roadhouse seriously. If we want time off from work, we have to request it in the leather-bound book behind the hostess stand two weeks in advance. And I didn't do that. The race Jeremiah wants me to run is in five days. Time to face the wrath of Stephanie.

I cross my fingers behind my back. She's busy reading a print-out of tonight's sales numbers—hopefully great numbers that'll put her in a good mood.

"Steph? If you haven't assigned side work for tonight yet, I'd be happy to refill the ketchup bottles."

Her gaze doesn't leave the printout. "What do you want?"

I take a deep breath. "Can I take Sunday morning off work?"

"What for?"

"There's this guy—"

She gapes and sets the sales numbers in a vat of sour cream. That's gotta be some sort of health hazard.

"You want to take off work to do something with a guy?"

"Yeah—" I'm about to explain about the race, but she cuts me off, grinning and pulling me into a side hug.

"You can do whatever you want, kid."

Well. That was easy.

What's not so easy?

My personal training session with Matt on Wednesday.

The gym he works at has an indoor track, and to make my heart stronger, he's making me do suicide sprints. He set five cones out on the track. The drill goes like this: run to first cone, run back to start, run to second cone, run back to start, and so on. To keep me distracted from his evil exercises, he always keeps a steady flow of conversation going, telling me about the house he and Kate just bought together for when they get married and listing the movies he wants to see, but after seven sets of suicides, salty sweat is pouring down my face and burning my eyes, and I'm hunched over on my knees, panting like a thirsty dog.

Matt hands me a cup of water, and as soon as I've sucked it down, he leads me back to the track for more jogging.

"I'm gonna die," I say after three miles.

"If you don't push yourself now, you won't make it through the whole race."

"I *will* finish it," I growl.

Matt grins. "That's what I like to hear."

After something like a gazillion sit-ups and push-ups and squats, my hip hurts like someone took a drill to it.

"I'm gonna be sick," I say, clutching my hipbone.

"Let's go stretch it out."

On a mat on the floor, Matt starts pushing on my thigh. That gives me an intense stretch, but it's odd having him kneel between my legs.

"This. Is. Awkward," I say, grunting.

Matt laughs, putting my legs into a pretzel-ish position, and pushes down on my knees. God, if I saw someone else doing this, I'd totally think it was foreplay. I decide to shut my eyes and pray for this to be over as soon as possible.

"Well, this sure is interesting."

I open my eyes to find Jeremiah. Without a shirt on. Watching his brother stretch me in a way that probably looks like dry humping.

"What do you need?" Matt asks his brother. "I'm working."

Jeremiah slips his ear buds out. "I had a question for Annie."

Matt looks from his younger brother to me. I'm still in the most. Awkward. Position. Ever.

"Are we on for Sunday?" Jeremiah asks.

"What's Sunday?" Matt says, raising an eyebrow.

"I invited Annie to run a 5K with me."

"Yeah, I can go," I say, which makes Matt fit to be tied.

"Why did neither of you ask me?" he grumbles.

"Because you'd get your panties in a wad," Jeremiah says.

"For the thousandth time, I do not wear panties."

"That's not what I heard."

"Guys," I say in a strong tone. Well, as strong as I can manage when my trainer is holding my butt off the ground and my legs are wide open, straight up in the air, while two brothers are arguing about panties. "Matt, is it okay if I run the 5K? I was going to ask you later today—I want to use it as my regular Sunday training run."

"You can do it as long as you don't push yourself too hard. Sometimes when people run their first race, they get excited, they hightail it, hurt themselves, and it messes up their whole training schedule."

"I won't let that happen," Jeremiah says seriously.

"You better not. Now, go away, Jere. We have to finish her workout."

"I'll pick you up on Sunday morning, Annie. I'll text you to figure out details."

"Okay," I reply breathily, as Matt makes a pretzel out of my legs again.

Jeremiah heads over to the weights, muttering, "His panties are so in a wad."

Matt tells me to sit up and do the splits, then plops down in front of me, doing the same. He takes my hands in his and pulls me forward so my nose is touching the mat.

"You should become a yoga instructor," I say, making him laugh.

"The quiet would drive me bonkers."

He helps me to a standing position and I adjust my tank top and shorts, getting rid of this awful wedgie. Unable to stop myself, I subtly gaze over at the weight room. Jeremiah's sitting on a bench doing bicep curls. A woman dressed like Workout Barbie is checking him out.

"Annie?" Matt says quietly, looking at his brother. "If you want him to leave you alone, just tell me. I'll make it happen."

"He's fine."

"But are you fine?" Matt touches my shoulder. "I know we've never talked about your boyfriend…but Jordan Woods told me what happened. And I want you to feel better…not worse."

"We're just friends…and I feel fine. I really do."

He grins and for a moment I'm jealous of Kate, that she's

marrying such a nice guy. I start to head for the locker room but turn back to Matt. "Why would I feel worse?"

He scratches his neck. "Jere's never had anything serious with anybody. He's an adrenaline junkie."

"What does that mean exactly?"

"It means that he moves from activity to activity, from person to person, always looking for his next challenge." A long pause. "It means that I don't want you to get too attached to him…"

Does Jeremiah consider me a challenge? When I went over to his house and sat on the porch with him, he told me how much he liked me. He seemed genuine. Am I just a game? I peer over at him. He's moved on to bench press, pumping a bar holding two giant weights. Jeremiah's so high-octane male, I have to catch my breath.

"We're just friends," I say. "That's what I need right now. A friend." I pause. "But why is he like this?"

"It's his story to tell."

And that's the real question. Do I want to hear the story? I don't want anything serious with him. I don't want drama. "Forget I asked, okay?"

Matt lets out a long breath, then gives me the high five I've come to expect at the end of our workouts. "I'll see you Saturday, then. You ready for our thirteen-miler?"

I nod, but I'm not so sure.

Thirteen miles. A whole half-marathon.

During his training, Kyle only went that far four times…

• • •

When I get home from the gym, I discover Mom left her apron and wallet on the kitchen counter.

I grab her stuff, climb in the car, and drive over to the Quick Pick. I used to bring her stuff over all the time, but since I was so nasty to her and said that unforgivable thing, my brother has taken on the chore. When I pull into the parking lot, I realize I haven't been here in months.

It's after 5:00 p.m., and a lot of people just got off work and stopped to buy groceries, so the lines are packed. I don't want to get Mom in trouble or hold up customers, so I grab some ibuprofen and Pepto from the medicine aisle and head toward cash register number two, where three people are in line ahead of me.

When Mom looks up from scanning some bananas, she gives me a surprised smile. I find myself smiling back, and when it's my turn to pay, she scans my items and bags them, then I hand over her apron and wallet.

"Thanks, sweetie."

"Mom?"

She tucks a brown curl behind her ear and looks up at me sadly. "Yeah?"

"Can you go shopping with me tomorrow, for school supplies? And go with me to do some other errands for college?"

Her eyes light up.

The next day, Mom helps me open my own checking account and takes me for some embarrassing vaccinations at the doctor, aka STD-prevention shots. Regardless of whether or not I'm having sex, my college won't let me start classes without them.

Then she and I go shopping at Target for school supplies and stuff for my new dorm room, like extra-long twin bed sheets and a shower caddy. It's hard to believe that in less than a month, my mom won't be sleeping down the hall from me every night. Nick and I won't battle-royale over the bathroom anymore. Mom won't be there to set my coffee to automatically brew. I'll miss that. I'll miss *her*.

"I hate this store," she says, pushing our red buggy with the wobbly wheel that screeches.

"You *love* this store."

"I hate it. I always want to buy everything. Those one-dollar bins are from the devil."

I pass her my shopping list. "It's your lucky day. I have to buy everything that has a purple checkmark beside it. You can pick it all out."

"What's this?" she asks, holding up the packet of papers.

"Kelsey made a PowerPoint presentation that lists the supplies each of us agreed to bring."

She abruptly halts the buggy. "Kelsey Painter?"

"Yeah…she's living in our suite."

"Are you okay with that?"

"Not totally…as long as she sticks to her room and I stick to mine, maybe we won't see each other much."

"I wish you girls could work through your issues…you used to be such good friends."

"I know!" I snap, and then feel guilty for lashing out at her again. I bow my head and she pats my back. "I'm sorry, Mom."

"Me too." Her voice is sad and that makes me feel like shit, considering she looked so happy when I invited her on my shopping trip.

"I want to fix things with Kelsey. I'm willing to work it out, but she never wants to talk to me. She wants nothing to do with me. Ever since she moved out of Oakdale, she's been a totally different person."

"When you met Kyle—"

"I don't want to talk about him!"

Mom ignores my outburst. "When you met him, you became a different person too, sweetie. But that doesn't mean you and Kelsey have to forget about each other."

I stop to examine hideous sandals adorned with yellow feathers. I'd never buy them—they are the ugliest things I've ever seen, but I need to concentrate on something before I explode. I can't control my breathing I'm so pissed.

"Why do you always have to bring things back to Kyle? Yeah, if I hadn't started dating him, maybe I would've had more girlfriends in high school. Maybe I would've joined a club or played a sport. Maybe I wouldn't have spent all my time doing home-work, working at the Roadhouse, and kissing him. But what's done is done."

"I know," she says, her eyes tearing up. "You don't know how often I think that. I'm sorry, sweetie."

"Can we finish shopping now, please?" I ask.

"Yes," she says in a thick voice, her eyes still watering. "But if you're really thinking of buying those awful sandals, I'm having you committed."

That's when we start giggling, and soon we're laughing like crazy, and when Mom finds a pair of the sandals with orange feathers, I'm pretty sure the entire store can hear us roaring. As Mom flips through the rest of the PowerPoint, she covers her mouth when she cracks up again.

"These suite rules are interesting. No cooking fish in the microwave?"

"You don't want to know."

"Cleaning day is every Thursday? And guys can't sleep over more than twice a week?"

Crap. I forgot that was on there. I can't believe I just handed the stupid thing over to Mom. My face burns hot with embarrassment.

"That rule is more for Vanessa than the rest of us because she's in a serious relationship with Rory Whitfield. Don't worry, guys won't be spending the night with me."

She gives me a knowing look. "What's this about you doing something with a boy on Sunday morning?"

"Stephanie has a big mouth."

Mom laughs again. "She's my best friend. Don't tell her something you don't want me to find out. So who is he? And why haven't your brother and I heard about him?"

"You asked Nick?" I exclaim.

"And he was no use. He didn't know a thing. Spill."

"My running coach's brother invited me to run a race with him this Sunday. I thought it would be good experience before the marathon."

Mom deflates and fans herself with Kelsey's PowerPoint presentation. "Your brother and Stephanie are gonna be so mad at me. They expected me to get some gossip."

"But there is none."

"Are you sure about that?" Her gaze shifts to my fingers. I stop playing with my necklace.

Why do moms have to be so observant?

The first time I slept with Kyle was his sixteenth birthday, after we'd been dating two years. I was three months older than him so I normally did the driving, but that night he drove us down to Normandy Lake—he'd just gotten his license that morning. I couldn't stop kissing his neck at stop signs and traffic lights.

"You're killing me," he moaned, laughing.

We went to his parents' cabin and made love for the first time in front of the fireplace.

"Happy birthday," I whispered when we were finished. I ran my hand over his short blond hair. The bristles tickled my palm. "I love you."

"I love you too." Then we curled up under a patchwork quilt on the couch and watched the Predators' game. He was a die-hard hockey fan, so he leaped to his feet and cheered when they beat the Blackhawks 2–1 in overtime.

"They won just for you," I joked.

"They could've lost for all I care," he whispered, softly running his knuckles against my arm. "You made my birthday perfect."

When I got home later that night, somehow my mother just *knew*. It must've been because I was playing with my necklace—it has always been my nervous tick. She didn't smile, and she didn't say anything except that she'd get me a doctor's appointment.

I've always been grateful I could talk to her about anything. But I can't talk to anyone about this. About how I fooled around with Jeremiah and it seemed different, it scared me, it made me feel like a bad person, it felt great.

But as she searches my face, I get the feeling she already knows.

• • •

When I get home, it's time to work out.

Matt's exercise schedule is intense. Some weekdays I run five miles. Others I run seven. Sometimes I don't have to run at all. Today is one of those days. But that doesn't mean I get to slack off.

Matt told me, "You need to work your heart hard. So even if you're not running, you need to ride a bike or swim or even go for a walk."

Since we don't have a garage, I keep my bike in my room. I bought it used a few months ago, specifically for training, but now I'm thinking I might ride it at college. Biking usually clears my thoughts just like running does. Tonight, however, after a day of shopping and that dreadful hepatitis B shot, I can't get my mind off leaving home next month.

It's a sweltering July evening, so hot the minute I step outside with my bike, sweat beads on my forehead. I climb aboard and start pedaling through Oakdale, passing by the basketball court where some of the neighborhood guys are playing a pick-up game.

My knee aches a little each time I pedal. Did I tweak something at yesterday's personal training session with Matt? I reach into my CamelBak's side pocket, pull out two ibuprofen, and swallow them.

I turn out onto the four-lane and work my way through town. I wave at Joe as I pass Joe's All-You-Can-Eat Pasta Shack, where I like to carbo-load on Fridays at lunch before my Saturday long runs. I zip past Madison Street Elementary, where I won the *Friendliest* superlative at sixth-grade graduation. Even after I graduated there, I would go swing on the swings and twirl around on the merry-go-round. At fourteen, when Kyle and I first started dating and needed our privacy, sometimes we'd go to the playground. I would sit on the swing, he'd twist up the chains and let go, and I'd fly around in a circle, squealing. Then we'd kiss as fireflies flickered on and off in the moonlight like floating Christmas lights.

It's weird to think that in a month, I'll be living in Murfreesboro, I won't be in Franklin, and I won't be a kid anymore. Leaving elementary school and going to middle school was a big change—I remember freaking out that we wouldn't have recess anymore. When would I play with my friends? I worried that girls coming from the other elementary schools would tease me about my non-name-brand tennis shoes. I worried about getting my first kiss, shaving my legs, wearing a bra, whether I'd remember my locker combo.

It all seems so not newsworthy now. So much has changed. The idea of leaving my safety net to go to college and being thirty minutes away from my mom is a lot scarier than buying a training bra. Going to college is sort of like starting kindergarten all over again.

What if I can't find a job in Murfreesboro and I go broke after one semester? What if my grades suck and I lose my financial aid? It's like the world is open to me, the sky is wide and blue, but clouds are threatening in the distance. I shake my head, push the clouds away.

I drop by the Franklin library for a new book. I decide on a thriller about two Secret Service agents (who are secretly having an affair) who discover the President is having an affair with the Secretary of the Treasury. Oooh, steamy. Then I hop back on my bike and pedal past Sonic, the place where kids from school hang out in the summertime.

"Annie Winters!" Vanessa waves from the back of Rory Whitfield's pickup truck. I shift into a lower gear and ride up to her. She and Savannah are lounging on the tailgate. Rory and Jack Goodwin are talking with a group of guys from the baseball team. And Kelsey and Colton are arguing over what they should do tonight.

"I want to go to Miller's Hollow," she says.

"Let's go to the movies," he says.

"That's silly. You'll fall asleep just like you always do."

"I won't this time," he replies, and I don't believe him one bit. Colton has always been a big fan of dozing during class. The boy could sleep through a rock concert.

"Seriously," Kelsey goes on, "only you could fall asleep during *The Fast and the Furious*. I mean, what boy does that?"

He scowls and she points a finger at him. They look like an old married couple.

"What's going on there?" I ask Vanessa.

She smirks. "Delaying the inevitable, as usual."

"Are they really not into each other?"

"I'm pretty sure they are, but she doesn't want to lose him as a friend, so she isn't willing to try anything. I think that's it, anyway."

I use my T-shirt to wipe sweat from my neck. "So what's up? I still got ten miles to ride before I'm done with my workout."

"It's amazing you're doing this," Savannah says. "I can't wait to see you run in the race."

"I'm coming to watch too," Vanessa says excitedly.

I swallow hard and dab my forehead with the back of my hand. "You are?"

"Of course," Vanessa says.

"Jack and I will drive down from Kentucky," Savannah says. She and her boyfriend are so in love, he decided to go to the University of Kentucky with her instead of Vanderbilt, so they could be closer. She got this incredible opportunity to teach younger kids how to become horse jockeys in exchange for college credit. She followed her dreams and her boyfriend supports her. I glance over at Jack Goodwin. Even though he's in a conversation, he keeps looking over his shoulder to check on her. Watching them kind of makes my chest hurt, and I sigh.

"You okay, Annie?" she asks.

"I'm good," I say with a wobbly voice. "I'm glad you're coming to the race." Honestly, I've been so focused on training and wondering if I can actually do this—run a full twenty-six miles—that I haven't even thought about who might show up on the day of. I figured Mom and Nick would be there, Kyle's friend Seth, and

Matt of course. Hearing that Vanessa, Savannah, and Jack will be there stirs a new kind of nervousness inside me.

"By the way, did you get Kelsey's PowerPoint presentation?" Vanessa asks.

"Yeah, that was something else," I reply.

"What PowerPoint?" Savannah asks, and by the time Vanessa gets done telling her about the no-fish rule and the color-coding of supplies, Savannah is cracking up.

"Kelsey, you need to get laid and get out of this drought already!" she shouts, dissolving into giggles with Vanessa. Kelsey crinkles her nose in reply and starts complaining to Colton about having to live with Iggy.

Vanessa said the same thing about getting laid to Kelsey when we met at the Roadhouse. Their inside jokes make me jealous. And Vanessa finishes nailing the coffin shut when she picks one of Savannah's long red hairs off her shoulder. Kelsey and I used to do that for each other. We joked that we groomed each other like monkeys.

"I need to finish my ride," I say quietly, placing one foot on a pedal.

"I'll text you about college stuff," Vanessa says.

I peek over at Kelsey. She sees me looking but pretends to focus on her cell phone. College sure will be *fun* if this is what I have to look forward to.

I suck it up and give her a wave, to show I want to put

everything behind us. A small smile appears on her face and she waves back, but then she turns to Colton to say, "Can we *pul-eese* do Miller's?"

"I swear, woman, you could start a fight in an empty house!" he replies. But as I start to ride away, I hear him calling out to the group, "Who wants to hit up Miller's Hollow?"

I'm glad I have a bike ride to finish.

When I get home, I fill a plastic baggie with ice for my knee, grab my cell and book, and head to the living room. Before I dig into the mystery I'm reading—think *Charlie's Angels* meets *The Da Vinci Code*, I swipe the screen on my cell to check my messages. I smile at Jeremiah's text asking me to call him.

"What are you doing tonight?" he asks once I have him on the phone.

"Nothing really," I say, settling onto the couch beside my brother, who shushes me, which is ridiculous because he's watching *Die Hard* for the thousandth time and knows every line by heart. I reach over into Nick's bowl and steal a potato chip.

"Do you want to go bungee jumping tonight?" Jeremiah asks.

He must be joking. "Uh, no?"

"C'mon! It'll be fun."

I prop a foot on the coffee table and drape the ice baggie over my knee. "Didn't you almost lose an eye doing that last year?"

Nick glances over at me, turns the volume down on the TV, and leans closer to the phone at my ear. I push him away.

"My roommate Mason and I are heading over to Pigeon Forge. They have a good bungee platform at Dollywood—it's completely safe and there's a balloon to land on, in case something goes wrong. They have safety certificates and everything."

"No way."

"It's only, like, a hundred feet high."

A gasp escapes my lips. That's, like, ten stories. Is he crazy? "That can't be safe."

"It's completely safe," Jeremiah says. "I've done it at this place at least five times."

I hate the idea of not being able to help him if something goes wrong. Because that's what would happen. Say he fell off the platform the wrong way. Or the bungee cord snapped. I wouldn't be able to push undo like on a computer.

"I can't," I say.

"You won't come?" Disappointment laces his voice.

"I don't understand why you're doing this. I mean, didn't your mom ask you not to? Don't you want to stay on good terms with your family?"

"I can't just quit cold turkey. And this is a perfectly safe way to have fun."

To get a rush, he means.

"Annie?" His voice wobbles over the phone. "The thing with my eye, it happened on a bridge and the cord was too long. What I did wasn't safe. I know that now."

"What about when you broke your arm and the bone grew back wrong? And going to the hospital three times in a month?"

No response.

I have nothing else to say either. This is too much. I like having him as my friend, but I hate the risks we're both taking. I burrow into Nick's side and he slides an arm around my shoulders, still entranced by *Die Hard*.

"Are we still on for the race Sunday morning?" Jeremiah finally asks.

I hesitate before saying, "Yeah."

He exhales into the phone. "I'll text you when I get back tonight."

"I think this is stupid."

"I'm trying, okay? But I need this."

I've never known anyone on drugs—well, except for kids at school who occasionally smoke weed, but none of the hard-core stuff. But that's what I'm thinking about when we hang up.

While *Die Hard* continues to entrance Nick, I use my phone to Google "adrenaline junkie," the term Matt used to describe his brother. I click on an article about how having sex, eating good food, doing things you love, *and extreme sports* pump dopamine into your brain. The article says that the effects of dopamine can be stronger than snorting cocaine. Wow. I scroll on, discovering that riding a bike and running can do the trick for some people, but others need bigger and better thrills to get an adrenaline rush.

Some pro athletes who went to the Olympics later suffered major depression and now turn to extreme sports or drugs in search of a fix for that lost adrenaline.

Another recent article says a man tried to break a free-diving record by going more than two hundred feet below the water's surface without any gear and died after he resurfaced. My heart aches for his family and friends…

The scariest part? The article says falling in love with the right person can trigger more dopamine than extreme sports and drugs combined.

A shiver races through me.

He made me feel so alive that day by the river. Yeah, the guilt ate at me, but I still get goose bumps just thinking about his hands on my skin and his lips warming mine. But that feeling is not worth the risk of losing somebody again. I need to know the people I care about are safe and sound. Maybe I shouldn't hang around somebody I could lose just like I lost Kyle.

I try to put Jeremiah out of my thoughts, but all night I'm on edge until I get his text.

Until I know he's all right.

Marathon Training Schedule~Brown's Race Co.

Name *Annie Winters*

Saturday	Distance	Notes
April 20	3 miles	I'm really doing this! Finish time 34:00
April 27	5 miles	Stupid Running Backwords Boy!!
May 4	6 miles	Blister from HELL
May 11	5 miles	Ran downtown Nashville
May 18	7 miles	Tripped on rock. Fell on my butt
May 25	8 miles	Came in 5 min. quicker than usual!
June 1	10 miles	Let's just pretend this day never happened…
June 8	9 miles	Evil suicide sprint things. Ran w/ Liza. Got sick.
June 15	7 miles	Skipped Saturday's run..had to make it up Sunday.
June 22	8 miles	Stomach hurt again. Matt said eat granola instead of oatmeal.
June 29	9 miles	Matt says it's time for new tennis shoes.
July 6	10 miles	Jere got hurt.
July 13	12 miles	Finished in 2:14! Only had to use bathroom once
July 20	13 miles	Halfway there!
July 27	15 miles	
August 3	14 miles	
August 10	11 miles	
August 17	16 miles	
August 24	20 miles	
August 31	14 miles	
September 7	22 miles	
September 14	20 miles	
September 21	The Bluegrass Half Marathon	
September 28	12 miles	
October 5	10 miles	
October 12	Country Music Marathon in Nashville	

Just a Friend

I put in my two weeks' notice at the Roadhouse today.

I never expected to work here while going to college since I'll be living over half an hour away, but it was harder to quit than I thought it would be. I've worked here since I turned sixteen.

Another ending in the last summer.

Stephanie gives me a hug. "You know you can work here over Christmas and spring break and you can come back next summer. We love you."

"I'll take you up on that, thanks."

In three weeks, I will move into the dorms at college and will have to find a new job. In three weeks, I start a new life.

During the Saturday dinner rush, I'm waiting at the window for Marty the line cook to scoop sides onto my plates so I can get this order out to one of my four tops.

"Hurry up, Marty! Did you have to dig the potatoes out of the ground or something?"

"Hold your horses." Marty plops mashed potatoes next

to a rib eye and scoops mac 'n' cheese onto a plate with chicken strips.

"Annie," Stephanie hollers back into the kitchen. "You got a group of guys waiting at your round."

I groan as I garnish my plates—lemons for the fish, honey mustard for the chicken strips. How many times is Nick gonna bring his friends to eat at my round? I hope he didn't bring Evan with him. After he sort of asked me out, I've been avoiding him.

I lift my tray above my shoulder and carry it out onto the floor, preparing to give Nick my evil eye. But when I pass my round, I nearly drop the tray.

Jeremiah is here.

With six guys I've never seen before.

"Annie," he calls.

"That's her?" says a guy wearing a ball cap backwards.

"Damn, she's hot," another one whisper-yells. He stole one of the coonskin caps off the wall and is now wearing it.

Oh Christ. This is gonna be a long night.

I drop off the food at my four top, quickly refill their iced teas, and get my two top another round of beers. Then I take a deep breath and head to the round.

I march right up, give them a basket of bread, and say, "Jere, this is my best table. You better leave me a big tip."

The guys hoot and holler, getting a kick out of me.

"Yes, ma'am," Jeremiah says, relaxing back in his chair.

"And you," I say, pointing at the boy who stole the coonskin cap from the wall. "Take that off right now. It's an antique!"

He sheepishly slips the cap off and hangs it back in its proper place.

"Do you have a sister?" another one asks, earning a prompt slap from Jeremiah.

He grins at me, cute as ever. He's wearing a black polo shirt and one of his knit caps. I'm beginning to think he sleeps in them. *What else does he sleep in?* I shake the thought from my head.

"You better behave, Jeremiah," I say. "I'm still pissed at you for last night."

He nods as the guys go "Oooohh." They think I'm playing, but I'm not. And Jeremiah knows it. His face fogs over and he worries his lip.

"I'm sorry," he says quietly.

I gently touch his shoulder to show him we're still friends. "I think you're dumb as hell right now, but I forgive you. I couldn't handle it if you got hurt. Now what do you want to drink?"

He lets out a deep breath. "Sweet tea, please."

A few of the guys are old enough to drink, so I wait for their beers at the bar, happy to have a chance to calm down. I steal cherries from the bar and pop them in my mouth, thinking. I'm happy Jeremiah's okay, but I want to punch his lights out too. I'm also glad he came to sit in my section at the Roadhouse. I don't like all these random emotions. My life is a damned clown show.

The atmosphere is a lot happier when I return to my round and start distributing glasses of tea and frosted mugs filled with frothy beer.

"Thanks, Annie," one of the guys says with a big grin. "I'm Jere's friend, Mason."

"I didn't know Jere had friends," I joke. "Did he pay y'all to come with him tonight?"

They howl with laughter at Jeremiah's expense. He scowls. "These idiots are in my fraternity. Can we have more bread, please?"

That empty basket had at least ten rolls in it!

"I swear, Jeremiah, all you do is eat."

"I'm an active guy. I need the calories. Weren't you starving after all that shuffleboard last week?"

"No."

"Well, I'm hungry. That's why I'm here—I'm starving."

"He's lying, Annie," a boy with black curly hair says. "He's here because he wanted to come see you."

Jeremiah throws a peanut at his head. And that starts a peanut fight.

Boys.

I go back into the kitchen. One of the prep cooks came down with a summer cold, so Stephanie has to fill in. Thank the heavens. The last thing I need is her discovering who the guy at my round is.

After I carry food out to my two top, I take orders at the

round. Jeremiah wants a bacon cheeseburger and fries with all the trimmings. Where does he put all this food?

"We're still on for the race tomorrow, right?" he asks.

"Yep. You're pickin' me up at five thirty a.m."

"You should just sleep over with Jere," Mason says. "You'd both get to stay in bed longer."

"Shut up, asshole," Jeremiah says, launching a peanut at his head. The other guys burst out laughing as my face burns up in embarrassment.

Another peanut fight ensues. They occupy my table for the rest of the night, raucously drinking beer after beer and flirting with me.

And leave a 60 percent tip.

• • •

When he told me to wear a white T-shirt, perverted things immediately jumped to mind.

But when Jeremiah hops down out of his Jeep and slowly walks to the door of our trailer, I know it wasn't because he wants to see me in a wet T-shirt—he's wearing a white tee and white shorts himself.

Nick stares out the window like a house cat stalking a bird. "This guy looks like an order of mashed potatoes."

"I still don't know why you're awake so early," I say.

Smiling, his mouth twitches. "You know why."

"Yeah, we're not missing this," Mom says, sipping from a coffee mug.

I swear. Nick goes camping every Saturday night with his girlfriend and Mom never climbs out of bed before noon on Sundays after working the night shift at Quick Pick. But here they are at 5:30 a.m., up early to see the guy taking me to a race.

"He's just a friend," I say softly.

Mom gently pats my back. "And I want to meet your friend."

Can Jeremiah see the three of us are staring at him out the window? If he can, he must think we're real creepers. He focuses on my front door and lets out a deep breath, as if he's nervous.

When he knocks, Nick and Mom rush to let him in. He grins when he sees me, but turns his focus to my mother, shaking her hand. "I'm Jeremiah Brown, ma'am."

"Call me Robin." I can tell she likes him right away, especially when he smiles.

My brother, however, is not as welcoming. He shakes Jeremiah's hand. Hard. "What time will Annie be home?"

"Ow. We should be back by nine. Unless she wants to get brunch."

"She wants to get brunch," Mom rushes to reply.

"Mom," I warn. *Please don't push me.*

"Or you can come home and eat with me," she says, and I give her a grateful smile.

"Text me on your way home," Nick says to me.

"Okay, *Dad.*"

Mom and Jeremiah snort at the same time, and Nick storms off to the kitchen in a huff.

"I'm sorry about him," Mom tells Jeremiah. "He's not normally like this."

"It's all right," he says in his slow drawl, laughing. "My little sister, Lacey, just turned sixteen. Her first date had to deal with me, my dad, *and* my brother."

But this isn't a date, I want to say.

Jeremiah tells my mother good-bye, saying he hopes to see her again real soon, and then we're off. We drive to downtown Nashville, over by the waterfront, where the Cumberland River looks green today, as always.

Before we get out of the Jeep, he pulls his hair back into a low ponytail. I swallow. I prefer his hair long and wild, but this look makes him seem harder, edgier. The muscle in his forearm flexes, showing off the crop circle tattoos. And that makes me think of his shoulder blade. Even though he has a shirt on, I can remember what the tattoo looks like. I still don't know what a black lightning bolt superimposed over a black circle means. Considering his mom is a youth pastor, I doubt it's a devil worshipping sign.

He catches me staring. "Yeah?"

"What's the tattoo on your shoulder blade mean?"

He looks at me like I sprouted an extra head. "You're kidding, right?"

I shake my head. "Is it a secret tribal sign or something?"

"It's The Flash."

"What?"

"I ought to take you straight home." He climbs out and comes around to open my door. "How do you not know who The Flash is?"

"It's a person?"

He gives me a withering look. "He's only the fastest, best superhero ever."

"Better than Iron Man?"

"Much better than Iron Man."

"But Iron Man is sexy."

Jeremiah considers this, tilting his head. "You know who's hot? Iron Man's assistant, Pepper…She kind of has your hair color." He tweaks my braid, and in a sneaky whisper he adds, "Well, it won't be that color for long."

"What?" I blurt.

He gestures at a large sign. The race is called *Color Me Rad*. A sea of white T-shirts fills my vision.

"Jeremiah Brown," I start, with hands on my hips. "What is this race exactly?"

He bites his lips together, obviously trying not to laugh. "Well, um, you see, as you run the course, you'll get sprayed with colored powder."

"Like baby powder?"

"It's more like Pixy Stix."

"How much colored powder?"

"Um, well, you won't have blond hair anymore and your shirt definitely won't be white…"

I laugh, then charge toward the registration line, leaving him to chase after me. I suck in a breath when I see the entrance fee is $25, but it turns out Jeremiah already covered my fee.

When I try to protest, he says, "My parents always say that if a guy invites a girl someplace, he pays for it. It doesn't matter if we're dating or not."

That's nice of him, but it makes me slightly uncomfortable. On the other hand, I severely wiped out my cash stash the other day at Target, so I will take this as a blessing.

"Thank you," I say.

His mouth twitches into a smile. "You're welcome."

Half an hour later, we're pinning numbers to our shirts with safety pins. My number is 5,094 and his is 3.

"What do the numbers mean?" I ask.

"Well, it's based on finish time. The faster you finish a race, the smaller your number is."

"So they think you have a chance at winning?"

He nods. On the way to the starting line, a couple of race organizers try to move Jeremiah to the first corral, but he says no thanks.

"Aren't you gonna run up front and try to win?" I ask.

"I'd rather run with you."

"You want to come in 5,094th place?"

His mouth quirks into a smile. "I don't care."

"Jeremiah? You make me happy."

"You make me happy too," he says quietly.

He kisses his lucky leather cord necklace, saying it's tradition, then the starting gun fires. The crowd roars. Everyone slowly begins to inch forward. I have a sudden fear that during the race, I'll get really tired and won't be able to finish. How embarrassing would that be? If I can't finish a measly 5K, how could I ever finish the entire marathon?

As we cross the official starting line, a burst of yellow powder blasts my face and shirt. I stop dead. It's like Big Bird blew up. Jeremiah dies laughing at my expression and tugs on my arm to make me start running.

I get what Matt said about wanting to run fast. The adrenaline, the cheers, the laughter—all of it makes me want to blast off. Then purple powder splatters us, topping the yellow.

"You look like Bart Simpson and Barney's love child," I say.

"That's just wrong, Winters. Wrong."

By the end of the race, we've gone from looking like Skittles to just plain dirty. The colors mixed together, creating a look I'd call *Blue Sewage*. I hold my hands above my head as we cross the finish line, where a final dusting of powder paints me orange. A year ago, I couldn't run half a mile. And I just finished my first 5K. I laugh, grinning up at the sun.

"Annie."

"Yeah, Jere?"

He lifts my braid up. "Your hair is green."

I grab his T-shirt in my hand and pull him closer. "You drive me insane."

He gives me a bear hug, and for the first time in a long time, I'm content, and there's nowhere I'd rather be.

Today's Distance: 14 Miles

Two Months until the Country Music Marathon

"Let's walk it off. C'mon."

Matt has a hand on my elbow. I feel queasy. Need to throw up. Need to throw up *now*. I vomit into bushes beside the trail. My vision goes hazy through my tear-filled eyes and acid burns my throat. Halfway through today's run, I had the worst bathroom experience of my life and I feel like I could have another any minute. How embarrassing.

"Drink this," Matt says gently, and I take the paper cup from his hand and sip. Lemon. Mmm. He gives me a towel to wipe my mouth.

"Hard," I say between sips. "The run was hard."

He squeezes my shoulders and smiles. "You did great. Just think, you can do fourteen miles. You're over halfway there."

"But what if, on the day of the marathon, my stomach gets screwed up to the point I can't finish?" I stopped three times today to use the bathroom. I couldn't keep up with Liza. It sucks running so far alone. And damn does it suck using porta-potties!

"I've never had a client with such a sensitive stomach," Matt says, scratching the back of his head. "And you've been taking Pepto?"

"Yeah."

"Maybe you should start eating white pizza, you know, without the sauce."

"That's sacrilege," I reply, making him laugh.

I finish my Gatorade, then Matt helps me stretch out my legs. He takes my ankle in his hands, pulling my leg toward his chest.

"Oww!" I say.

He lets go immediately. "Where does it hurt?"

"Left knee and thigh."

"The knee's a little swollen. How long's it been hurting?"

"It bothered me when I was biking the other night. But today...a few miles?"

"Did you walk on it or keep running?"

"Kept running." I understand now why Jeremiah wants to push through the pain. I can't imagine giving up now, not after all this training.

"Next time it hurts, stop and walk for a couple minutes, okay?" Matt helps me bend it back and forth. "Bridget, fetch me an ice pack, please."

While she's doing that, he lugs two big binders out of his truck, flipping through both of them. He pulls out the waiver form I signed when I joined his team. I feel a sudden rush of fear that maybe he'll tell me this is it. That I need to stop running. That he doesn't want to lose his 100 percent race-day success rate. That I won't get to run the marathon in honor of Kyle. But then I get a hold of myself. He's just looking at my insurance information, for God's sake.

The other binder reminds me of my brother's baseball card collection, but it's filled with business cards instead of Topps.

Matt whips one out. "I'll call this orthopedist today and try to get you an appointment. He might be able to see you first thing Monday if I call in a favor."

"Do you think it's that serious?" I ask quietly.

"I don't know. But we're not messing around with it. You've worked too hard to have something eff it up now."

My hand shakes as I take the card from him. "Will the visit cost money?"

"This guy takes your insurance. I can come with you if you want me to. We'll make sure we adjust your training correctly if we need to."

"That'd be good, thanks."

Matt won't let me leave until my leg is good and iced, so I'm still here when Jeremiah finishes his twenty-four mile run in which he paced two men. Of course he freaks out when he sees my leg propped up.

"Let me see it," he demands.

I yank the ice pack away and he gently runs his fingers over my kneecap, making me shiver.

"It's swollen, all right," he says softly. "Some people's knees just aren't cut out for long distances. The wear and tear over time makes it harder to run."

"But they keep running?"

He nods. "Sure, they get braces, start doing new exercises to strengthen the muscle around the knee. Some people eat a lot of fish."

I scrunch my nose, thinking of Iggy. "Fish?"

"It's good for your knees. Now keep icing it. I'm sure it'll feel better later—I can tell nothing's seriously wrong with it."

"Jere, you ran on a sprained ankle. You're not pushing me, are you?"

"That's different. I'd never do anything to hurt you." His eyes bore into mine, then he suddenly digs his phone out of his pocket and swipes the screen on. "Are you working tonight?" he asks casually, not taking his eyes off his phone.

"Why? You gonna come hog my best table again?" I ask.

"No way. My friends already won't stop talking about how hot you are. They need to get lives."

His friends have been talking about me?

"Actually, I'm not working tonight. It's my brother's birthday, so I'm going with him and his friends to Normandy Lake. I promised him I'd go camping."

"That sounds fun."

"Want to come?" The words spilled out of my mouth before I

even thought them through. It felt natural, I guess. Still, his eyes flash at the invitation.

"Yeah, sure. It'd be fun to hang out with my friend Winters." Wrapping an arm around my neck, he gives me a noogie.

After lunch, which I can't manage to keep down thanks to my stomach issues, Jeremiah picks me up in his Jeep and drives us out to Normandy, a lake with a white sand beach and ample camping area. I rarely see him wearing anything but mesh shorts and worn T-shirts that date to the prehistoric era, so it shocks me to learn he owns khaki shorts, a button-down shirt, and aviator sunglasses. And even more shockingly, he's wearing them.

"How's the leg?" he asks as he helps me out of his Jeep.

I downed a bunch of ibuprofen, so it's not hurting anymore. "It only bothered me when I was running this morning."

"I bet I'm right about the long distances. You'll just have to be careful as you run more and more."

"We'll see what the doctor says on Monday."

"I bet you twenty bucks I'm right."

I huff. "You're making my injury into a game too?"

"I thought you wanted to beat me at something. I'm just trying to be a good friend and give you opportunities."

"Opportunities, my ass."

"That language of yours is not very ladylike."

"Ahem." My brother clearing his throat interrupts our argument. Jeremiah and I look up to find Nick and his friends gaping at us. Evan's face goes splotchy, as if invisible fairies just pinched his cheeks, and when he fiercely shakes Jeremiah's hand, a look of pain crosses Jeremiah's face.

"What is up with the guys in your life squeezing my hand off?" he mutters, wringing his fingers out.

"Just protective, I guess."

"Yeah? Well I'm gonna have to stop shaking their hands or I won't have a hand left to beat you at badminton later."

I chuckle.

Evan brought a girl, Alisha. She's my age and I know her from school. Always hung around the shop class guys. She definitely notices that Evan keeps looking at Jeremiah and me; while she's collecting firewood for our campsite, she keeps snapping sticks in half and dramatically throwing them to the ground. Doesn't she know she has nothing to be jealous of? I've never wanted Evan.

"C'mon," I tell Jeremiah. "Let's set up our tent."

Setting up the tent consists of me doing all the work while Jeremiah stares at the rods, trying to fit them together and repeatedly reading the instructions. It baffles me that a country boy like him can't put a tent together.

Then we decide to go for a swim. Inside the privacy of the tent, with Jeremiah waiting outside, I change into my blue-and-white checkered bikini. When I step back out to give him a turn to change, he gives me a once-over, then suddenly pulls his aviator sunglasses off and cleans the lenses on his shirt. Evan gazes over from the picnic tables, where he's sitting with Alisha. She definitely notices him looking, but I pretend not to.

Jeremiah ducks into the tent to change into his bathing suit. Two minutes go by before I hear a thrashing sound and a curse.

"What's going on in there, Jere?"

"I'm not used to changing my shorts while sitting down! You try it."

"I just did it a couple minutes ago."

"But I'm taller than you."

"Jesus," I mutter.

He emerges a couple minutes later wearing long, navy blue board shorts, nothing else, and leaving little to the imagination. Holy ab muscles.

We doggy paddle out to the rope line that encircles the swimming area. I throw one leg over a buoy and pull myself onto it. He does the same, facing me, shaking the water out of his crazy hair. Swiping the wet bangs off his forehead, he swiftly looks me up and down.

"What?" I ask.

"I like your bikini. It reminds me of these supper napkins my mom has."

I roll my eyes. "You sure know how to make a girl feel special, Jere."

"I notice anything that has to do with my mom's cooking."

"Boys."

I take a deep breath and look around, enjoying the blue water and thick trees. The forest here is so massive it's a creature unto itself.

We sit in silence until Nick, Kimberly, and their friends cruise up on her father's speedboat.

"Want to come on the boat?" my brother calls. Jeremiah leaps off his buoy and climbs up the boat ladder before I can even respond. Soon we're speeding around the lake, and after he gets his fill of driving the boat, Jeremiah wants to water ski. And of course he's awesome at it, ripping up the waves.

"Does he have to be so good at every sport?" I grumble to Nick.

"He's making the rest of us guys look bad, but I'm glad you brought him," my brother replies, squeezing my shoulder.

At sunset, I sit on a smooth log to watch the blue sky change into purple and gold. Jeremiah joins me, carrying two cans of beer under his arms and a plate of sliced watermelon that we immediately dig into. I rip huge chunks off with my teeth, wiping the juice from my lips with the back of my hand.

He daintily eats his piece as I chow down. "Don't eat the seeds! You'll grow a watermelon baby."

I spit a seed near his foot to piss him off and he laughs. The surface of the water was so busy earlier today when everybody was boating and splashing, but now it's a calm blue, just like Jeremiah and me. I like being around him because I don't have to worry about filling the silence. We just *are*. I study him out of the corner of my eye. Half of his crazy brown hair is pulled back with a band; I never thought I'd be into the ponytail look on guys, but it seems I am. He hasn't put a shirt on yet, so I discreetly check out his skin. The Flash tattoo on his shoulder blade. The lifetime of scars and bruises spotting his arms and back, even though he's only twenty.

"I can't believe how nice it is out here," he says, toeing the white sand. "I never knew this beach existed."

"Not many people do, I think. It's private. My brother's girlfriend's father works at the Air Force base, so that's how we're allowed to use it."

He pops the cap on his beer and sips. "Kimberly seems nice."

"You just like her because she gave you beer and pulled you around on her boat all afternoon."

"You caught me," he laughs. "I loved water skiing. I've never gone before."

"But you looked like a pro out there! How is that possible you're good at every sport?"

"That's just silly. I stink at ballet—my little sister tells me that when I try to copy her moves."

I snort, nearly choking on a watermelon seed.

Jeremiah slaps my back. "I told you not to eat the seeds, Winters."

I spit another one at him and he smacks it away like a pro.

"How'd you get into extreme sports anyway?" I ask quietly, wondering where the adrenaline junkie-ness came from.

"I started trying to beat myself at stuff. To work harder. To learn more about my body and mind and their limits."

I pop open my beer and take a long sip, processing what he said. The beer makes me feel a little lightheaded considering I couldn't keep food down after my run earlier. "When did you start doing this?"

He toes a twisty root sticking out of the ground as he takes a drink of beer. "After high school, I reckon. I played soccer my whole life...and then I didn't make it onto a college team...I needed something to do with my time."

Is this what Matt didn't want to tell me? Is that why Jeremiah hasn't been truly happy in a while?

"So you were trying to get a scholarship or something?"

He nods slowly. "My best friend, Trent, and I grew up playing together. He was a whole hell of a lot better than me, but I still thought I had a shot. He got a scholarship to play for Auburn, and I got nothing...I spent too much of high school dicking around."

The boy can run a sub five-minute mile. "I'm sure that's not true."

"It is. I never pushed myself hard enough. I was too busy messing around with girls and acting all important. And Trent worked hard and left me behind."

"Do you still hang out?"

"Not often—he's four hours away and always has practice and games or whatever."

I won't ask Jeremiah if he misses his friend. That's obvious.

But I wonder if it's a lot more than missing his friend. Maybe he misses the opportunity he never had. Maybe he felt like he had to prove he was just as good as his friend.

"What was the first crazy sport you tried?" I ask.

"I went BASE jumping off Fall Creek Falls on my eighteenth birthday. It was wild."

Holy crap. That must be a few hundred feet tall! And he just jumped off the waterfall? I shake my head at the craziness while he smiles at the memory.

"But you're not doing crazy things like that anymore, right?"

"My mom gave me a choice: my sports or my family. I'm still pissed at her for that... She hasn't even acknowledged how good I'm doing—noticed that I haven't done anything really dangerous in a while. It's like she's still punishing me for stuff I did last year."

"But, um, aren't you still bungee jumping? And white water rafting?"

"I've cut back, but I still need to do some stuff."

How in the world did Jeremiah's thinking get so jumbled? He said he couldn't just quit cold turkey. Is bungee jumping at Dollywood his version of giving up cigarettes and starting the patch?

"But when will you stop all this? How will you know when you've, like, accomplished enough?" I ask.

He wipes the condensation off the rim of his can, his hand

shaking as he thinks. "I'm not sure that I have any specific goals or anything. I just know I need to feel a rush."

"But you're great at racing, right?" I ask.

A curt nod. "I won my age group at the Marine Corps Marathon last year. Finished in two hours and forty-seven minutes!"

"And that's not enough?" I exclaim.

"Like, after I finish a race, I mentally feel a sense of accomplishment, but I'm already thinking of another challenge that's harder or more unique that I can train for and compete in."

"If I dared you to swim across the English Channel, would you?"

"Sure." He doesn't miss a beat.

"Would you walk on hot coals like people on the Discovery Channel?"

Another long sip of beer. "If an expert was here to show me how to do it right and not hurt myself bad, then sure."

"But why would you want to hurt yourself like that?"

"It's not about the pain, Annie. It's about the challenge." He focuses on my face, and the combination of the sun setting over his shoulder and the serious look on his face makes my vision go spotty. I squint and look at the far banks of Normandy.

"When you put it like that, I feel like I haven't done anything."

"Would you stop saying silly things? Hardly anybody has the guts and the strength to do a marathon. And you're working hard to get what you want."

It's nice hearing him say that if you work hard, you can do

anything you want. I like knowing I can control my future. All those years ago when I did the Presidential Fitness Test, I never imagined I could run fourteen miles one day. But I did. But there also needs to be some sort of balance, right? I don't want Jeremiah to take it too far. I could beg him to stop. But then would he be pissed at me like he's pissed at his mom? Considering we aren't together or anything, do I even have the right to try to help him?

He goes on, "And how can you say you haven't done anything? I saw you waiting tables. It's crazy that you can carry ten drinks on one tray above your head."

The rest of the evening is pretty laid back. We sit around with my brother and his friends, telling stories, roasting marshmallows, and emptying a cooler of beer. The sweet summer air reminds me of what life used to be like before. Tonight almost feels like that. Well, except for Evan and Alisha giving me weird looks for their own different reasons.

At about midnight, Jeremiah announces he needs to sleep if he's going to get a workout in tomorrow, so I say good night as well and duck into our tent. I thought it might be awkward sharing a tent with him, but I like being with my friend. It's nice not being alone. In our side-by-side sleeping bags, Jeremiah looks over at me with a smile. "Good night, Winters."

"Good night, Jere."

But neither of us can sleep. He can't get comfortable on the ground. My stomach still hurts from today's run, and being in the same tent makes me want to curl around his body and rest my head on his chest. Not to hook up or anything—just to be warm. But I don't want him to think I'm starting something. His breathing hitches each time I move a muscle.

On top of that, Nick and his friends are still raucously drinking beer and telling raunchy jokes.

Jeremiah checks the time on his phone. 2:00 a.m. "God, are they ever going to shut up?"

"Not likely," I say. After camping, Nick never rolls home before dinnertime on Sundays.

"I knew I should've set this tent up farther away."

"You mean *I* should've set the tent up farther away?"

He grumbles.

"I don't get it. How can a country boy like you not know how to set up a tent?" I ask.

"My brother and I always wanted one growing up, but we never had the money. My dad's a teacher and my mom's a pastor and they had five kids. Things like tents came second to putting food on the table." Jeremiah starts chuckling.

Not having money doesn't seem like something to laugh about. "What are you thinking?" I ask.

"When my brother first got together with Kate, he was working at a camp. And he didn't know how to set up a tent either—this camp had fancy cabins, so when he and Kate would sneak out at night to fool around, he'd just drag this giant parachute out onto the grass and they'd sleep on it."

"Wait. The big parachute like we used in gym class as kids?"

"That's the one." Jeremiah laughs again. "Matt says she found it very romantic…Of course, she found out the truth later on that fall—they went camping and she had to set up the tent because he didn't know how."

I grin at that, snuggle deeper inside my sleeping bag, and shut my eyes. This morning's run exhausted me and I'm begging for sleep to come, but I can't seem to pass out—I'm too wired thinking about my leg, wondering if it's really hurt or if I just worked it too hard today. And what the hell is up with my stomach? My body hurts everywhere.

That's when I hear them talking.

"Who is this guy?" Evan asks. "He didn't go to our school, right?"

"Nah," my brother responds. "Jere lives over in Bell Buckle."

"Are they dating?"

"I don't think so," Nick says.

"Is she ever gonna date again?" Alisha asks.

"Did you see that guy's scars?" Evan asks. "I mean, you can't possibly let a guy like that hang around your sister."

Jeremiah tenses up in his sleeping bag next to me, going still as a possum playing dead.

"I think he's sexy," Kimberly announces in her

I've-had-a-ton-of-beer voice. "Goooo, Annie!" Great, we've moved on to the cheerleader voice.

"Can we find something else to talk about besides my baby sister's love life?" Nick asks.

"I'm just kind of surprised," Evan replies. "I mean, I thought I might have a shot."

"What?" Alisha hisses.

Nick groans. "That better be the beer talking, dude."

"I like her," Evan continues.

"Oh God," I mumble. Jeremiah stays still as a log.

"But I haven't asked her out because I never saw an opening after Kyle died, and now she shows up with this random guy none of us has ever heard of before?"

"Let's not talk about Kyle," Nick says.

"It's pretty pathetic Annie's still swooning over him," Alisha says. "What's it been? Like, a year?"

I rush to cover my mouth.

"Shut up," I hear my brother hiss. "Evan, if Alisha can't keep her mouth shut, take her home."

Somebody murmurs something I can't hear.

"I don't care how late it is," Nick says. "She shuts her mouth or she goes home."

Jeremiah sits up straight and jerks the tent zipper down, ready to pounce. I reach out and grab his shoulder, shaking my head, silently telling him it's not worth it. I'm not messing up Nick's birthday because some stupid bitch is stupid.

I suck in a deep breath, pulling my lower lip between my teeth. I clamp down on it to feel the pain.

Jeremiah re-zips the tent and looks at me sideways. "I like your brother. But if that girl had said something about Lacey or Jennifer, I would've dunked her head in a toilet and given her a swirly. Clearly Nick is more diplomatic than I am."

I snort into my pillow, wanting to give Alisha a swirly myself. She doesn't have a fucking clue what it's like to lose the person you talked to every day for three years.

That's the hardest part. For everyone else, life goes on. But for me, part of me is stuck in limbo with Kyle…and I kind of want to stay there. I miss him. It's my fault he died. I suck in another deep breath, hoping it will tide me over for a while. I don't have the energy to breathe.

"You all right?" Jeremiah murmurs, lying back down next to me.

"No one ever says shit like that to my face," I whisper. "That they think I'm pathetic. But they have no fucking idea."

The sound of crickets chirping fills the silence.

My little rant felt good.

Jeremiah folds his hands behind his head and stares at the tent ceiling. "They're just jealous."

"What is *that* supposed to mean?" I exclaim.

"You've been in love. They're probably jealous of that. I am…"

"You've never been in love?"

"Nope."

I pause. "But you want to be?"

"Who doesn't?"

Talk about something you don't hear guys say very often. "You haven't met anybody?" I ask, propping myself up on an elbow.

He rolls over onto his side to face me. Then slowly shakes his head. "I've dated a lot," he admits quietly. "And like, sometimes I feel a rush at first, but then it goes away…even when I don't want the feeling to go away, it does."

"So you've never been close with a girl?"

"What's your definition of *close*?" he asks with a nervous laugh.

"Like, you keep a spare toothbrush in her dorm room. Or you scratch her back for her." I groan. "God, I miss the back scratches."

"Don't they sell backscratchers so you can scratch your back yourself?"

"It's not the same," I pout.

"Is this your way of saying you want me to scratch your back?"

"Would you mind?" I ask hurriedly, flipping over to face away from him. "Top left."

He chuckles, then gently scratches my left shoulder blade.

"Now go down," I say. "Now to the right. Now to the left. Go up a little. Now down. To the middle of my back. Right there. Yes. Now up."

"Yeah, I can see how this is so much more efficient than a backscratcher," he says sarcastically.

"Go back up and to the left. Yeah, there," I groan.

"Jesus. This is gonna take all night."

"Do you have somewhere else to be?"

"Nope." His fingers go still on my shoulder. "So can I get one of these back scratches next?"

• • •

On Monday when I meet Matt at the doctor, his eyes immediately dart to my knee.

"It doesn't look too swollen," he says, falling into step beside me as we walk through the parking lot.

"Hello to you too."

"How do you feel?"

"It doesn't hurt today."

He drags a hand through his dirty blond hair. "I'm anxious to see the X-rays."

"I hope it's like what Jeremiah said, that I might be overusing it. I don't think I've torn anything or sprained it. It only hurts when I run for a long time."

Matt glances at my face as he opens the door to the orthopedist's office. "He told me he went camping with you on Saturday night."

"It was fun," I say, and I smile until he gives me a look. "We're just friends."

"I know, I know, Jere's told me that about fifty times."

How often do he and his brother talk about me? And why? Yeah, we're attracted to each other, but we really are only friends.

"Just be careful," Matt adds.

"We're fine. You should trust your brother more."

He smiles at me sideways. "You're right."

We sit down in a waiting room filled in equal parts with fish tanks and anatomical posters of hips and knees. After I fill out paperwork on a clipboard, the nurse leads me into the X-ray room. I wore shorts today, so I don't have to bother with a gown. I climb onto the table and answer the questions about whether I could be pregnant. The X-ray technician asks me three times if I'm sure, and I'm tempted to yell that I haven't had sex since October…since the night I lost Kyle.

"There is absolutely no way I could be pregnant."

The look on my face makes her back off. Finally. She takes the X-rays, then leads me back to the exam room, where Matt is texting. "Jere says to call him after we're done here," Matt says, pocketing his phone.

I take a deep breath. Dealing with that X-ray technician upset me, and I'm worried about my knee. It started hurting a few minutes ago. Or am I just imagining that?

The door opens and the doctor walks in, reading a chart. "Annie Winters? I'm Dr. Sanders."

"Hi," I say, shaking his hand. Matt and the doctor nod at each other. Dr. Sanders hangs my X-rays up over the fluorescent light, and Matt stands to study them.

"And you're having trouble with your left knee?" the doctor asks.

"Yep."

"I'm not surprised. Your chart says you're running forty miles a week."

"That's right. To train for the Country Music Marathon in October," I say slowly.

The doctor takes my foot in his hands and pulls it toward his chest, extending my leg. I wince. "What have you been doing to alleviate the pain?"

"Icing it, stretching it, and taking ibuprofen."

"You've been taking ibuprofen?" Matt blurts.

"It's a good anti-inflammatory," the doctor says.

Matt stares at my torso. "But sometimes it causes stomach problems."

What? I've been taking it for months. Could ibuprofen be the reason my stomach is wrecked after every long run?

"Why didn't you tell me you were taking ibuprofen?" Matt asks.

"I didn't know it was such a big deal. I mean, you've given me Tylenol before. I figured ibuprofen was okay."

"Tell me everything you swallow from now on, okay? And no more ibuprofen. Hopefully there's no permanent damage to your stomach lining."

"Okay," I whisper, touching my stomach. I'll stop taking it

right away, but if I don't take an anti-inflammatory, will my knee hurt worse? "Dr. Sanders, what about my knee?"

"I can see the swelling. It's coming down, but it'll go back up when you do another long run."

I suck in a gasp as the doctor keeps talking.

"It's the way your knee is shaped. Your bones are misaligned, and when you overuse it, the nerves in your kneecap get aggravated. We call it runner's knee. It's not meant for long distances."

"That's what Matt's brother said," I say with a shaky voice. "What can I do?"

"The best thing to do is rest it. Work on your core strength. Maybe run the race next year."

"I can't!"

"She can't," Matt repeats after me.

"I have to finish this."

The doctor gives me a long look, then studies my X-ray again. "There are a few things we can try. I'll get you fitted for a brace that'll keep your knee from moving from side-to-side. That'll help the nerves. But you need to keep it pointed straight all the time, understand?"

I nod, internally freaking out. I have enough trouble reminding myself to keep my feet facing forward! And now I have to remember for my knees too?

"And Matt can work with you on some exercises to strengthen your knee and thighs. That'll help." He pulls a deep breath and scribbles something on my chart. "But, Annie? I have to tell you, I'm not sure if your knee will make it through the race."

I drop my face into my hands. I think of Mr. and Mrs. Crocker. Of Connor and Isaac. Of Seth. All the people that Kyle cared about most. They were all so excited when they heard I was finishing the marathon on his behalf. How shitty would it be if I failed? If I disappointed them?

And as much as I hated it at first, running and training have become a huge part of my life. I've made friends with Jeremiah and Matt and Liza. Who am I without this training program?

Matt squeezes my shoulder as I tell the doctor thank you. We make our way out of the office to the parking lot, where Matt grabs my shoulders and turns me to face him.

"Listen, Annie. I'm no doctor, but I want you to know that whatever you decide, I'll be there every step of the way."

I wipe a tear from my eye before it trickles out. "But what about your one hundred percent race-day success rate?"

He waves a hand at me. "This is all up to you. I'll do everything I can to get you there. But you have to keep talking to me. Tell me everything you put in your body."

"I can do that."

I say good-bye to Matt, then sit in my driver's seat, grip my steering wheel, and stare at a redbrick building.

I can't give up now. *I already let Kyle down once.*

After I turned down his proposal, he dumped me, and I

thought nothing could hurt worse than that. Mom kept encouraging me to ask old friends to hang out or to spend time with my brother and his friends, but all I did was curl up on the couch and watch reruns of *Friends* and *Law & Order*, anything to get my mind off him. Every time I saw him at school, his face looked ghost white, like Elmer's glue, and I never saw him smile anymore. How could he stand it? I couldn't even fall asleep at night.

A few weeks later, he skipped his mom's Sunday family dinner and came to my trailer. "I wasn't thinking. I made a mistake."

"When you asked me to marry you?"

His deep chocolate eyes lit up. "No, that wasn't a mistake. It was a mistake when I broke up with you."

He promised not to propose again until I was ready, and we crawled under the covers and made up, showing how much we loved each other. The terrible feelings weighing my body down floated away as he kissed me everywhere. His mother would've flipped out if she'd known we were doing it during her weekly turkey dinner.

When we were finished, he pulled his polo shirt back on and zipped his jeans. "I have to go home before Mom sends out a search party."

"You just want leftovers," I teased.

"Damn straight." He loved his mother's cranberry sauce and mashed potatoes.

We kissed good-bye, and that was the last time I saw him.

If I hadn't said no to his proposal, he never would've come to my house that Sunday evening to apologize. He wouldn't have missed his mom's dinner.

He would still be alive.

It's my fault.

In the present, I forget to blink until my eyes start burning. Decide to call Jeremiah. He answers on the first ring.

"What'd the doctor say?"

"What you told me. That some knees aren't made for long distances. That maybe I should quit."

"What do you wanna do?" Jeremiah asks.

I sniffle and wipe my nose. There's only one answer. "I need to finish this for Kyle."

A long pause. "Then let's get you there."

PART III

A Beginning

MOVE-IN DAY

Two Months Until the Country Music Marathon

"He'll be here."

Mom glances down at her watch. "He's five minutes late."

"And he's never been late before," I reply. "I hope nothing's wrong."

Mom and Nick share a look.

"What?" I ask.

"Nothing," they say in unison.

"Can't we just start moving your stuff inside?" Nick asks. "We'll leave all the heavy boxes for Jere to carry."

"Two more minutes." I check the time on my phone and look to make sure he didn't text. He didn't. "Fine, let's go."

Nick leads the way through a busy courtyard up to the dorm where I'll be living. It's five stories high and made of brick. A group of smokers is lounging on benches. Kids are tossing a Frisbee. The courtyard is full of laughter. And yelling. And whooping.

Mom sees the smile on my face and wraps an arm around me. "I'm so, so proud of you."

Hearing that makes me happy and sad at the same time—sad

because now that we're finally getting along, I'll really miss her. A piece of me wants to stay home and commute to school, but I need some newness in my life. And some time apart might be good for us.

"Annie!"

We turn around to find Jeremiah sprinting up.

"I'm so sorry I'm late." He swallows hard. "I misestimated how long it would take to walk here. I didn't factor in welcome-back-to-school gridlock."

"What does that mean?" I ask.

"It means that everyone and their mom stopped me to talk about nonsense. I barely escaped Gloria, the little old lady who runs the copy center at the library. They have a new high-volume color printer, by the way."

Nick stares him down. "You're carrying the heavy stuff, Brown."

"You got it."

After Jeremiah gives Mom and me quick hugs, we head inside my dorm and check in. The front desk guy makes me fill out an emergency-point-of-contact form and sign for keys to my room and mailbox. He also hands over a huge student-life policy package, complete with all the rules of dorm living.

"This code of ethics booklet is bigger than a Bible," I mutter to Jeremiah.

"It probably has more rules than the Bible too," he replies. "I bet we'll break every one this year."

Mom and Nick share another look. Ugh. Maybe I can't wait for them to be gone.

My room is on the fourth floor. When I step off the elevator, I find a common room with a big screen TV and cushy sofas. A girl is arguing with her mother about who accidentally left one of her bags at home in Alabama. Two girls who seem to be new roommates are fighting over who gets the top bunk. They are so loud you could probably hear them on the other side of campus.

A guy wanders down the hall wearing *only* a white towel tied around his waist. Jeremiah doesn't find this odd at all, but Nick looks like he might kill the guy, and Mom does a double-take, blushing. I pucker my lips and make a kissy noise, to tease her, and she scowls at me. When I see the monstrous safe sex bulletin board, Mom and I both start blushing. Is that a bucket of condoms hanging on the wall? A little sign announces, *Take as many as you need!*

Noted.

I stick my key in the lock to my room. This is where I'll be living until next summer. Here goes. I push the door open and discover I'm the first person here. Nick and Mom come in and look around at the tiny kitchenette and bathroom that links my room to Kelsey's.

She and Vanessa texted me earlier, saying they'd be arriving in the late afternoon. I'm glad I got here before Iggy. This is so overwhelming I need the time alone to adjust.

"Want me to start moving your stuff?" Jeremiah asks, and I nod. He and Nick disappear out the door and I try to decide which bed I should take. The one closest to the door? Vanessa would probably like the window. No reason to start the year off with a fight like those girls in the hall.

I set my backpack down on the bed by the door and check out my closet, desk, and dresser space.

Jeremiah, a guy I thought was the epitome of muscle, staggers through the door, weighed down by a box of my stuff. "Oh my God, Annie, what's in here?"

"Books, I think."

"Did you pack an entire library?" He lurches to my desk and sets the box down. On the next trip, he brings a heavy box of my clothes. Sweat gleams on his forehead. I give him a break after he hauls my printer upstairs.

While Mom sits on the floor refolding all my clothes that got jostled in the box, I'm busy working to fix a bulletin board to the wall. Jeremiah takes the hammer and nails from my hand and swiftly hangs it. Hooray for my own personal handyman!

"Thanks," I say, sorting my small pile of pictures I'm planning to tack up.

Jeremiah lifts a worn picture of me, Mom, and Nick at the *USS Alabama*, the big World War II ship that's docked in Mobile.

"Don't ever go on a ship like that in July," I say. "We boiled in there."

He smiles and sets the photo down. He shuffles through the stack until he comes across a picture of me and Kyle from Thanksgiving the year we convinced our families to eat together. In the photo, I'm feeding Kyle a bite of pumpkin pie and he's cringing.

"He hated pumpkin pie," Mom says, refolding a tank top. "But he ate it that time because Annie tried to make it."

My spine stiffens as I glance at Jeremiah's expression: interested, but nervous.

"That was the worst pumpkin pie I've ever had," Mom adds.

"Mommmm," I whine.

Jeremiah makes a face. "Please don't ever bake pumpkin pie for me, Annie."

I shove his arm, making him laugh. Then he focuses on the picture again. "His name was Kyle, right?"

I nod and take the photo from his hand. I need to sniffle, but I don't let myself. I should be able to look at a fucking picture without becoming a geyser. I slowly pick up a thumbtack and hang the photo. Let out a long breath.

Jeremiah grabs another picture and a thumbtack and pins it to the middle of the board, lopsided.

"No," I say. "That looks terrible."

"It looks fine," he grumbles and hangs another picture in a not-pretty way.

"Ugh. Would you go get the rest of my heavy boxes already?"

Mom sniggers. Jeremiah and I both turn and give her a look. She clears her throat, then goes back to folding clothes.

It doesn't take much longer to unpack the car and lock my bike up outside on the rack, and soon, it's time for Nick to go meet his girlfriend. It's time for Mom to head on back to the Quick Pick. And it's time for me to start my new life.

Jeremiah must sense that I want to say good-bye to my family alone. "I'll catch up with you later, okay? Text me if you want to hang out."

I nod slowly. "Thank you for helping us."

"I wouldn't have missed it." He gives me a quick side hug and goes into the hallway, looking over his shoulder at me. My room suddenly feels darker. I need to pick some flowers or hang posters on the wall or fish my cows out of the closet at home.

"You're coming home Labor Day weekend, right?" Mom asks.

I nod. "I might come home before then though, you know, if I need to."

"Call me anytime, okay?" Nick says. "Day or night. I'll be here."

"Thank you."

My brother gives me a big hug. "I love you."

"I love you too."

Then it's time to say good-bye to Mom. And that's when I lose it. Tears streak down my face. It sucks that something so exciting is so sad. She embraces me and smooths my hair. She opens her mouth to speak, and I expect that she'll say she loves me.

That she's proud of me. To go after my dreams. Or she'll quote some "deep" line from that book everybody seemed to receive as a graduation gift, *Oh the Places You'll Go* by Dr. Seuss.

But she doesn't.

A smile appears on her face. "Have fun."

• • •

My quiet lasts approximately half an hour.

And then the Vanessa-Kelsey-Iggy hurricane makes landfall. Squealing ensues. Parents are everywhere. Vanessa's ridiculously hot brother, Ty, moves all her stuff in. He's a 6'4" NFL quarterback. The result is that girls we've never met are lined up outside our room to sneak a peek. He doesn't seem to notice.

"Where do you want your TV?" he asks Vanessa.

"Over there?"

After he's deposited the TV on top of her dresser, he looks out the window. "You've got a nice view of the quad," he says.

"Thanks for giving me the window, Annie," Vanessa says, smiling. "You didn't have to do that."

"That's really nice of you," Ty says with a grin that probably makes girls throw their panties at him.

Colton arrives, because he can't seem to keep away from Kelsey to save his life, and fan-boys over Ty, giving him a high five and singing his praises.

"Dude, that pass you made last year in your game against the Seahawks was insane."

"Thanks, man," Ty says.

"Colton, you're just as bad as the girls swarming in the hall," Kelsey says.

"What girls?" he asks seriously. He goes to the door and peeks out. "Oh. Girls. Hello." He shuts the door and sits back down beside Kelsey on Vanessa's bed.

Vanessa gives me a look and whispers, "He's got it bad."

Colton can't sit still. "I can't believe we're actually here. I mean, we get to do whatever we want now." My mom has never been overly protective of me because she always wanted me to understand the real world, but Colton's dad is the mayor of Franklin. That means Colton has always been under close scrutiny.

"No curfew!" Kelsey squeals.

Colton stifles a yawn with a fist.

"Not that you'd be able to stay up past ten p.m.," Kelsey says.

"I could!" he replies, and much eye rolling ensues.

"Your curfew is still midnight," Ty says to Vanessa, who sarcastically blows a kiss back at her brother.

Iggy flits into our room, sticking a hand out to Ty. "Are you our RA?"

"What?" Ty says, narrowing his eyes.

"Our resident assistant. You look like an authority figure."

Vanessa mouths, "Authority figure."

"Are you kidding me?" Colton asks. "You don't know Ty Green?"

Vanessa collapses into a fit of giggles and Ty checks his

phone, not amused. "C'mon, Vanessa, I told Papa we'd have dinner with him."

Kelsey and Colton leave next. He says he needs Kelsey's help getting his room set up.

Iggy decides to go join the Baha'i Faith Club, whatever that means.

And I'm alone.

It's only 7:00 p.m. I do need to get to sleep early tonight considering I have a sixteen-mile run tomorrow. Only two months until the marathon. But 7:00 p.m. is way too early to pack it in. Laughter and music fill the hallways. I suddenly feel panicky, like I don't know who I am or what I'm supposed to do. Can you lose your identity in a place that you don't understand?

Do I even have an identity?

Would Kyle have helped me move in today? Would we have gone to dinner in Murfreesboro or explored campus together? Or would he have had to work at the fire station? If I had said yes to his proposal, I might not even be here. We probably would've gotten a place to live together by now.

If I'd never met Kyle, would I be out with Kelsey right now…?

Through watery eyes, I look around my new, empty room. I definitely need posters asap.

I swipe my phone and look at the screen. No texts. No emails.

I start typing: Got 16-miler tomorrow. Wanna carbo-load with me?

• • •

Sixteen miles.

If I finish, this will be the farthest I've ever run. I'm wearing the new knee brace Dr. Sanders prescribed—a thin band stretches around my knee that helps keep it in place, but now I have to think about foot placement all the time. I can't let myself fall. I can't step the wrong way. I can't slip on a rock or it's all over.

We're running the full length of the Stones River Greenway twice today. I'm aiming to finish in three hours, which is a hell of a long time to stare at the same scenery. Who ever knew blue skies could get old? At least the Greenway has a few beautiful waterfalls and wooden bridges to keep me entertained.

"So what'd you do last night?" Liza asks, swinging her arms back and forth.

"Ate some spaghetti with Jeremiah Brown. You know, Matt's brother? You've probably seen him on the trails pacing other runners."

"Oh, he's *cute*, Annie. Are you guys dating?"

"No. We're just friends."

She pulls her sunglasses down and glares at me. "Seriously? Just friends with a boy who looks like *that*? Have you seen him?"

Yes. Yes I have.

Since nearly everybody in Franklin knows what happened to Kyle, and Coach Woods told Matt what happened and he told his brother, it's weird I have to explain this. This is the first time I've had to, actually. "Look, I'm still getting over somebody."

"Bad breakup?"

I sip some water from my CamelBak and stare straight ahead. Point my toes. Swing my arms. Thirteen miles to go. A half marathon. *Breathe, Annie, breathe.* I sniffle.

"Sorry, I didn't meant to pry," Liza says softly.

One foot after the other. "It wasn't a breakup...he...he passed away. I'm running the marathon for him."

A long silence unfolds between us. And even though I don't believe in the afterlife, I pretend that Kyle is up there with the sun, telling it not to overheat me on the day I'm running a sixteen-miler. Giving me the strength to push through the next thirteen miles.

Liza props her sunglasses on top of her head so we can see each other. "I take it you don't want to talk about it?"

No, I don't talk about him.

"There's nothing left to say."

We run for a half mile in silence. For six whole minutes. I start to feel panicky that I'm going to lose my running partner. Why would a glamorous, successful woman like Liza want to hang around an eighteen-year-old with loads of baggage? I'm sure she has more important things to think about, like her sexual harassment case and being a powerful woman and saying the word penis way too often for her liking.

"I didn't tell you the whole truth about why I moved here," she says finally. "My firm did want me to try this harassment case, but the real reason I decided to start over is because my boyfriend dumped me."

"What?" I exclaim. Liza is beautiful, nice, and funny as hell. If a guy dumps her, what hope is there for the rest of womankind?

"He was an ass. Well, not when we were together, but after. He said I was too focused on my work. He didn't understand why I worked such long hours."

"You wanted to be successful."

"Yeah…I wanted a partnership at my firm, but what does that really mean?"

Talking about such adultish things makes me a little uncomfortable, because what if I don't understand something or I say something stupid? But I'm glad Liza feels I'm mature enough to confide in. "Um, I don't know much about being a lawyer, but isn't that, like, the top? Isn't a partnership the thing to achieve?"

"You're right, it is. But what about everything else?"

"Like what?"

"Like being happy. Like lying in bed on a Sunday morning with somebody you love? Or going to the beach? Or starting a family?"

Kyle always liked the little things in life: going to his dad's cabin at Normandy, running the mile for the Hundred Oaks track team, playing Legos with his little brother, watching TV with me. He wanted to become a firefighter, to help people, plain and simple.

Liza keeps talking, "I worked all day every day, even weekends. I had no time for my boyfriend. No time for my family.

I wasn't healthy. I hadn't been to the doctor in years and I was living off coffee and takeout. And yeah, I made partner, but when I got there, I realized I had nothing else except for money and a fancy title. And it didn't make me happy. Everything is about balance...it took me so long to figure that out."

For my entire life, my mom has been pushing me to go to college, to make a name for myself. And I am going to do that. But what if, when Kyle proposed, I had truly been in the moment? Truly thinking about what he was asking and what it meant for us, for me and the boy I loved so much—what would that have meant for me? All decisions are different in hindsight. Maybe all we can do is make the best decisions we can in the moment, using the best information we have right then. But still.

What if Kyle hadn't broken up with me? What if he'd let my rejection stew for a day and then moved on? What if he'd apologized a couple days later? A week. What if he'd apologized the morning after the night he died?

Is life one big long *what if*?

I've been blaming myself entirely for his death for months... but Liza is right: everything is about balance. It wasn't just me that could've done something differently. Kyle could have too.

But that doesn't mean I've gotten over him...I don't think I ever will. I loved him too much.

I need to change the subject before I start crying. "So what's up with Andrew?" I ask.

She glances over at me. "He asked me out after our fourteen-miler last week."

"And?"

"I said I'd think about it."

"Oh."

"Right now is Liza time. I'm running this marathon because I want to get in shape and do something I've always wanted to do. It's not a reason to meet guys. Taking time for yourself is always okay."

I grin. "That's really cool."

This past year has been Annie time. I felt guilty about that sometimes when my mom, or my brother and his friends, would invite me out and I didn't feel like leaving the couch, but I don't feel bad anymore after hearing what Liza said. Sometimes you just have to do what's best for you. For me that's going to the drive-in, our spot, and popping popcorn in my mouth, watching nineties movies. But I do like the idea of trying to find a new balance—one with college, family, a job, and friends. Something more than what I had in high school.

"Maybe I'll say yes after the marathon is over if either of us is still interested," Liza says.

"So you are interested!"

"Have you seen Andrew's shoulders and chest? Damn. And he's a cop."

I laugh.

"I can't say I haven't sneaked a peek at Matt's little brother," she says. "He has nice shoulders too."

Yes, I know. I've seen them. Touched them. Squeezed them.

"I feel like a cradle robber saying that," Liza adds, laughing.

"Nah. But you do seem a bit obsessed with shoulders." That reminds me. "Oh my God, yesterday when I moved into the dorms, a guy was walking around in only a towel. He had nice shoulders."

"God, I miss college."

The sixteen miles are long and hard. When I first started running, I would get a great lead and then a metaphorical piano would fall on me, but I've learned to pace myself. I'm learning my limits.

Sometimes I have to slow down so Liza can catch her breath, and sometimes she does the same for me when the lactic acid buildup makes my legs burn. She needs to walk for five minutes between miles twelve and thirteen. My stomach feels better since I gave up the ibuprofen, but I still need to use the porta-potty twice. Liza waits for me outside each time—I think she appreciates the break from running. We stick together, and it makes me feel a little better knowing that, even at thirty-two, Liza hasn't figured her life out yet.

Maybe you don't have to figure life out at all.

Maybe it just *is*.

Marathon Training Schedule~Brown's Race Co.

Name *Annie Winters*

Saturday	Distance	Notes
April 20	3 miles	I'm really doing this! Finish time 34:00
April 27	5 miles	Stupid Running Backwords Boy!!
May 4	6 miles	Blister from HELL
May 11	5 miles	Ran downtown Nashville
May 18	7 miles	Tripped on rock. Fell on my butt ☹
May 25	8 miles	Came in 5 min. quicker than usual!
June 1	10 miles	Let's just pretend this day never happened...
June 8	9 miles	Evil suicide sprint things. Ran w/ Liza. Got sick.
June 15	7 miles	Skipped Saturday's run...had to make it up Sunday.
June 22	8 miles	Stomach hurt again. Matt said eat granola instead of oatmeal
June 29	9 miles	Matt says it's time for new tennis shoes.
July 6	10 miles	Jere got hurt.
July 13	12 miles	Finished in 2:14! Only had to use bathroom once ☺
July 20	13 miles	Halfway there!
July 27	15 miles	Humidity just about finished me off. Time 3:06.
August 3	14 miles	Hurt knee. Overdosed on Pepto.
August 10	11 miles	Wore new knee brace—it messes with my gait.
August 17	16 miles	Didn't get enough sleep in dorms.
August 24	20 miles	
August 31	14 miles	
September 7	22 miles	
September 14	20 miles	
September 21	The Bluegrass Half Marathon	
September 28	12 miles	
October 5	10 miles	
October 12	Country Music Marathon in Nashville	

Iggy Strikes Again

You have got to be kidding me.

It's noon when I get back from my sixteen-mile run, and Vanessa is still sleeping away.

I dope up on Pepto, wishing I could take ibuprofen, and collapse onto my bed with an ice pack on my throbbing knee. I close my eyes, planning to relax for a few minutes before grabbing a shower. I smell like a locker room.

Two hours later, I wake up in a puddle of water. My shorts are soaked and my skin itches. I fell asleep with the ice pack on.

"Oh good, you're awake!" Vanessa says, pulling her headphones off. "We didn't want to check out campus without you." I shoot her a death stare but she's having none of it. She shoos me. "Shower. Now. Go!"

I'm groggy as hell as I climb into the shower and lean my head against the tile. Today's run just about killed me. This feels worse than any hangover I've ever had.

When I'm shampooing my hair, I accidentally slip on the suds but catch myself using the bar before I crash to the floor. *Please don't let me pass out in the shower.* I can barely move. Spots flash across my vision. Is this what every Saturday is going to be like until the marathon is over?

After somehow slipping my noodle-like arms and legs into clean clothes, Kelsey, Vanessa, Colton, and I decide to check out the *Welcome Barbecue* on the quad. Loud music blares and kids are doing everything from playing catch to lounging on picnic blankets. An ambitious guy is already campaigning for the Student Confederation President election in October. Girls are sunbathing in bikini tops, wearing headphones. The whole scene makes me happy—I've never seen so many people in my life, and hanging out with the girls makes me feel a zing inside.

The four of us load our plates with barbecue and potato salad, squeezing past other hungry kids. Someone jostles my elbow and I nearly drop my paper plate as we grab seats on the grass in front of the communications building.

Colton fist-bumps me. "Now that is what I'm talking about. Three barbecue sandwiches *and* a hot dog?"

"I'm starving," I say, taking a big bite of the hot dog.

"Ugh," Kelsey says. "I have heartburn just looking at Annie's plate."

I slurp some water in response.

"If this won't end your drought, I don't know what will," Vanessa says to Kelsey as they gaze around at the guys.

Colton says in a deadpan tone, "I've never seen so many hot girls, myself."

"So go talk to one," Kelsey says.

"Then who would carry your Coke and silverware while you're trying to balance your plate? You never would've made it through that buffet line without me."

Kelsey pops a bite of potato salad in her mouth. "True. You're a good manservant," she says.

"And you're a pain in my ass," Colton replies.

"Why don't y'all just do it already?" Vanessa blurts.

"Not gonna happen," they say simultaneously, but the minute they stop talking, he pulls her hair out of her face so it doesn't fall in her potato salad and she wipes crumbs off his chest.

We finish eating and go in search of dessert. On our way to grab cookies from the buffet, we pass a bunch of Delta Tau Kappa guys wearing T-shirts with their letters embroidered across their chests. I spot Jeremiah standing with two guys, chatting up a couple of girls. I haven't seen him yet today because he ran in a race instead of pacing somebody...I kind of missed him. His pretty blue eyes meet mine. "Annie," he calls, holding up one finger.

Vanessa grabs my elbow. Kelsey's mouth drops open.

"You know somebody in DTK?" Colton asks in a rush. "That's the fraternity I want to join. But it's hard to get into unless you're a legacy."

"What does that mean?" I ask.

"Unless, like, your father or brother or cousin or somebody's in it, it's hard to get in. It's the best fraternity on campus."

"What's so important about being in a frat?" I ask. I haven't actually talked to Jeremiah about it yet.

"Good connections for jobs after school," Colton says. "My father still plays golf and does business with people from his fraternity. But they don't have a chapter of Kappa Theta here at MTSU. That's what my dad is."

"Why didn't you just go to school where your father went?" I ask.

Colton glances at Kelsey, not answering my question.

Finished with his conversation, Jeremiah jogs up, his light brown hair bouncing everywhere. "Hey," he says to me. "So your run went well this morning?"

"I finished in three hours, five minutes."

He beams, crossing his arms. "Nice. How's the knee? Did you get a good stretch in afterward? Or do you need a partner stretch now?"

"For the hundredth time, I do *not* need you to partner stretch me." Ever since Jeremiah caught Matt doing those weird pretzel stretches with me, Jeremiah's been offering to "partner stretch" me.

"How was your race?" I ask, thrilled to see he's in one piece—no cuts, no bruises, all limbs intact.

"Not bad. I came in second place. Won a thousand dollars.

226

That ought to cover my books for this semester." I give Jeremiah a quick congratulatory hug and he tweaks my braid, like he likes to do.

"I haven't been to the bookstore yet," I say. "That's really how much they cost?"

"It depends."

Vanessa loudly says, "Ahem." She, Kelsey, and Colton are watching us like we're a movie.

"Oh," I say. "I'm sorry. Guys, this is Jeremiah." I introduce him to the girls and Colton and everyone shakes hands. Vanessa and Kelsey start sniggering like eighth graders and making eyes at the two of us. Jere laughs at that. I get a hankering to kill them all, Jeremiah included.

"So you're in DTK?" Kelsey asks him.

"I am."

"What year are you?" Vanessa asks.

"I'm a junior."

She mouths at me, "He's a junior!"

"What's your major?" Kelsey says. Every person I've met in the past day has asked that question, and it's starting to get real old because I have no real answer. Undecided but maybe physical therapy? Vanessa is majoring in accounting and Kelsey is thinking about journalism.

"Jere," I say, rescuing him from the inquisition. "Colton is really interested in your fraternity."

Jeremiah looks over at Colton, sizing him up. "You're a friend of Annie's? She hasn't mentioned you before."

Colton's face starts to fall, but I speak up even though we've never hung out much. "Yeah, we went to high school together," I say. "I've known Colton forever."

Kelsey gives me a grateful look. No matter how much she and Colton try to play down their feelings, it's obvious she cares deeply for him. They've been great friends ever since Kelsey moved into his neighborhood.

"We're having a back-to-school party at the house tonight," Jeremiah tells Colton. "We're not starting rush until next month, but you should come to the party. Get to know some of the guys." He walks over to another boy and grabs a couple fliers from him, then hands one to Colton.

"Thanks, man."

Jeremiah offers the other flier to me, his eyes flickering to mine. "I hope you can make it. And Vanessa and Kelsey too."

I look at the piece of paper. *DTK: Back-to-School Beach Bash. Beach Volleyball Tourney. Bathing Suits Required!!!*

"We'll be there," Kelsey says in a rush.

"Nice meeting you, Jere!" Vanessa says, then links her arm through mine and starts power-walking me toward the dorms. I glance over my shoulder at him and he waves.

Kelsey grabs my other elbow and hauls me even faster. Colton stays behind, continuing to talk to Jeremiah.

"Where are we going so fast?" I ask.

"You've been holding out on us, little missy!" Vanessa says.

"Who was *that*?" Kelsey says.

"Jeremiah Brown."

"And who is Jeremiah Brown?"

I take a deep breath. Kelsey and Vanessa are all over me. "Why do you want to know?"

Vanessa gives me a look. "Who doesn't love girl talk?"

"Let's talk about you and Rory then," I say.

"Bo-ring," Kelsey sings. "They've been doing it for ages."

Soon we're back in our suite, piled on Vanessa's bed. Kelsey is so excited, she seems to have temporarily forgotten our falling-out.

"How'd you meet Jeremiah?" Vanessa says. "I love his crazy hair."

"And he has a great body," Kelsey adds.

"And those tattoos on his arm! Oh my God, that's hot—"

"He has The Flash on his shoulder blade," I say. "The comic superhero guy."

Kelsey and Vanessa giggle. "You've seen it?" Vanessa asks.

My lips begin to tremble.

"Spill already," Vanessa says.

"I met him running on the trails."

"He seemed interested in you today."

I know he's interested, I want to say. But I can't. If I wasn't so nervous to talk about this—about my feelings for Jeremiah, about how I'm not over Kyle, about how I'm worried to death

Jeremiah's going to hurt himself—it might feel good to have a girl talk.

When I was little, when Kelsey's mom took care of me at night while my mother worked, Kelsey and I had slumber parties all the time. We draped sheets over the dining room table and pretended to camp out and talked about everything. But our conversations grew different as we got older. We went from talking about Barbie, to learning cursive, to who had gotten their periods, to who we wanted our first kiss to be. That's what today feels like, and the excitement makes my heart pound faster. But back then, even though I freaked out over every little last thing, nothing was truly at stake.

Everything is at stake with Jeremiah. I don't want to lose him to some crazy sports accident. I don't want to lose him as a friend, either. And like Liza said, sometimes it's okay to be single. That's what I need.

"Do you have a cute bikini for the party tonight?" Vanessa asks me. "If not, I bet one of Kelsey's will fit you. Maybe the orange one with white polka dots?"

Kelsey nods quickly. "I've got a cute white sarong to go with it—"

"I'm not going," I interrupt.

Vanessa slaps the mattress. "You have to go! I couldn't believe the tension between y'all today."

"That's precisely why I don't want to go."

"What aren't you telling us?" Kelsey asks slowly.

I fall over onto a pillow. "I hooked up with him."

"What? When?" Vanessa squeals.

"Right after graduation. Um, when we were running."

"You hooked up while running?" Kelsey asks, furrowing her eyebrows. "How does one hook up while running?"

"I thought only, like, Cirque du Soleil performers could do stuff like that!" Vanessa says.

I roll my eyes. "We were running on the trails by the Little Duck River and then we went down by the water."

Vanessa and Kelsey glance at each other.

"So why haven't you mentioned him?" Kelsey asks.

I pull myself into Indian style. "He didn't call afterward..." *And then I found this ring in Kyle's bedroom.* "And I just felt..."

The girls stare, waiting for me to finish.

"It felt wrong." Saying that is sort of a lie, but the emotions are too complex to figure out.

"But do you like him?" Vanessa asks. "I could tell something was up between you guys."

"We're friends."

My heart beats faster and faster when I think back to that moment on the banks of the river. Yeah, I'd never felt so turned on, so out of control, but lust and love are two different things. Love is far more dangerous.

"He's not for me," I say.

The girls let out sighs.

"We're still going to this party, right?" Vanessa holds up the DTK flier.

"Yeah, maybe we'll meet other guys there," Kelsey says. "And we can both get rid of these droughts."

"I don't think Annie has a drought," Vanessa says. "She hooked up like a circus performer while running, remember?"

I swat her with a pillow.

"Was the hookup fun?" Kelsey asks with a hopeful gleam in her eye.

We're back in seventh grade again, chatting about our crushes, back when we always told each other the truth—our deepest secrets and fears and hopes and dreams.

That's why I admit, "Jeremiah was really good."

And they squeal.

• • •

I'm not sure how, but I manage to convince Vanessa and Kelsey that I'm not ready for a party at the DTK house.

"My muscles are killing me from this morning's run," I say, which isn't remotely a lie.

The girls exchange looks but ultimately give in. Vanessa did find me zonked out in an ice-pack puddle earlier today, after all. "Text us if you change your mind," she says, checking her bikini in the mirror for the nth time.

"Is Rory gonna be pissed when he hears you went to a party without him?" I ask.

"Nope," Vanessa says confidently. "I already texted him a picture of me in my bathing suit. He's very happy now."

"Ugh, I do not want to know what that means," Kelsey says.

"Hey, you try having a long-distance relationship. It's tough having my boyfriend two hours away."

After one last quick mirror check—Kelsey adjusts the straps on her orange polka-dotted top and Vanessa adds another layer of lip gloss—they are out the door. I let out a deep breath.

I decide to read some of Mom's book I found on the coffee table at home, a medical thriller about how a rogue FBI agent teams up with a hot doctor to stop a worldwide plague, then wash my face and start getting ready for bed. I roll my shoulders and stretch my arms. This morning's run did a number on my poor body. I change into matching pink pajama shorts and a tank, then sit down on the rug and attempt to stretch out my legs. The long run made them stiffer than steel. I lean over onto the floor, pressing my nose to the rug. That's when someone knocks on the door.

"Who is it?"

"Jere."

Did he come to drag me to the party?

"Come in."

He walks in and finds me pressing my face to the floor. "Is this your way of saying you want me to partner stretch you?"

I sit up straight, and the sight of him wipes the scowl clean off my face. He's wearing long red board shorts, a cheesy neon green tank, and flip-flops. Sunglasses sit perched on top of his head. I don't know if his outfit makes me want to die laughing or fan myself. It's ridiculous, yet ridiculously attractive too.

"What are you doing here?" I ask.

"I'm here to beat you at something else. Now, I know you're interested in being a nurse, but I think I can hold my own." With a wicked grin, he holds up the board game Operation.

"Bring. It. On."

We sprawl out on the floor with the game between us. I go first, carefully extracting the butterfly from the cartoon man's stomach. Then Jeremiah plucks out the broken heart. My turn to get the wishbone.

"Why didn't you come to the party?" he asks quietly.

I glance up. *Because you scare me.* "This morning's run was hard. I just wanted to relax and not have to be social."

He opens a bag of Swedish fish he brought and offers me one. I choose an orange fish. "I wish you had come—I wanted to show you around our house…but this is good too."

"Yeah, most guys I know *love* playing Operation on Saturday nights."

He chuckles. "You know what I meant. I like hanging out with my friend."

"I like hanging out with my friend too."

Soon it's down to the wire. If I remove the wrenched ankle

without hitting the board, I'll win. I worry on my lip, my hand shaking as I descend toward the ankle. I grab the wrench with my tweezers and slowly start to pull up when I bang against the board. It buzzes loudly.

"Dammit!" I say, and before I can even pout, Jeremiah plucks the wrenched ankle out with the tweezers, winning the game.

"Arrrgggh!" I pound my fist on the floor, cracking him up.

With the game over, we decide to watch a movie. He scrolls through my iTunes while I flick off the overhead fluorescent light and turn on my desk lamp.

"What is all this crap?" he says. "*Dirty Dancing? The Notebook? Legally Blonde? Twilight?!*"

"Hey! Those are good movies."

"Oh my God, *Sisterhood of the Traveling Pants?*"

"Jeremiah Brown."

"*A Walk to Remember?!*"

"If you don't behave, I'm gonna send you right home."

"Yeah, that's the scariest threat ever. You'd be sending me to a bathing suit party."

"I know you'd rather stay here with me."

Crap. Where did that come from?

"Fine," he says with a smirk. "We'll watch *Mean Girls*, whatever that is."

He positions my laptop at an angle where we can both see it, then lies back on my bed, pulls his glasses from his pocket, and slips them onto his nose. I sit Indian style and lean over onto my knees. The room is quiet, except for the movie, our breathing, our laughing.

Jeremiah folds his hands behind his head. "Man, these girls are bitches."

"I know, genius. That's why it's called *Mean Girls*."

Without a warning, he yanks me back against his chest. "Watch the movie with me," he whispers.

"That's what we're doing." Deep down I know what he really means, and that makes my heart beat wildly, but I can't decide if that's a good or bad thing. My thoughts and pulse are racing.

He arranges me under his arm, and I wrap my trembling hand around his middle, cozying up to him. He feels warm, but I'm shaking like it's snowing. It's hard work to control my breathing. We lie together in silence for what feels like hours just watching the movie, until I feel him dragging his fingertips gently up and down my arm. Up and down my spine. Is his hand shaking?

Is this what adult relationships are like? You just touch someone without first laying down the boundaries? I mean, I've never been in a relationship except for with Kyle, and it was slow moving and had barriers to cross. First handholding, first kiss, first make-out session, first time he took off my shirt. And with Jeremiah, I feel lost, like during personal training when I don't know what the next exercise will be. It's scary not knowing what's coming.

I'm not ready for a new relationship. I don't know if I'll ever want one again. I don't want to have that conversation with Jeremiah. But I don't want him to stop tracing his fingertips up and down my arm, either. It feels soft and smooth and tingly. And being pressed up against him is *sweltering*.

That's when the door opens to reveal Iggy holding what appears to be a mandolin.

"Kelsey, are you in here? Did you steal my cheetah-print bra— Oops. I didn't know you had somebody over, Annie. Why didn't you tie the jump rope to the door?"

"Jump rope?" Jeremiah asks, lifting his head to get a look at her.

"Did somebody steal the jump rope?" she asks, pushing her glasses up on her nose. "I knew this would happen. I can't wait to tell Kelsey."

"Iggy," I say, choking back a laugh. "Could you please excuse us? We're watching a movie."

Her mouth forms an O. "I get it. I'll put the jump rope on the doorknob for you."

"No!" I say.

"Fine." She slams the door shut.

Jeremiah raises an eyebrow. "Is the jump rope your suite's code for sexiling?"

I swallow hard. "Yeah."

"Mason and I have a code too," he says. "We're supposed

to knock five times. If one of us has a girl over, we yell 'Get lost, loser!'"

"Why don't you hang something from the door? Kelsey says that's what people normally do."

"Your roommate Iggy got it right. One time Mason hung a sock on our doorknob. Someone stole the sock…and I walked in on him and some girl butt naked."

"Ew."

"You're telling me." Jeremiah takes his knit cap off, tosses it on the floor, and runs a hand through his messy hair, not meeting my eyes. His Adam's apple shifts as he swallows. "Want to finish the movie?"

"Um, sure."

We lie back down on the bed. And my heart starts rocketing out of my chest toward the moon. My breathing becomes labored. Not taking his eyes off the screen, he pulls me onto his chest and squeezes my shoulder. And I want him so bad I can feel it in my bones. I can feel it in the tips of my toes, in the palms of my hands, in all sorts of other tingly places. He caresses my back. I feel dampness between my legs. It would be so easy to take what I need from him, but that's not fair because what if he wants more than just the physical?

Frankly, I shouldn't even let him touch me. I'll just end up hurting him.

I gently push him away. "My roommate's gonna be back soon."

We sit up together, the tension hanging over the room like a haze, and right then, Vanessa opens the door. A bright smile flickers on her face when she sees us together. "Whoops! Sorry to interrupt." She closes the door and disappears within seconds.

Jeremiah glances over at me, smiles, and drags a hand through his hair. He digs his phone out of his pocket of those bright red shorts and checks the screen. "I probably should go. Got an early run tomorrow."

"But you raced today!"

He shrugs. "I gotta train hard if I want to keep winning."

"I don't know how you do it."

"What? Run?"

"Do all these crazy races. I mean, I hurt so much after every single long run, and you do them constantly."

"It's my job."

I shake my head, incredulous. "How far are you running in the morning?"

"Ten miles, but then I'm doing a few hours of training on a bike. I'm planning on trying a motocross race soon."

I've heard Nick and Evan talk about those races because they repair bikes down at Caldwell's. Sometimes people fall off and break their legs. Sometimes they get run over by other contestants. Sometimes they get thrown thirty feet. Sometimes they die.

I sit up straight, my body rigid as a brick wall. "Jeremiah, why would you do that?"

"I have to find new stuff to do." He pushes a strand of my hair behind my ear and touches my neck.

"You don't have to do anything," I say quietly. "Why can't you just keep doing regular races?"

He starts tapping his foot nervously. "Because they aren't as much fun for me anymore. I need more. Not even marathons challenge me."

I clench my fists. "So you don't think doing the Country Music Marathon is worth anything?"

"I didn't say that at all," he replies in a soft voice. "Hardly anyone has what it takes to do a marathon. And you're tougher than nails. You keep getting faster and faster, and I can tell how strong you are. You are going to pimp the Country Music Marathon's ass."

"Uhh." I mouth "pimp the Country Music Marathon's ass," making Jeremiah laugh quietly. "I don't even know what that means," I say.

"Neither do I."

I pinch the top of my nose. *Breathe.* I care about my friend. I really do. I don't want to see him hurt. I can't lose someone else. "I really wish you wouldn't do this motocross thing. Please, Jere."

He lifts his knit cap off the floor and puts it on. "It sucks that you're trying to tell me what to do."

That makes me feel shitty. But he's right. I'm the last person who has the right to tell him to change. It's not like we're dating.

"But I'll do it for you," he says sincerely. He turns his gaze to me, to my lips, and I know what he's thinking. Me asking this of him will make things a lot more serious between us. Do friends change who they are at their core for each other? That's not healthy. But neither is motocross…

"You don't have to quit on my account. I just want you to take care of yourself, Jeremiah."

"I will." He pats my hand and stands up to collect Operation. "This was fun. You want to hang out tomorrow afternoon when I get back?"

"Okay."

"I'll text you."

I walk him to the door, where he gives me a quick hug good night, and when I curl up in bed later, I can still smell his cologne lingering in the air.

College is Drama

"Let's get matching sweatshirts!"

"No, Jere," I say. It's Sunday afternoon, Jeremiah arrived at my dorm room unscathed, and now we're at the school bookstore. "We're here to buy my books."

He picks up an MTSU snow globe and shakes it. "C'mon. I'll get a blue one and you'll get a red one and then we'll match like old people on the beach."

"Fine, we'll get matching sweatshirts as long as yours is pink." That shuts him up.

The bookstore is huge and books are piled everywhere. I touch my throat. It's a little overwhelming. I take my course and book lists from my purse and begin searching through the stacks.

"Here's your biology book," Jeremiah says and drops it into the basket he's carrying for me. Holy crap, it's $100!

Most of my general education courses this semester involve science and math, but for some unknown reason I have to take an art class. The art history textbook costs $175, is bigger than a large pizza box, and must weigh twenty-five pounds. I place it back on the shelf—I can't afford that whatsoever. I guess I'll check online later to see if I can get it for cheap on eBay. Otherwise, maybe I'll have to find a different type of art class. But paint supplies and brushes and canvas can't be cheap either.

In the line to pay for my biology and calculus books, Jeremiah examines all the crappy trinkets and goodies they try to get people to buy while waiting. I bet he would love joining Mom for a fishing expedition through the $1 bins at Target.

"Oh, check this out," he says. He finds an MTSU troll keychain with pink hair. "You need this."

"I don't need a troll doll," I say with a laugh.

"You're getting it." He tosses it into the basket.

The girl behind us, who only has one book in her hand, glances into our basket. "Don't tell me you're actually buying your books?" she asks, incredulous.

"Why wouldn't I?" I say.

"Who actually reads their books for class? You should only bother reading if you have a test coming up or a paper to write. And then you could just borrow the book from somebody in class or the library."

I peer up at Jeremiah to get his opinion. He shakes his head at the girl. "Annie, the biggest problem you have with buying these books is hauling them back to your dorm. They're heavy as hell."

"That's not a problem. That's what you're here for." I nudge his side, making him laugh.

The girl behind us huffs and starts playing with her phone, taking quick peeks at Jeremiah. He yawns, ignoring her. I bet she wishes she hadn't tried to embarrass me now.

"Besides," Jeremiah starts, "you can sell these books back to the bookstore at the end of the semester, and you can use the money for Christmas presents."

"Good to know," I say. "Will you help me carry the books back at the end of the semester too?"

"Of course. And then you can turn around and buy my Christmas gift. I got a hankering for some matching sweatshirts."

I playfully smack his arm and the girl behind us huffs again. She must be jealous of happy people. I smile at Jeremiah, who's busy looking at a rubber chicken wearing a tiny MTSU jersey. He really does make me happy. Being around him clears my head just like running does.

When we lug my bags of books through my bedroom door, we discover Vanessa chatting with Rory over the computer. Thank God they aren't having Skype sex or something.

I plop my keys and new troll keychain down on my desk. Jeremiah insisted on buying it for me. He named it Jay-Z for some unknown reason.

"What is that?" Vanessa ask.

"A troll keychain," I say. "Named Jay-Z."

"Isn't it awesome?" Jeremiah grins.

Vanessa holds the troll up to the screen. "Ror, isn't this keychain hideous?"

"No, he's right—it's awesome," Rory replies. "Can you get me one of those, babe?"

Vanessa takes Rory and her computer into the kitchenette. I think she wants to give us alone time.

I turn on some music and take the books out of my bags to line them up on the bookshelf. Jeremiah turns his attention to his phone and starts texting away. When he plops down on my bed, his track pants ride up, revealing a thick white bandage wrapped around his lower leg.

A bandage…

I rush to kneel next to it. "What happened?" I gently touch the bandage and he winces. Whatever the injury is, it's tender.

His face flushes as he bends to remove my hand from his leg. "It's nothing."

"What did you do?"

"What you told me not to do," he says quietly.

"Motocross?"

A curt nod.

How stupid of me to think he'd show up unscathed. When has he ever been known to do that? "Tell me what's wrong with your leg," I say, staring at the bandage.

"Burned it on the bike."

I clench my eyes shut. Goddammit. What if he breaks his leg next time? Or loses it? I bury my face in the heels of my hands until I feel him gently touching my shoulder.

"I'm all right. I accidentally knocked my leg into the metal when I was getting off. It was an amateur move. Probably because I am an amateur—"

"Are you going to do motocross again?" I interrupt.

"No. If it upsets you, I promise I won't."

"How can I believe that?"

"Because this is better than motocross."

"What is?"

A pause. Drums his fingers on his knee. "Just sitting here with you."

God…hearing that is scarier than him BASE jumping off the Empire State Building.

"Hey," he says quietly, sliding off the bed to sit next to me on the floor. Our shoulders touch. A shiver slivers up my spine. "My leg'll be fine."

"Jere? I think you should go."

"Why?"

A tear trickles out of my eye. I quickly brush it away. "This is too much."

"I promise I'll never do motocross again—"

"That's not it!"

He cups my cheek with his hand, and my stupid cheek leans

into him without my permission, and then our foreheads are pressed together. Our breathing races. He smells so good.

But the bandage on his leg kills the mood.

"I think you should go," I mumble.

Jeremiah pats my thigh twice, then checks his phone. "I have to go anyway. My fraternity has its chapter meetings on Sunday nights, and I have to put on my good shirt and tie."

He stands, stretches out a hand, and lifts me to my feet before walking to the door. "I'll text you."

I shake my head at the carpet. "Please don't."

His face crumples. "Annie, it was an accident. It won't happen again—"

"You don't understand. I don't want to lose you—"

"You won't—"

"How can you be so sure? I've already lost…" My voice trails off.

"Do you want to talk about him?" Jeremiah asks quietly, looking unsure.

"No, I don't. How can you not understand how your doing motocross makes me feel?"

"How am I supposed to know how you feel? You never talk about him and what happened. I don't even know how he die—"

"I'm not talking about him!"

"Friends tell each other how they feel. And we're friends, Annie. You're one of the best friends I've ever had." Jeremiah's voice is soft.

"I don't want to lose you—"

"So you're pushing me away? Just like my mom?"

"I need to be alone. Please."

He shuts his eyes and lets out a long breath. "Fine. I guess I'll see you around."

And then he's gone.

• • •

College is different.

At home, I went to my room when I needed alone time. Now I have a roommate with an addiction to online videos. Every five seconds, Vanessa wants to show me a cat riding a Roomba, a whale chasing a boat, or a goat bleating like Taylor Swift. When Vanessa's not YouTube-ing, she's Skyping with Rory. She stays up until 3:00 a.m. most nights, doing everything from fixing her hair to doing sit-ups and weird yoga poses, and I like to be in bed by 11:00 p.m. in order to go running in the mornings before class. Sometimes I just want complete silence so I can read my trashy medical thriller. (Why can't the doctor and the rogue FBI agent just do it already?!)

On my fourth night in the dorms, I decide to buy earplugs. I love Vanessa because she's so nice, but God, having a roommate can be annoying. It could be worse, I guess. I could have Iggy and her mandolin.

But even if Vanessa were silent, I'd still have the crazy screaming people in the hallways to contend with. Two guys got into an argument because one drank the other's Snapple. A couple broke up in the common room because he cheated with the girl who runs the projector in his film class. Our neighbors live for blasting electroclash music. Kelsey and Iggy got into a fight because Kelsey didn't clean her hair out of the shower drain.

"Do you think hair clumps are against the Baha'i faith or something?" I asked Vanessa, who sniggered.

Classes are different from high school too. Instead of having homework every single night, we have a few major tests and term papers per semester. Only five hundred kids went to Hundred Oaks, but here at MTSU, I'm in a psychology lecture with over three hundred. At least Colton is in the class with me. That makes it not so overwhelming.

The reading assignments for all classes are long and tough. Sometimes I have no idea what I'm reading. Sometimes I wonder if I'll make it through four years of this crazy hard coursework. I make plans to go visit my teachers during office hours.

After classes on the first day, I went to the Professional Health Sciences office. I saw online they were hiring for a part-time office assistant. Vanessa suggested that instead of changing my major from undecided to physical therapy or nursing right away (apparently her brother changed his major, like, three times and warned her not to worry about it until later), I should try to get a work-study job at the school, so I can see what it's like *and* start earning money. I'd been stressing about how to pay for books along with Matt's training program dues for this October.

The physical therapy office itself reminded me a lot of the gym where Matt works. The place was full of mini trampolines, medicine balls, and nutrition posters. I met a nice guy, Michael, who rocks these red-rimmed rectangular glasses and has black studs in each ear.

"I'm here to apply for the job?" I said with a shaky voice.

He smiled as he handed me an application, and I filled it out. After I talked with the office coordinator, explained that I've been working steadily as a waitress for over two years, and told her how important exercise has become to me, she hired me on the spot. Sure, with the office's minimum wage I won't be making good money like I did at the Roadhouse, but I feel great that I have a way to make some cash and will hopefully learn something too.

I love the late afternoons after classes when the heat has died down. Vanessa, Kelsey, and I like to lie out on towels on the quad, just talking and studying. They giggle when guys whistle at us. And even though Kelsey and I haven't talked about our past, everything seems okay. I love having friends again.

I keep wishing Jeremiah would walk by and challenge me to a game of Parcheesi or something. But he doesn't.

Jeremiah and I only text each other twice during my first week, and we never make plans to meet up again. I texted to see if he wanted to run together one morning or evening and he replied: We don't run the same speed. It makes no sense to train together.

I took a literal step back when I read that text. Fine, I thought. He's right. I would just slow him down.

But honestly? I scared him off. He isn't jumping to see me anymore. I find myself looking for him on campus, at the gym, at the bagel place, on the quad between classes. With 30,000 kids at this school, it seems impossible to just run into him. How is it possible that I miss him so much...but I'm scared of him at the same time?

Mom always said I depended on Kyle too much: *a guy should fit into your life, Annie, not become it.* I don't want to depend on Jeremiah like that. I go to dinner with Kelsey, Vanessa, and Colton every night, and on Wednesday, I grab a coffee with Michael after he trained me for my new job.

But I still miss my friend.

Maybe that *rush* Jeremiah told me about applies to friends too. Maybe he lost that feeling of flying with me. Maybe that's why he's barely paid attention to me this week.

I mean, I asked him to give up something he loves just because it scares *me*. Me, somebody who has given him nothing except friendship. Am I being selfish? Yeah. But I don't want him to get hurt.

On the Friday night before my first twenty-mile run—the farthest distance Kyle ever ran—instead of carbo-loading with

Jeremiah, I find myself driving back to Franklin to the drive-in movie theater. *Grease* is playing tonight. Kyle and I loved watching this movie together. I loved the songs and he loved when Sandy wore the hot leather outfit and smoked a cigarette at the end.

God, I miss the way things used to be. I buy a small popcorn, sit on the hood of my car, and use my thumb to wipe away the tears.

Marathon Training Schedule - Brown's Race Co.

Name _Annie Winters_

Saturday	Distance	Notes
April 20	3 miles	I'm really doing this! Finish time 34:00
April 27	5 miles	Stupid Running Backwords Boy!!
May 4	6 miles	Blister from HELL
May 11	5 miles	Ran downtown Nashville
May 18	7 miles	Tripped on rock. Fell on my butt
May 25	8 miles	Came in 5 min. quicker than usual!
June 1	10 miles	Let's just pretend this day never happened...
June 8	9 miles	Evil suicide sprint things. Ran w/ Liza. Got sick.
June 15	7 miles	Skipped Saturday's run..had to make it up Sunday.
June 22	8 miles	Stomach hurt again. Matt said eat granola instead of oatmeal.
June 29	9 miles	Matt says it's time for new tennis shoes.
July 6	10 miles	Jere got hurt.
July 13	12 miles	Finished in 2:14! Only had to use bathroom once
July 20	13 miles	Halfway there!
July 27	15 miles	Humidity just about finished me off. Time 3:06.
August 3	14 miles	Hurt knee. Overdosed on Pepto.
August 10	11 miles	Wore new knee brace—it messes with my gait.
August 17	16 miles	Didn't get enough sleep in dorms.
August 24	20 miles	Need lifetime supply of Pepto & ice packs. Stat!
August 31	14 miles	
September 7	22 miles	
September 14	20 miles	
September 21	The Bluegrass Half Marathon	
September 28	12 miles	
October 5	10 miles	
October 12	Country Music Marathon in Nashville	

THE WIN

"Annie, please come with me," Colton begs, and I keep shaking my head.

It's Saturday evening after I've completed my first twenty-mile run. I haven't been able to keep a bite of food down all afternoon, and I iced my knee three times and took an extra strength Tylenol. Vanessa is busy hooking up with her boyfriend in our bedroom, so Kelsey let me camp out in hers.

And Colton freaking wants me to go to a DTK party and put in a word for him with Jeremiah, who currently doesn't want anything to do with me.

"Please?" Kelsey asks me quietly.

With my bedroom being commandeered by Vanessa and Rory, it's not like I have much else to do.

"Okay," I finally agree, mostly because Kelsey asked me to. And if I'm being honest, because I miss Jeremiah and want to see how he's doing.

She opens her closet. "We need to make ourselves hot asap. Colton, get out."

He grins at her. "I'll go change my shirt and meet you back here."

Kelsey and I turn up the music real loud while we get ready, straightening our hair, slipping into various outfits. She dances around the room, sliding lip gloss on, and I limp around like I just had my hip replaced.

"I have no idea where I'm going to sleep tonight," I say, popping two more Tylenol. "Maybe I should go back to Franklin. I bet Vanessa and Rory won't come out of there before noon tomorrow."

"I bet they don't come out until he has to drive back to his school…maybe you should stay with Jere tonight."

I ignore Kelsey and go back to trying on her clothes. I settle on a pair of jeans, a black halter top, heels, and bangles, rocking an arm party.

Kelsey nods at my outfit approvingly. "That's really cute. Do you like these?" She wiggles her butt in her tight pink shorts, and that starts us laughing. This reminds me of playing dress-up in her mother's closet when we were little. It's crazy that we're all grown up with somewhere to go finally.

"Oh my God, this is nuts." Kelsey starts telling me about how Iggy talks in her sleep. "This is just a guess, but I think she has a crush on this guy she knows, Jason Bulger."

"Why?"

"Because sometimes in the middle of the night, she starts yelling in her sleep, 'Bulger! Bulger!'"

I crack up along with her, and by the time Colton comes to pick us up, Kelsey and I are laughing our asses off. The side of Colton's mouth slips into a smirky smile when he sees how happy she is.

When we arrive at the party, cars are everywhere, so we have to park down the street. But I can still see that the DTK house is huge. A tall fence encircles the property. Or should I say palace? This place is like a castle, with its ivy covering the brick walls and the fancy fountain…with a statue of a mermaid naked from the waist up. Hmm.

We walk in the door and immediately a guy hands us each a plastic cup and a Sharpie to write our name on it. Then we get drinks.

This is nothing like high school parties, where boys jump off the roof into the pool and everybody gets smashed and hangs all over everybody, using alcohol as an excuse for hooking up. Sure, people are drinking here, but they aren't loud. Well, the beer pong tournament is noisy, but most people are sitting on couches, slowly sipping their drinks or making out in dark doorways. The music isn't blaring. Who ever thought a frat would be somewhat classy? I use the word *somewhat* because I'm sipping box wine out of a plastic cup.

Mason, one of the guys who came to the Roadhouse and also Jeremiah's roommate, hustles up to me. "Annie!" He gives me a noisy kiss on the cheek, making me grin. What a goofball.

"You got enough to drink?" Mason asks.

"I do, thanks. Have you met my friends Kelsey and Colton?" They all shake hands, and another guy who came to the Roadhouse approaches—the doofus who stole the coonskin cap off the wall and wore it. Mason introduces him as Fisher. I'm not sure if that's his first, last, or nickname (because he's good at catching bass or something?).

Fisher points at me. "We met you at that restaurant! You're Jere's friend."

I nod, wondering if that's still the case. Are you still friends if you go from talking every day for nearly two months to sending only two texts in one week?

"Where *is* Jere?" Kelsey asks, sipping her beer.

"Last I saw him, he was in our library," Fisher says. "With his ex, Gina."

I choke on my wine.

Mason pushes Fisher's shoulder. "Dude, shut up." He gives me a worried look as I cover my mouth to cough—wine is stuck in my throat. "Don't mind Fish, Annie. He doesn't know whether to check his ass or scratch his watch."

Jeremiah has an ex? He's here with a girl...?

Kelsey lays a hand on my arm. "Want to go home?"

Her concern makes me smile, and I pat her hand, but deep inside I feel a low darkness starting to spread. "I'm fine. You should go dance with Colton."

After giving me a long look, she and Colton start moving to a fast song, getting lost in each other.

"Do you want to dance?" Mason asks me, looking awkward. Fisher has vamoosed.

"I'm cool," I say, and Mason lets out a long breath of air, muttering something about needing to check the keg.

All alone, I find myself wandering toward the back of the house, looking for the library. I can't help it. I have to know what's up with Jeremiah. I need to know if I screwed up our friendship.

I pass by a billiards room with three pool tables, then a den full of cushy sofas. I come upon a room with lots of desks and shelves filled with books. I bet this is where DTK guys study. I hear a noise and gaze to the right. Jeremiah.

He's sitting with a pretty girl on a leather sofa. Smiling at her. She touches his arm and returns his stare. Seeing them together makes me choke again.

He jerks his head when he hears me cough. My heartbeat races and I feel panicky. Seeing him with another girl sucks. I have no right to him, I know, but still. This really does suck. My hands shake. I make a break for the door.

"Hey, wait up," he says breathlessly, rushing toward me. "You came to our party."

"I did." I look past him to where the girl is still sitting on the couch. I wipe my damp palms on my jeans. The darkness inside me starts to spread. "I didn't mean to interrupt."

He glances over his shoulder but turns right back to me. "You aren't interrupting. Gina and I are in the same Ethics of Education class. We were talking about this paper we have to write for the midterm."

"Oh." *I thought she was your ex.*

"But you came," he repeats, a grin spreading across his face. He rubs his hands together. "How about a tour?"

Gina stands and stalks over to him, wobbling on her four-inch heels. "So that's it, then?"

"We can talk about the paper on Monday. Talking about schoolwork on a weekend is a crime."

"It is not," Gina says.

"I'm sure it is in some states. People outlaw all sorts of shit. Like, in Minnesota, it's against the law to eat ice cream on side-walks on Tuesdays."

Gina glares. "But we were talking!"

"We'll talk on Monday." Jere takes my hand, leaving her behind, and leads me to a rear staircase. His dark jeans, knit cap, and snug gray tee make my mouth go dry.

"I should go back to my room—I mean, home," I say. Even after a week, my new room doesn't feel like *home*.

"You can stay right here with me."

"You were with a girl. I don't want to interrupt."

His expression is soft and kind. "You didn't interrupt."

"Fisher told me she's your ex." I stare at the hardwood floor.

He doesn't say anything back, and when I finally look up at him, I find a wicked smirk.

"We dated for a couple weeks last winter, but we didn't mesh... Are you jealous?"

"No!"

"I think you're jealous," he whispers. He nods at my fingers, which are currently playing with my necklace.

I cross my arms. "Nope. You should go right back to whatever you were doing with Gina."

"You are *so* jealous."

I change the subject. "This is not what I expected a frat house to look like."

"Oh?"

"Where's the waterslide? Where's the body shot area?"

"That happens later in the evening," he jokes. "Want that tour now?" He takes my hand in his and leads me to the backyard. They do, in fact, have a pool, but no waterslide. Probably couldn't afford one after buying that naked mermaid statue. Eye roll. They also have lots of picnic tables, lounge furniture, and tennis and basketball courts. Inside the house: a huge kitchen with an island, a meeting room, and a dining room with five long tables that easily seat a hundred people.

"What is this? The Great Hall at Hogwarts?" I say, making him chuckle.

He leads me to the foyer, where Mason and Fisher are passing out cups and hitting on girls. When they see Jeremiah holding my hand, Fisher silently mouths "Yes!" at Mason.

"How many guys live here?" I ask.

"Forty. We have over a hundred members, but some of the older guys live in apartments or in houses off campus, and freshmen usually live in the dorms."

Running his hand along the bannister, he leads me up a wide staircase to the second floor. Composite pictures of pledge classes cover the walls. Jeremiah points out his brother Matt's class that graduated a few years ago.

"We all share bathrooms up here, so if you need to go, use the one for girls downstairs. It always has soap and toilet paper."

"How do I know which room it is?"

"It has a sign on the door that says *Sheilas*."

"Like at Outback Steakhouse?"

He cocks his head. "I think we stole that sign from there, yeah."

Jeremiah pushes open his bedroom door. It's set up kind of like mine: two twin beds, two dressers, two desks. How is it different from my room? Socks, T-shirts, boxers, and shorts are everywhere.

"Sorry for the mess," he says. "I would've cleaned up if I'd known you were stopping by."

"It's okay. I have a brother, you know."

"A brother who would kill me if he knew you were in my room right now."

"Yeah, he would." I look at the pictures of his family taped to the wall. I laugh at one where Kate is shooting a water gun at him. Another shows Jennifer sitting on his shoulders at a zoo. And then I see the medals and trophies.

"There must be a hundred medals here," I exclaim, examining one from the New York City Marathon.

"I get 'em at the end of most races. I save them."

The room is quiet, minus the sounds of the party downstairs. I lean up against his desk. "I probably should head back to my dorm. I'm tired."

"Don't go," he says in a quiet voice.

"Why not?"

"We still haven't talked about why you were jealous tonight."

"God!" I growl. "Do you have to win at everything? Can't you just let it go?"

"Nope."

"I'm not a prize to be won, Jeremiah. I'm worth more than that."

He stalks toward me and pins me to the desk. His hips press against mine, stealing my breath. "What's that supposed to mean?" he snaps.

"Your brother told me you don't do serious relationships. Are you just trying to win me? Then forget about me?"

He takes a step back, nearly tripping over a heavy hiking boot. His nostrils flare. "How could you question our friendship?"

"I'm—"

"No. Let me get this out." He paces the room. "I care about you. I care about you like I've never cared about anybody before. More than my family. More than my brother."

I close my eyes and grab his desk chair to hold myself up.

He goes on, "I've wanted you since the moment we met."

My instincts tell me to rush out of the room, but the tug to stay with him is too strong.

"I never wanted a relationship with a girl before you," he goes on. "My life moved too fast to slow down for anybody. But this entire summer I've been going slow. I've been waiting for you. And I can wait as long as you need. I can't say I know how you feel or tell you how to feel better, but I can wait. I'll be your friend.

"But don't insult me. I haven't been with another girl since I met you. I don't consider you some prize to be won."

By the time he's done speaking, he's panting and there's a vulnerability in his eyes I've never seen before. It scares me. But it also knocks something loose.

He can wait.

"Jere?"

"Hmm?"

I reach a hand out to him. "I'm sorry. Can you forgive me?"

"Always."

We stand quietly, staring at each other, holding hands.

I ask, "If I'm ready for some things with you, but not other stuff, will you be mad?"

Searching my eyes, he gently rubs his thumb against my palm. "I'm ready for whatever you're ready for."

I take a deep breath. "I met Kyle after I smashed him in the head with a volleyball." Jeremiah dips his head and smiles sadly, listening as I tell the story of my first love. I describe our first fight—how Kyle had signed up for the Homecoming kissing booth, not understanding we were in a real relationship and people in relationships don't kiss other people in kissing booths, even if it is for charity.

"Dude had cojones," Jeremiah jokes, and I smack his arm. He sets his hands on my waist and pulls me close, as if he's scared I'm going to get away. "Tell me more."

"I liked silence and he always had to fill it. He was a terrible backseat driver—he would stomp an imaginary brake when I was going too fast. He smacked his cereal and it drove me nuts. He proposed to me...and I said no, but I would've eventually said yes. He was mine and I was his."

I choke up, and Jeremiah pulls me into a long hug. "Thank you for telling me about him."

I wipe tears off my cheeks. "I miss him."

"I know you do, darlin'." His voice is soft and sweet. I press my palms to his chest, and my own feels lighter. *He can wait for me.*

"I know a game I can beat you at," I say, gently sweeping my fingers across his T-shirt.

"What's that?" he asks, peering down at my hands.

"The first person to kiss the other wins."

I quickly press my lips to his. A short peck. A short peck that feels like a supernova. When he opens his pretty blue eyes that pierce mine, his breaths are short and shallow. He wraps his hands around my waist. Lifts me onto his desk. Parts my knees and slips between my legs.

His mouth dips to my ear, his breath tickling me. "You won."

Our lips meet again, and it's slow, and sweet, and nothing at all like our rushed number down by the river this past June.

And then his lips tell me not to think anymore, to just do what I want to do, and I whisper okay. I cup his cheeks with my hands, enjoying the way his stubble scratches me, and his hands move up and down my back, softly exploring and making me warm.

He lifts me and slips his hands under my bottom to carry me to his bed. I wrap my legs around his waist and we plop down on his quilt together, continuing to kiss. I pull his knit cap off his head and toss it to the floor.

I discover he's chatty in bed. He talks about everything, from how he likes the taste of my lips to how he wishes the guys would shut up downstairs to how he wishes I'd stay the night and go running with him in the morning.

"But you're so much faster," I say between kisses. "You said in your text that it'll mess up your training."

"Who cares?" He pulls me on top so I'm straddling him, and I can feel his hardness pressing against me through his jeans. He can't take his eyes off my black halter top.

I haven't *just* made out like this in years. Sure, I've already seen Jeremiah without any clothes on, but there's something exciting about just kissing and not knowing what's next.

"I care about you so much," he says breathily. "I've wanted you since the moment we met—when you yelled at me for running backwards."

"I was scared you couldn't forgive me," I reply, running a fingertip around his crop circle tattoos. "I was worried our friendship was over."

"All that matters is that you came back."

We kiss until our lips are raw and my clothes are twisted around my body. He rolls off me, smiling lazily. His light brown hair is a disaster: I ran my hands through it while we were kissing and now it's sticking up everywhere.

He gently drums his fingers on my stomach. "So you kissed me first. That means you finally won fair and square."

"I did," I say with a laugh.

"Will you stay the night?" he asks quietly, nervous and wanting. When I don't immediately respond, he adds, "I'll take you to Bacon N'Oatmeal in the morning after we run."

I laugh, sticking my tongue out. I may be new to college, but there are some things everybody knows about. Bacon N'Oatmeal is this total dive diner right off campus. Kids go there to nurse their hangovers with greasy eggs and sausage.

"I don't think you're allowed to go there without a hangover, are you?" I ask. "I bet the food is terrible sober."

He props himself up on an elbow and flirts, "But I will have a hangover. An Annie hangover. I'm drunk off you, baby."

"Oh my God, you did not just say that!"

Jeremiah collapses into a giggle fit worthy of his ten-year-old sister. "You should've seen the look on your face!"

I hit him over the head with his pillow, and then it's time for bed. He turns his back while I change into one of his T-shirts. He changes into a pair of Nike mesh shorts and a tee that says *Bell Buckle Ten Miler 2005*. I'm shaking as we crawl under the covers. What would Mom say if she knew I was spending the night in his bed?

After quickly punching out a text to Mason telling him not to come back tonight, Jeremiah reaches past my shoulder to turn off his lamp, then spoons me. The party downstairs is still going strong, but the sound of his heartbeat is louder, especially when I twine my fingers with his and kiss him good night over my shoulder.

A Change of Pace

"Somebody didn't come home last night," Vanessa sings.

For lunch on Sunday, I go to the dining hall with Kelsey and Vanessa, and Vanessa wants to know everything.

Kelsey points at me with her fork. "You disappeared upstairs at the party pretty quick."

"Did you and Colton have a nice time?" I ask to delay this conversation.

Kelsey shakes her head. "I started talking to this guy John about an econ paper I have to write—he's a TA in my class. Colton didn't bother to let me introduce him, so I guess he assumed I was interested in John…" She takes a deep breath. "So Colton left the party with some floozy."

"I'm sorry, Kels," I reply, unable to believe Colton would leave with another girl. Vanessa gives her a side hug while I wonder if he only pretended to hook up. I can't imagine him having eyes for anybody else, not even, like, a Victoria's Secret model.

Kelsey shrugs. "So what happened with Jeremiah?"

I push salad around on my plate. "We kissed."

"And then you slept over?" Vanessa asks hurriedly.

"Nothing really happened. We just made out."

"Are y'all together now then?" Kelsey asks.

I shake my head. "He said he could wait until I'm ready."

"But you are ready to sleep over and kiss him?" Kelsey goes on, sounding pissed.

"What's your problem?"

"My problem is that you're leading him on."

"I'm not leading him on. I've been honest with him this entire time. If anybody's leading somebody on, it's you with Colton."

She scowls, and it wouldn't surprise me if steam came out of her ears. "You really like Jeremiah. I don't see why you can't admit it."

"I don't see why you can't give Colton a chance."

People at the surrounding tables have stopped talking. A small crowd stands nearby, listening in.

"Chick fight," a random guy says, bumping fists with a friend.

"Ugh," Kelsey exclaims.

Vanessa shoos the eavesdropping guys away, then picks up her tray. "Y'all need to talk. And I've got a study group for world politics." She leaves us there alone.

"Look," I say. "I'm sorry if I went too far with Colton. I shouldn't guess to know how you feel."

"You're right. You shouldn't. We haven't been friends in years."

I rip the crust off my sandwich. I had hoped that we were getting back to where we once were. Before high school. Before life took over.

"I'm sorry I stopped coming over to your house back then, but I want to be your friend now," I say.

"Why? Why am I suddenly good enough for you? Is it because your boyfriend's gone? Is that it?"

Did she really say that?

"No, Kels." I take a shaky breath through my anger. "It's because I've missed you for a long time. Since eighth grade, when you became better friends with Vanessa than me. I missed you even after you told everyone that I started dating Kyle even though you liked him. You know I wouldn't have done that, Kelsey. Why did you wait to say something until Kyle and I had been going out for months? We were in love by that point... and I wouldn't dump him for no reason, for a friend who hadn't spoken to me in forever."

"Because...I wanted to hurt you," she says quietly. "Your life was so perfect...and you just left me behind for a boy."

"I felt like you left me behind when your mom got married and you moved into a new house while I was still in Oakdale. I didn't feel good enough for you anymore."

We sit in silence, pushing our salad around on our plates.

I pull a deep breath. I should've tried harder to keep our friendship back then. "I want to be friends. Here, right now. I care about you. I don't know how I'm going to make it through college without my friend."

"I missed you too. I still do."

"Then let's start over."

There's a long pause before she picks her fork up and scoops her rice. "So you spent the night at Jeremiah's?"

"Yes."

"I slept over in Colton's room on Friday. That's why he got so pissed I was talking to my TA."

I slap the table. "What? How did we not know this? How did Iggy not let it slip?"

"I told her that gossiping goes against the Baha'i faith."

I snigger. "Is it?"

"I have no idea." Kelsey laughs and sips her Diet Coke.

"So you slept over with Colton? But you're not together?"

She shakes her head.

"Have you kissed?"

Another shake of the head. "I don't want to lose him as a friend...not like I lost you."

"I don't think you'll lose him," I say quietly.

"But it's a big risk."

"I know what you mean. I never thought I'd lose him..."

"Kyle?"

I nod slowly. "But I'm glad I didn't miss any of the time I had with him. If I'd been worried I'd lose him, maybe I wouldn't have dated him. And I never would've had all those other moments."

Realizing this, my body feels lighter, feels stronger, like I could go out and run a marathon right now.

"But you aren't with Jeremiah yet?" Kelsey asks. "I can tell you like him."

"I do…but he does all these adventure races and goes bungee jumping and does other crazy stuff…and I'm worried something will happen to him."

"So you're telling me to risk being with Colton, even though it could ruin our friendship, but you won't give Jere a chance? Why not enjoy what you have now?"

"Why don't you enjoy what you have with Colton?"

We laugh together.

"I'm sorry…" Kelsey says. "I shouldn't have spread that rumor that I liked Kyle."

"Forget about it. We're starting over."

• • •

Sunday night, Jeremiah shows up at my dorm room.

I let him in and the door clicks shut behind him. He's wearing a white button-down shirt, a skinny plaid tie loosened at the neck, and gray pants, aka the nice outfit he bought for fraternity meetings. He's carrying a box of mac 'n' cheese, a stick of butter, and a carton of milk.

"What's going on?"

"I thought I'd cook you supper."

A smile breaks out on my face. How cute is this? A guy cooking me mac 'n' cheese.

I lead him into the kitchen, where he gently pushes me against the counter and drops a kiss to my lips. "You think one box is enough for us?" he asks, looking at it dubiously.

I run my fingers over his slim hips. "I'm sure that's enough."

"But normally I eat a box all by myself...I don't share."

"Well, I'm honored you'll share your macaroni with me. Maybe I've got something we can pair with it."

"Maybe we can pair it with kissing."

How cheesy, I smile to myself. But I can do cheesy as long as it involves kissing.

He steals one, and another, and butterflies flutter around in my stomach. I really get into it, and I'm fixing to pull Jeremiah out of the kitchen into my bedroom and under the covers when Kelsey and Colton stumble out of the bathroom together. Neither is wearing a shirt.

"Uh, hi," I say. Kelsey and Colton burst out laughing. Jeremiah and I stand there, wide-eyed. I figured they might get together soon, but this is *soon* soon. It's only been a few hours since Kelsey and I spoke about her taking a risk. At least she has a bra on.

"What happened to the drought?" I ask with a sly smile.

"It's over!" Colton says, making Kelsey laugh again, and then they start kissing like there's no tomorrow.

"Y'all want some macaroni?" Jeremiah asks, raising his eyebrows.

"Maybe later," Colton says. "I'm not done with Kels yet."

She laughs and I say "Blech" because that is way too much info.

"Did you talk to him yet?" she asks me, and I shake my head. "Get to it." She grabs the jump rope and ties it to her bedroom door before they disappear inside.

"Well then," I say.

Jeremiah stares at the jump rope for several seconds, then shrugs. "I'm glad we don't have to share our macaroni with them," he says in his drawl. "I was getting worried about portion sizes."

I grin, shaking my head. I leave Jere to watch the water boil and start searching through my fridge for something to pair with the macaroni. "How about we boil these hot dogs too?"

He points at me with a plastic spoon. "Now you're talking."

When the food is cooked, we sit on my bed Indian style and watch Sunday Night Football together. The official season hasn't started yet, but Jeremiah insisted on watching because it's the Titans. I'm pretty interested myself because Coach Woods's older brother plays for them. I smile to myself, realizing I never would've met Jeremiah if not for her. I probably wouldn't be training for a marathon anymore, either.

"What was Kelsey talking about?" Jeremiah asks, spooning noodles into his mouth. "She asked if you'd talked to me about something yet."

I chew my macaroni. "It was nothing."

He taps his bowl with his fork. "I don't believe that."

"You are the nosiest boy I've ever met."

"Tell me what Kelsey meant, or I'm stealing the rest of your mac 'n' cheese."

"That's evil." We eat in silence for a minute or so until he speaks again.

"So they're together now? How did that happen?"

"I told Kelsey she needed to take the risk with him."

A knowing smile appears on his face. "And she...wanted you to take a risk with me?"

How did he figure that out? "You said you'd give me time," I say quietly, digging my thumbnail into my palm.

He runs a hand through his hair and takes a deep breath. "I can."

I can't define what we are or how I feel. I thought Kyle was my one and only. And now there's Jeremiah...and I like being with him.

But I'm still not sure I'm ready to risk going after something more.

• • •

"Matt!"

He sprints to me from the mile marker nine water stop. "What's wrong? What's the matter? Is it your knee?"

When I reach him, I grab his arms. "I need Vaseline. Now."

He bites down on his lips but can't contain the burst of laughter that erupts from his mouth. He digs in his pack and pulls out the glorious Vaseline. I grab it. Rush off the trail. Hide behind a tree. Scoop the gunk out and rub it between my legs, sighing loudly.

"Annie?" Concern fills Matt's voice.

"If you tell your brother about this, I'll kill you!"

He laughs. Hard.

Today we're running twenty-two miles, our longest distance before the marathon next month. I've done thirteen miles already—nine to go.

After slathering Vaseline everywhere, I join back up with Andrew and Liza on the trail. They are both sniggering at my chafing incident. I scowl at them. Andrew started running with us a couple weeks ago. He even gave up his iPod. Now he entertains us with stories about his little boys from his first marriage and his job working as the sheriff over in Smyrna.

"Wait," I say. "You got a 911 call because someone lost their python in their house and then it turned up at the Walmart?"

"In the produce section," Andrew says. "I thought I was gonna have to shoot the thing but animal control arrived just in time. Now people want to sue Walmart for undue stress, even though it's not their fault somebody lost their python."

"Liza's a lawyer," I say. "She can handle it all."

"I'm an employment lawyer," Liza says. "I only deal with human animals."

Matt's assistants have tables set up every couple miles along the path. I find myself slurping water and pouring it down the inside of my shirt to stay cool. I eat Jolly Ranchers. Swing my arms back and forth. At about mile fifteen, I need to eat something more substantial or I won't make it another mile, much less seven. From the side pouch of my CamelBak I pull out an energy gel pack. I haven't eaten one of these before. Matt says the trick is to eat little bits at a time so I won't get sick; with my weak stomach, I can't take any chances. I rip the pouch open. Gooey, sticky stuff oozes out and coats my hands.

"Oh gross," Liza says, giving the gel pack a dirty look.

I lick a tiny bit off my thumb. "It doesn't taste too bad. It's kind of like super sugary honey." Over the next mile, I finish eating the gel pack but with no trashcans in sight and not wanting to litter, I stick the gooey wrapper in my CamelBak. I groan at the mess it will make.

"Ugh, this is terrible," I say, trying to lick the stickiness off my fingers. I pray that a water stop is coming up, so I can wash my hands. I would wipe my hands on my shorts but I don't want an even bigger mess. Then my stomach starts churning.

I clutch my side. "Oh no."

"Your stomach?" Andrew asks.

I nod. Thank the heavens there's a porta-potty at mile marker five. I jog ahead of my friends and then I'm sprinting, totally out of breath, knee on fire. I need the bathroom. Need the bathroom now.

Gotta go, gotta go, gotta go.

I barely make it. Andrew and Liza are nice enough to wait for me while I go to the bathroom. Ever since I gave up ibuprofen for Tylenol, I haven't had to go as often, but it still happens. Just my luck I need to go during a twenty-two-miler. I hate my weak stomach.

I hit an all-time low scraping the energy gel gunk off my fingers with toilet paper. Little bits get stuck to my hands. Sweat rolls down my face. Gross. It's so damned hot in the porta-potty and my stomach hurts and I can't tell if I need to vomit or use the bathroom. I'm a sweaty, disgusting mess. Ugh.

"Thanks, y'all," I say when I'm done. "I don't think I could finish without you."

Andrew pats my back. "We couldn't finish without you either, Annie."

For the final five miles, we don't talk at all. None of us has the energy. I can't run fluidly anymore—I'm doing a sort of limp run. My knee throbs. Dr. Sander's voice fills my head: *"I have to tell you, I'm not sure if your knee will make it through the race."*

The 0 mile marker comes into view. I let out a sob.

"Thank God!" Andrew gasps.

Cheers erupt as we pass the mile marker. I walk it off for about thirty seconds but then I start to collapse. Matt grabs my elbows. Holds me up. Lowers me to a beach towel. It feels like a hundred bees are stinging my legs at once. Sweat streams down my face, burning my eyes.

I start crying. Liza sprawls out on the towel next to me. Andrew bends his head between his knees. I lean to my side and vomit all over the pavement. *Not again.*

Matt unsnaps my knee brace and Bridget hands him an ice pack. A peeled banana appears in my hand. Thank goodness. I don't think I could've peeled it myself. I stuff it in my mouth, nearly choking on it. I just got sick but I could eat an entire grocery store. Matt lifts a cup of lemon Gatorade to my lips. I take a sip but end up spilling the rest all over my blue tank top. The yellow blends with the blue to make a gross-looking green spot on my chest.

He moves to help Liza stretch and Bridget is making Andrew take Tylenol. This is crazy. If I barely made it through twenty-two miles, how will I survive twenty-six?

Kyle never even made it to twenty-two miles. The furthest he ever ran was twenty. Just thinking of that makes the tears pour down my face even harder. He never made it here. I'm not sure I can make it again.

"Matt, I can't," I ramble. "I can't do the race. How am I gonna run four more miles? It's too much. It hurts. It hurts."

"Annie, you got this," Matt replies softly. "I won't let you hurt yourself. Your knee's barely swollen today. Our exercises are paying off—"

"I can't," I say through my tears. "My stomach. I can't."

Two hands grasp my ankles. Jeremiah kneels in front of me. "Annie. You are not quitting. You can do this, understand?"

Snot is pouring out of my nose.

"Annie," Jeremiah says again. His voice sounds far away. "Drink this. Now."

Another cup appears in front of me. "I can't. I can't. It hurts." My stomach feels like it got turned inside out. I lean over and get sick again, right in front of him. I clutch my side. He suddenly stands up. I grossed him out.

But then I feel him sitting down behind me, stretching his legs to cradle mine. His arms circle my middle. "I've got you. Relax." I lean against his chest, working to catch my breath. Matt glances away from examining Andrew's ankle and smiles when he sees his brother with me.

Jeremiah whispers in my ear, "You are going to finish this for him. You *will*."

That just makes me cry harder. I blink away my tears, staring at Jeremiah over my shoulder.

"Kyle's counting on you, Annie."

Marathon Training Schedule~Brown's Race Co.

Name *Annie Winters*

Saturday	Distance	Notes
April 20	3 miles	I'm really doing this! Finish time 34:00
April 27	5 miles	Stupid Running Backwords Boy!!
May 4	6 miles	Blister from HELL
May 11	5 miles	Ran downtown Nashville
May 18	7 miles	Tripped on rock. Fell on my butt
May 25	8 miles	Came in 5 min. quicker than usual!
June 1	10 miles	Let's just pretend this day never happened...
June 8	9 miles	Evil suicide sprint things. Ran w/ Liza. Got sick.
June 15	7 miles	Skipped Saturday's run..had to make it up Sunday.
June 22	8 miles	Stomach hurt again. Matt said eat granola instead of oatmeal.
June 29	9 miles	Matt says it's time for new tennis shoes.
July 6	10 miles	Jere got hurt.
July 13	12 miles	Finished in 2:14! Only had to use bathroom once
July 20	13 miles	Halfway there!
July 27	15 miles	Humidity just about finished me off. Time 3:06.
August 3	14 miles	Hurt knee. Overdosed on Pepto.
August 10	11 miles	Wore new knee brace—it messes with my gait.
August 17	16 miles	Didn't get enough sleep in dorms.
August 24	20 miles	Need lifetime supply of Pepto & ice packs. Stat!
August 31	14 miles	Ran w/ Liza & Andrew
September 7	22 miles	Holy crap! Time 4:35. I ran for 1/2 a school day!
September 14	20 miles	
September 21	The Bluegrass Half Marathon	
September 28	12 miles	
October 5	10 miles	
October 12	Country Music Marathon in Nashville	

The Bluegrass Half Marathon

Three Weeks Until the Country Music Marathon

I bounce up and down on my toes.

Liza, Andrew, and I are in the corral for people aiming to finish the Bluegrass Half Marathon in two hours and thirty minutes. Excitement ripples through the crowd and people cheer for no reason at all. The race starts in less than ten minutes and I can't wait.

Jeremiah slips into my corral and kisses me. "Good luck, Winters. I'll meet you at the finish line."

"You too," I reply, and he smiles over his shoulder at me before disappearing toward the first corral where the best runners have gathered.

Liza and Andrew start making embarrassing "wooo!" noises at me.

"I hate y'all," I grumble, and they laugh.

"Are you guys together yet?" Liza whispers to me.

I shake my head. Jeremiah and I have been making out and sleeping over with each other for a month—never going further than second base, but I'm still not ready for a relationship with a guy who lives on the edge. The space between us makes me feel safe…and a bit antsy. It would be nice to tell him how much he means to me—that maybe there is more than one person for everybody—but I feel that would cement us together. I don't think my heart could survive losing another person so special to me…

"You need to get on that," Liza adds, nodding in Jere's direction.

"You're one to talk," I whisper back, throwing a glance at Andrew.

I've been at college for a month and a half. It's only three weeks until the Country Music Marathon, and today is the last time I'll run a long distance before then. Matt says it's time to taper off, so we'll be in good shape for race day.

I totally get why people run races. After months and months of hard work, the excitement is like nothing I've experienced before. It's the night before Christmas.

A gun fires. Runners cheer. The crowd edges forward, and it's so cramped, it takes a little while before we can start jogging. But then it's hard to keep my pace in check—so much adrenaline floods my body, I want to take off like a bottle rocket. It's a good thing Liza and Andrew are here with me to control my pace.

When I was a kid running laps around the playground in gym class, I thought running was the most boring thing ever. But running a race is not boring. Not boring at all.

"Oh. My. God," Liza says, pointing at five Speedo-clad guys with American flags painted on their faces.

"How is running in those comfortable?" I blurt.

"I don't know, but it's plenty comfortable for me to look at. Not to mention patriotic." She laughs naughtily. I make a gagging sound. I did not need to see that.

Crazy people are wearing crazy costumes. One guy is dressed as a fairy? Another is wearing a pink gorilla suit. A group of guys in Batman masks cut holes in their shorts so their butts are hanging out. They call themselves the Bare Butt Batmans.

Liza loves them, of course.

Three miles into the race, as beautiful vistas of the Great Smoky Mountains come into view, a man in front of me trips. "Pothole!" somebody yells, and I hop over it just in time. Other runners grab the man who tripped and help him to the side of the course. My heart doesn't stop pounding hard for a few minutes. What if I had fallen in the hole two weeks before the full marathon? What if I'd twisted my knee? An icy chill rushes through me.

I love the bluegrass bands stationed along the course. We cross over creeks and the Watauga River, passing factories, barns, and cornfields. A pastry chef gives out cookies when we run past her restaurant on Main Street and the three of us have never been so excited to see dessert. The sun soars higher and higher in the sky as the race goes on, but I never feel truly tired. I only have to stop to use the bathroom once. All my training pays off.

I cross the finish line in 2:35 and do a silly pose for the automatic camera taking pictures of runners. Andrew high-fives Liza and me, and she and I hug. We scream "wooo!" together and bounce around like kids at recess, proud we finished. Compared to the twenty-two mile run we did two weeks ago, this race was a cinch.

It was a rest day.

A race volunteer hangs a medal around my neck and another drapes a crinkly silver cape around my shoulders. It looks like aluminum foil but feels soft and keeps me warm. My heart starts to slow down as I weave through the crowd to find what I need most: a snack.

Andrew, Liza, and I grab bananas off a table, then head to the tree where Matt's large blue flag hangs from a branch. It lets our team know where to meet.

I walk up to Bridget. "Hey, have you seen Jeremiah? Or Matt?"

Her eyes are bloodshot. "They went to Vanderbilt hospital."

"What?" I drop my banana on the ground. "Why?"

"Jeremiah got hurt during the race. He fell off a bridge—"

I don't even stop to hear the rest. I grab my bag from the storage truck, pull out my car keys, and sprint to the parking lot.

• • •

This race was supposed to be safe! How could he fall off a bridge? Was it the long stretch over the Watauga River at mile eight? Did the medics rescue him and take him by ambulance before I even reached that part of the race? I didn't hear any sirens or see any police cars blazing by.

A memory flashes in my mind. Sirens blaring during a thunderstorm. The moment, an hour later, when Mr. Crocker knocked on my front door to tell me *he* was gone.

I drive to Nashville as fast as I can, speeding through yellow lights, barely stopping at stop signs.

I never got a chance to tell Kyle good-bye. That I loved him.

On his way home from my place our last night, after we made up and got back together, there was a torrential downpour. He saw a car veer off the road into a ditch, and when he rushed out of his car to help the elderly man who'd crashed, another car slipped off the road and hit my boyfriend. During his eulogy, his brother Connor said Kyle died just the way he would've wanted to: helping somebody.

• • •

On the last night, Kyle and I stood in the doorway of my trailer.

Nick sat a few feet away watching the World Series on TV. The noisy game and noisy rain made it hard to hear what my boyfriend was saying.

"I'll pick you up for school," he said, kissing me for what must've been the hundredth time that night. I would never get tired of his kisses. His chocolate brown eyes were happy when he said he'd buy me a chai latte before he picked me up in the morning.

"How can you leave during the middle of the game?" Nick asked.

"No more baseball for me this year. I can't believe we lost to Philly in the playoffs again," Kyle replied.

"And you call yourself a baseball fan."

I knew it wasn't about the baseball at all. My brother liked having another guy around the house and it thrilled him I was getting back together with my boyfriend after a month apart.

"Maybe you should wait for the rain to clear out," I said when the rain started pelting the roof. "Call your parents and tell them you're staying here until the storm is over."

He kissed me. "I'll be fine."

I handed him a newspaper to cover his head and he dashed into the night. He honked, and I waved from the porch, not caring that I was getting all wet.

"Bye, Annie!" he yelled out the window.

I smiled, filled with hope. We were back together. Everything was going to be just fine.

• • •

At the hospital, I park in an area that clearly says "no parking" but I don't care if I get towed. I jet into the emergency room. The front desk lady tells me he's in room five. Before she can even ask if I'm friend or family, I sprint down the hallway, my sneakers squeaking on the hospital floor. *Can't breathe. Can't breathe. Can't breathe.*

Tears are gushing down my face when I find Matt and their father. Mr. Brown is pacing back and forth. I rush up to Matt and hug him. When I pull away, Mr. Brown gives me a weak smile and hands me a Kleenex. Thanking him, I take it and wipe my nose.

Matt rubs his thumb over the medal hanging from my neck and smiles. "You finished."

Who cares about me right now? "How is he?" I start to open the door but Matt grabs my arm.

"I wouldn't go in there if I were you."

Ignoring him, I shove the door. I have to know. I can't lose him. I can't. The door swings open.

"I told you, I'm not wearing the gown!" Jeremiah shouts at a nurse. He's cradling his arm. "You don't need to take my shorts off for this procedure."

"Sir, this is hospital policy. You will wear a gown!"

All the air rushes out of me when I see he's okay. I charge him. Hug his neck. Plaster my lips to his. With one arm, he yanks me up against his chest and deepens the kiss.

"That was nice," he murmurs when we break apart. "What was that for?"

"I thought you were dying!" I desperately pat his chest and legs and face. All intact. When I grab his shoulders, he cringes and yelps in pain. "Are you okay?"

"I'm fine, Annie. Why would you think I'm dying?"

"I heard you fell off a bridge."

"A footbridge," he says with a laugh. "Some asshole cut me off during the race and I fell into a creek. I think I dislocated my shoulder."

I press my forehead to his as tears continue to fall down my face. Happy tears. My body sags against his. My hands shake. I process what he said.

A footbridge? Considering all his crazy BASE jumping stunts and motocross and bungee jumping, it never occurred to me he could get hurt during a regular race. A race that I just ran myself. Anything can happen. Anything. Anytime, to anyone. We have to live now. Now, now, now.

"I love you," I blurt, and a rush of white-hot heat fills me.

His blue eyes light up. "I love you too."

And I love this moment. Love it. Laughing, we start kissing again. I get into it and accidentally jostle his shoulder, making him yelp for a second time.

"That's it," says the nurse. "It's time for your X-rays. Now put that gown on."

"I don't need a gown! You're X-raying my shoulder, not my butt."

"Jeremiah Brown," I say. "Put that gown on right now."

"No."

"Right. Now."

"Fine," he grumbles, untying the drawstring on his shorts one-handed.

"I like her," says a voice from the hall.

"Daaaad," Jeremiah whines. I can hear Matt laughing.

"I'll be in the waiting room, okay?" I say, and Jeremiah grabs my half-marathon medal and pulls me close for another kiss.

"I love you."

I laugh. "You already said that."

"I've never said it before. I like it…I think I'll keep saying it."

We grin at each other, and relief flows through my body until the door slams open, startling me. I jump. Mrs. Brown appears, her short brown hair disheveled, her face streaked red with tears. Clearly she also got the message that Jeremiah fell off a bridge. Why did no one bother to clarify what kind of bridge it was?

She rushes forward and hugs her son hard. "Thank goodness you're all right," Mrs. Brown says, and the nurse tsk tsks. She's probably never seen such commotion over a dislocated shoulder.

"I wish you'd stop racing," she says with a trembling voice.

Over her shoulder, Jeremiah rolls his eyes at me. "It was a regular half marathon, Mom."

"I can't stand this," she says, releasing him from the hug. "Every time I answer the phone, I worry someone is calling to tell me you're hurt…or worse. I got six calls from the hospital last year. I don't want to pick you up from the hospital anymore, son—"

"It could've happened to anybody," I interrupt. His mom meets my gaze, and I want to dare her to say something else to me, a person who's suffered a huge loss. "Jeremiah was doing the safest race ever. He just got the short end of the stick on this one."

"But he has the worst luck when it comes to sports. Why can't he just join a Bible Study?"

Jeremiah looks completely appalled by that idea, and that

makes me laugh. I can't deny he takes risks, but I'm not going to swaddle him in bubble wrap to keep him safe.

"Please stop doing this to me," she says, and I can see in her glistening eyes how much she loves him. "Please."

"Mom," Jeremiah starts, "it's not fair to make me decide between my family and doing something I love. You know I've cut back. I can't truly feel anything unless I put myself out there."

"Agreed," I say with a smile. He gives me a grateful look.

"It sucks that I'm trying to make you happy so you'll let me come around the house and see my sisters…and you haven't noticed that at all. I've given up a lot."

His mom ruffles his hair and shuts her eyes. "I appreciate that you're taking better care of yourself. I don't like the things you do…" She pauses to glance over at me. "We can talk about this more later."

He grins. "I'm definitely willing to talk. We can discuss how I want to go skydiving again."

"Young man, that is not the kind of discussion I was thinking of."

"But PopPop got me another gift certificate!"

Matt and his father enter the room to join the argument about whether Jeremiah can go skydiving again, but I just hold his hand, thinking about what he said.

If you don't put yourself out there, if you don't take risks, you can't truly feel.

And I'm ready to feel again.

...

"So we're gonna try this?"

"Yeah, let's see where it goes," I reply.

"Thank the Lord," he says with a smile, sweetly kissing my cheek. I turn to catch his mouth with mine, grasping his T-shirt in my hands, careful to mind his sling.

The morning after my first official half marathon, we're lounging in my bed, discussing a relationship. Vanessa is visiting Rory in Knoxville, so Jeremiah slept over and we had the room to ourselves. I took care of him all night, giving him his painkillers and icing his shoulder. He liked having his own personal nurse. And I liked kissing him constantly. I couldn't keep my lips off him.

Speaking of. I cozy up and slip a hand under his T-shirt, touching his rock-hard stomach. His pretty blue eyes light up and I know I love this guy. I press my lips to his, kissing him deeply, then trail kisses down his neck and lower. Soon he stealthily steals my pajama bottoms, which takes skill considering he only has one arm right now. I steal his shorts in retaliation, leaving him in black boxer briefs. Then he pulls me on top with his good arm, throws my tank top on the floor, and gently dips his hand into my pink panties. And wow it feels great.

I look into his eyes and catch him grimacing.

"Does your shoulder hurt?"

"Like hell. But I don't care right now."

He moans as I slip my hand inside his boxer briefs, moving

my hand up and down until he wants me back on top. I love feeling him pressed up against my body, and I sort of hate that we're separated by underwear as we take care of each other's needs. I rock against his hips until I'm seeing spots, pressing my forehead to his when tingles fill both our bodies.

"Yeah, a relationship sounds just fine," I say, working to catch my breath.

"I reckon this means I finally get to take you on a real date, huh?" he responds with a lazy smile.

"You'd better."

"How about tonight?"

"Can't. Kelsey and I are grabbing dinner at the dining hall and then seeing that new Brad Pitt–Angelina Jolie movie where they're cyborgs trying to kill each other. It's girls' night."

He grins at that. "How about roller blading this afternoon, then?"

"We are not going roller blading with that shoulder a mess like it is."

He laughs, tangling his feet with mine. "Just kidding."

I drag my fingertip up and down the surgical scar on his arm and bury my face in the warm hollow of his neck. "You're gonna take it easy for a while, right?"

"I can't move my arm. I don't think I have a choice but to relax."

"Until you find some new crazy stunt to try next week, you mean," I say with a laugh.

"I'm not doing any more stunts."

I can't control what might happen. All I can do is live. "I don't want you to give up what you love for me."

"That's not it." He shakes his head. "Don't you understand how you make me feel?"

"You told me you love me—"

"I'm going to show you how much you make me feel. You're gonna feel it yourself."

"How?"

"Do you trust me?"

• • •

My body is shaking, my nerves crackling. Sweat pours down my face. I feel like I'm on a beach in a storm and lightning might strike any second.

"Next!" a worker says, and I step forward. Cords and clips dangle off the harness tightly strapped around my body.

I can do this. I can do this.

The zip line employee helps me up onto the wooden platform attached to a tree. I look down into the vast canyon below me filled with pointy rocks and trees.

"I can't do this."

"Getting up here is the worst part," the worker replies. "It's perfectly safe, I promise."

I believe him. Regardless that he's willing to take big risks, Jeremiah would never put me in danger. I let out a deep breath.

The worker hooks me to a trolley, tells me to sit down in my harness, and pushes me off the platform.

Wait. He pushed me off the platform!

I scream, holding on to my rope tight. Wind smacks my face. I soar over the canyon. Fear ices my body and my heart leaps to light speed.

"Slow down, slow down!" the guy waiting on the other platform yells. I press the lower line, and I jerk to a stop right in front of the tree trunk.

"Holy shit," I blurt as the guy reaches out and pulls me from the air onto the platform.

"You did good," the worker says with a bright grin, hooking my rope to the tree so I don't fall into the canyon I just crossed. I gasp when I look down. "We're over three hundred feet high and the line you just zipped is three hundred and fifty feet long. It's our most challenging obstacle."

"Why in the world would you make us do the hardest line first?"

"It's all easy peasy from here on out." The worker fist-bumps me.

I zip three more lines, each one leaving me shakier than the last. I like the feeling of stress bleeding away when I'm back on solid ground. Not sure I could do this on a daily basis, though.

After the final line, I trudge up the hill to a smiling Jeremiah. I'm at a total loss for words, overwhelmed by the experience I just had—placing all my trust in some ropes and people I don't know. We stand in silence as he helps me remove my gear. With his good arm, he unsnaps my harness, letting it fall to the deck. Careful to mind his sling, I wrap my arms around his neck and hug him until my heart begins to slow. He massages warm circles onto my lower back.

"Well?" he finally asks.

"That was nuts." I touch fingers to my neck to feel my out-of-control pulse.

"Did you feel the adrenaline?" he asks.

I nod. Right now I could lift a car if I had to. "I can see why you're into it."

He unsnaps my helmet, then looks at me with mischievous glittering eyes. His lips meet mine, and he slips his good hand behind my neck. "I never knew what an adrenaline rush really was until we met. When I first saw you? That was the day all my running finally paid off—because you were on the trails. You make me feel three times the rush of skydiving or bungee jumping…I felt the biggest rush of my life when you said you love me."

I hop up on tiptoes, bury my hands in his crazy hair, and capture his lips with mine. My stomach leaps into my throat.

When we finally stop kissing each other, he holds me close. "So how about some lunch?"

I draw tiny circles on his chest with my fingertips. "Vanessa is still in Knoxville visiting her boyfriend…how about we go back to my room?"

His eyebrows pop up when he realizes what I'm offering. "You're sure?"

I answer with a kiss that leaves us both breathless.

Marathon Training Schedule~Brown's Race Co.

Name *Annie Winters*

Saturday	Distance	Notes
April 20	3 miles	I'm really doing this! Finish time 34:00
April 27	5 miles	Stupid Running Backwords Boy!!
May 4	6 miles	Blister from HELL
May 11	5 miles	Ran downtown Nashville
May 18	7 miles	Tripped on rock. Fell on my butt
May 25	8 miles	Came in 5 min. quicker than usual!
June 1	10 miles	Let's just pretend this day never happened...
June 8	9 miles	Evil suicide sprint things. Ran w/ Liza. Got sick.
June 15	7 miles	Skipped Saturday's run...had to make it up Sunday.
June 22	8 miles	Stomach hurt again. Matt said eat granola instead of oatmeal
June 29	9 miles	Matt says it's time for new tennis shoes.
July 6	10 miles	Jere got hurt.
July 13	12 miles	Finished in 2:14! Only had to use bathroom once
July 20	13 miles	Halfway there!
July 27	15 miles	Humidity just about finished me off. Time 3:06.
August 3	14 miles	Hurt knee. Overdosed on Pepto.
August 10	11 miles	Wore new knee brace—it messes with my gait.
August 17	16 miles	Didn't get enough sleep in dorms.
August 24	20 miles	Need lifetime supply of Pepto & ice packs. Stat!
August 31	14 miles	Ran w/ Liza & Andrew
September 7	22 miles	Holy crap! Time 4:35. I ran for 1/2 a school day!
September 14	20 miles	Knee brace is The Devil
September 21	The Bluegrass Half Marathon	Finished in 2:26! Won a medal!
September 28	12 miles	Tapering off
October 5	10 miles	Almost there!
October 12	Country Music Marathon in Nashville	

It's Time

"Did Jeremiah tell you? His frat accepted Colton into the pledge class."

"That's great!" I say to Kelsey. She and Vanessa are driving me back to Franklin for dinner. We're going to Joe's All-You-Can-Eat Pasta Shack so I can carbo-load before the marathon tomorrow.

Kelsey and Colton have been dating for nearly two months, and contrary to the bathroom incident in which they weren't wearing shirts, they've been taking it slow. But it doesn't surprise me when she says they finally went all the way.

When Jeremiah and I got back to campus after zip-lining, we sprinted to my dorm. We couldn't get there fast enough. We stumbled from the elevator to my room, tugging at each other's clothes, nearly trampling a freshman guy, kissing the entire way. In my room, he tripped over Vanessa's shoe, lost his balance because of his shoulder, and landed on top of me. Our heads clonked together and we groaned.

The very sweet, very unsexy memory makes me laugh to myself. "I've been sleeping with Jeremiah too."

Vanessa bounces up and down in her seat. Kelsey honks the horn, squealing. I kind of want to squeal myself. I love spending time with my friends.

About five minutes out from Franklin, I whine, "I'm so hungry."

"I swear, Annie, I can't believe how much food you eat," Kelsey says.

She's right. For lunch today, I ate an entire large pizza by myself. With my training schedule, I wake up hungry and go to bed starving, no matter how much I eat.

When we get to Joe's, I hop out of the car and jog to the entrance, preparing to order tortellini. We walk in the door, the little bell jingling, and tons of people yell, "Surprise!"

A huge banner hangs on the wall: GOOD LUCK, ANNIE!

Kyle's best friend, Seth, rushes up and hugs me. "I hope you don't mind…we just wanted to show you how excited we are."

My eyes welling up with tears, I gaze around at the crowd I wasn't expecting. Mom and Nick are here, along with Jeremiah. Vanessa, Rory, Kelsey, Colton, Jack, and Savannah. Coach Woods. Stephanie, my manager from the Roadhouse, and some other people who work there. My old principal, Dr. Salter. A bunch of guys from the Hundred Oaks track team. Men from the fire department. Even Liza and Andrew are here, beaming at me.

Kyle's parents, Mr. and Mrs. Crocker. His little brothers.

I swear, it's like the entire town is here. To support me. To remember Kyle.

My heart lurches when his parents come over to me.

"We're so proud of you," Mrs. Crocker says, giving me a big hug.

His father says, "We'll be there tomorrow at the finish line."

"Daddy got us a fog horn to blow when you run by!" Kyle's little brother Isaac says.

"I can't wait," I say with a laugh.

I introduce Jeremiah to Mr. and Mrs. Crocker as my boyfriend. Mr. Crocker slips a comforting arm around his wife and gazes at her until she nods as if to say, *Yes, I'm all right*. Then they both shake Jeremiah's hand and ask how college is going. Mrs. Crocker makes me promise to drop by the house during Thanksgiving break next month.

Coach Woods is digging into a massive plate of spaghetti. I walk over to her table to thank her for coming. She swallows and lets out a loud groan. The guy she's with says, "Don't eat so fast or you're gonna bust a lung."

"Shut up, Henry."

"Um, hi, Coach Woods, thanks for being here."

She looks up with a smile. "Annie, hi. This is my boyfriend, Sam Henry. Henry, this is Annie, my former student."

The picture of him on her desk at school doesn't do him justice: her boyfriend is hot. Way to go, Coach Woods.

"Good luck tomorrow," he says, grinning.

"I can't wait to see you run," Coach Woods says. "I'm so proud of you. Matt says you're in really good shape to finish."

"I am," I say. I've never worked so hard in my life.

"Need any pointers?" Henry asks.

"She does *not* need pointers from you," Coach Woods says.

"Sure she does. You know where the beer stops are, right?" he asks with a wicked gleam in his eye.

Coach Woods groans again. "You're gonna get me fired one of these days, Henry."

"I do know where the beer stops are," I say. "Miles sixteen and twenty-two."

"Matt's got you trained up well, I see," Henry replies, stretching his arms across the back of the booth. "I wish I could come to the race, but I have to work."

"What do you do?" I ask.

"I just got on with the Titans as an SEC scout."

"The best job ever," Coach Woods says. "Basically he watches college football games all the time."

"How can I get that job?" I ask, making them laugh.

After I've said hi and thank you to everybody, I join Jeremiah over at a big round table with my friends. Jack Goodwin and Savannah are down from Kentucky. Rory drove over from Knoxville and is currently kissing Vanessa's neck. We all roll our eyes at that and tell them to get a room. Kelsey holds Colton's hand and he's so busy staring at her, he keeps missing the straw as he tries to take sips of his drink.

"Now that Colton's pledging my fraternity, I can ask him to do anything," Jeremiah whispers in my ear, playing with my braid. "I could make him feed you spaghetti."

"Oh stop," I say. "Don't torture my friend."

Later in the evening, Jeremiah comes back to my trailer with us. We sit at the kitchen table because he wants to go over the course maps with me for the gazillionth time. But I quickly learn that "go over the course maps" is code for making out, because he won't stop stealing kisses. It's fun, but I can't get something out of my mind.

"I need to do something," I say quietly.

"Let's do it then."

"Alone."

He stares into my eyes, fiddling with his leather cord necklace. "Okay."

"I'll be back in a little while if you want to stay here. You and Nick can see what's on TV."

"Cool."

"*Die Hard*'s on," Nick announces.

"You watch that every day—"

"I love that movie," Jeremiah interrupts me, flopping down on the couch beside my brother.

With a deep breath, I grab Mom's keys and borrow her car.

It's time.

I go to the drive-in. Our spot. I sit on the hood of the car and eat popcorn, watching *Titanic*. I'll never forget all the moments we shared, good and bad, sad and funny. All the wonderful time we spent together. Every moment means the world.

I'll never forget you.

• • •

A noise jolts me awake. My eyes blink open to find Jeremiah sneaking into my room at home. He crawls onto my bed, laughing, and touches his nose to mine.

"I thought you went home?" I hiss. "You can't sleep over. My mom'll kill me."

"I forgot to give you something before the race."

He clasps something around my neck. I gaze down to see it's his lucky leather necklace. Our eyes meet, then he kisses my fingers.

"Love you," he says. "Sweet dreams."

"Love you too."

He scrambles off the bed and tiptoes out into the hallway. Then I hear him getting in trouble.

"I sent you home an hour ago, young man," Mom says.

"I forgot to give Annie something."

A loud snort. Nick. "She needs her sleep for the race!"

"Okay, okay, I'm going," Jeremiah says.

"I better not see you again tonight, Jeremiah Brown," Mom says.

"You're as bad as Annie!"

I laugh myself to sleep.

But I don't sleep well. I keep waking up every hour because I'm scared my alarm clock won't go off. When it finally rings, Mom and Nick rush into my room.

"Just wanted to make sure you're awake," she says, and it nearly makes me cry because she believes I can really do this.

I grab a shower to wake myself up, pull on the clothes I laid out the night before: my favorite pink shorts and the panties that never ride up. I safety pin my race number to my white tank.

I ride to Nashville with my family, just the three of us. Nick drives and Mom mans the radio. They both took off work. My knee shakes the entire drive.

After getting good-luck hugs from my mom and brother, I join my team under the tree with Matt's blue flag. Andrew has an arm around Liza's waist, and they both hug me.

Matt smiles around at those of us who made it to today. "I'll see you all at the finish line," he says without a trace of doubt in his voice. And then it's time for us to head to our corrals.

But I have one final thing to do: I slather Vaseline all over my thighs.

"Another Vaseline convert," Matt says, chuckling. "Told you it'd help with the chafing."

"I don't think I'm comfortable with you talking to my girl about chafing," Jeremiah says as he walks up to our team.

"I'm her coach. It's well within my bounds."

"And I'm your brother. It's well within my bounds to knock you upside the head."

And of course, the brothers start in on each other. Jeremiah grabs Matt in a headlock and Matt jabs at his brother's stomach. I roll my eyes.

An announcer's booming voice tells us to report to our corrals. The cool air seems to still. I begin to follow Andrew, but Jeremiah takes my elbow.

"Good luck," he says, quickly pecking my lips. He tweaks my braid, then walks off with his brother, waving at me over his shoulder.

I weave through the crowd to my corral.

I check my shoelaces one last time.

Make sure my official timer is attached to my shoe.

Shake out my legs.

Slip Kyle's red Nike headband on.

A gun fires in the distance. The crowd inches forward. Cheers echo in the park. And I'm off.

And as I cross the starting line, I picture Kyle's face and say thank you for helping me get through this. *Thank you for all you've given me.*

And when I look up at the gray sky, light breaks through a cloud and I feel the sun on my face.

Marathon Training Schedule~Brown's Race Co.

Name *Annie Winters*

Saturday	Distance	Notes
April 20	3 miles	I'm really doing this! Finish time 34:00
April 27	5 miles	Stupid Running Backwards Boy!!
May 4	6 miles	Blister from HELL
May 11	5 miles	Ran downtown Nashville
May 18	7 miles	Tripped on rock. Fell on my butt
May 25	8 miles	Came in 5 min. quicker than usual!
June 1	10 miles	Let's just pretend this day never happened...
June 8	9 miles	Evil suicide sprint things. Ran w/ Liza. Got sick.
June 15	7 miles	Skipped Saturday's run..had to make it up Sunday.
June 22	8 miles	Stomach hurt again. Matt said eat granola instead of oatmeal.
June 29	9 miles	Matt says it's time for new tennis shoes.
July 6	10 miles	Jere got hurt.
July 13	12 miles	Finished in 2:14! Only had to use bathroom once
July 20	13 miles	Halfway there!
July 27	15 miles	Humidity just about finished me off. Time 3:06.
August 3	14 miles	Hurt knee. Overdosed on Pepto.
August 10	11 miles	Wore new knee brace—it messes with my gait.
August 17	16 miles	Didn't get enough sleep in dorms.
August 24	20 miles	Need lifetime supply of Pepto & ice packs. Stat!
August 31	14 miles	Ran w/ Liza & Andrew
September 7	22 miles	Holy crap! Time 4:35. I ran for 1/2 a school day!
September 14	20 miles	Knee brace is The Devil
September 21	The Bluegrass Half Marathon	Finished in 2:26! Won a medal!
September 28	12 miles	Tapering off
October 5	10 miles	Almost there!
October 12	Country Music Marathon in Nashville	Signed up for San Francisco Marathon!

ACKNOWLEDGMENTS

I'm a lot like Annie. When I was little, I used every excuse I knew to get out of running in gym class. I'd say I had a cold. A sprained arm. "My asthma is acting up and I forgot my inhaler today." I just didn't like running. It made me tired and sweaty and out of breath, and all the other kids were so much faster than me. It felt like it would never end.

Even when I got to high school and started playing varsity soccer, I never wanted to run laps before and after practice. "You mean to tell me after we've been kicking a ball around for an hour, you want me to run two miles?!" Again, even in high school, I had excuses. "My ankle hurts." "My asthma is bothering me."

It wasn't until after college that I decided to really get in shape. I started eating right, started exercising several days a week, and I bought some books that taught me how to run. Running is something that humans are designed to do. Like talking, eating, and sleeping, running is a part of the human experience. But as you probably saw from Annie's story, learning to run long distances is not an easy feat. The book I read gave tips on how to build up my mileage over time, much like Annie does in the book. It took me about a year to train, but I was eventually able to work up to 26.2 miles. I am of the opinion that if you want to run a marathon, you can—you just have to work hard and read magazines and books to learn how to train correctly.

I ran the Marine Corps Marathon in 2005. And it was the toughest thing I have ever done in my entire life. Some people think running is something you do on your own, but it requires a support team—people to keep you hydrated and fed, and to cheer you on.

Writing a book is a lot like training for a marathon. It takes lots of focus and practice. And I couldn't do it without a lot of help from family and friends.

My husband, Don, helps me through every book I write—with his knack for understanding human character and pointing out my wordiness, I couldn't do this without him. He's always great at getting me out of the house when I have writer's block and need to clear my mind. Thanks for being my biggest fan.

Thank you to the Longstreths, Kenneallys, and Beggans for always supporting me.

A huge thanks to Julie Romeis Sanders, who helped me take this book from a shell of a story to something much bigger and stronger. I am in awe of how you recognize the important threads of a plot and know how to pull them out and enhance them.

To my beta readers, your feedback and insights were, as always, super helpful: Jessica Spotswood, Tiffany Smith, Trish Doller, Sarah Skilton, Natalie Bahm, Lena Thomsen, Kari Olson, Jen Fisher, Andrea Soule, Mickey Reed, Jessica Wallace, and Robin Talley (you finally got your Ping-Pong book).

The personal thoughts and feelings about extreme sports given to me by Hannah Maier and Scott Vetere were invaluable. Darryl Jones, trainer extraordinaire, taught me so much about working out in the gym and the human body in general. All of you helped me to understand Jeremiah Brown's character.

To Duffy Winters, one of the biggest YA fans I know, thanks for letting me use your last name! And to Bob Nardo, you probably don't remember them, but a lot of the conversations we had in college about life and death helped me shape this book.

Sara Megibow, you have always been my biggest advocate—I couldn't ask for a more committed agent. Thank you to Aubrey Poole and Todd Stocke for your thoughtful edits and tireless advocacy on behalf of this book. I continue to be amazed by the team at Sourcebooks: Dominique Raccah, Sean Murray, Derry Wilkens, and Jillian Bergsma. Thank you to Leah Hultenschmidt for launching my career.

Many thanks to my fans—none of this would be possible if not for you. Keep working hard and believing in yourselves and going after what you want.